ATLAS *of* UNKNOWABLE THINGS

ATLAS *of* UNKNOWABLE THINGS

McCORMICK TEMPLEMAN

ST. MARTIN'S PRESS
NEW YORK

First published in the United States by St. Martin's Press, an imprint of St. Martin's Publishing Group

EU Representative: Macmillan Publishers Ireland Ltd, 1st Floor, The Liffey Trust Centre, 117–126 Sheriff Street Upper, Dublin 1, DO1 YC43

www.stmartins.com

Designed by Devan Norman

Library of Congress Cataloging-in-Publication Data

Names: Templeman, McCormick author
Title: Atlas of unknowable things / McCormick Templeman.
Description: First edition. | New York : St. Martin's Press, 2025. |
Identifiers: LCCN 2025017950 | ISBN 9781250393494 hardcover |
    ISBN 9781250393500 ebook
Subjects: LCGFT: Horror fiction | Paranormal fiction | Novels
Classification: LCC PS3620.E464 A95 2025 | DDC 813/.6—dc23/
    eng/20250414
LC record available at https://lccn.loc.gov/2025017950

Our books may be purchased in bulk for specialty retail/wholesale, literacy, corporate/premium, educational, and subscription box use. Please contact MacmillanSpecialMarkets@macmillan.com.

First Edition: 2025

10 9 8 7 6 5 4 3 2 1

FOR JAMES AND PHOEBE—
YOU MAKE MY LIFE SO HAPPY.

AND FOR UNCLE CASEY. I MISS YOU DEARLY.

With relief, with humiliation, with terror, he understood that he also was an illusion, that someone else was dreaming him.

—JORGE LUIS BORGES, "THE CIRCULAR RUINS"

CONTENTS

I

VISITORS FROM UNSEEN REALMS

1.1

THE SUPERNATURAL

A marveilous newtrality have these things mathematicall, and also a strange participation between things supernaturall, immortal, and intellectuall, simple and indivisible, and things natural mortall, componded and divisible.

—JOHN DEE, SIXTEENTH CENTURY

Consider for a moment, the Latin root of the word *monster*: *monere*, to warn. Monstrosity in its essence is another word for a warning. As such, what a society considers monstrous is often both a signal and an outgrowth of its own particular prejudices. But beneath that, can we find deeper roots in the belief in the mythic? And is it possible to perceive a glimmer of the factual and historical within mankind's persistent attraction to the supernatural?

These were some of the topics of the dissertation I once intended to write. That original manuscript was meant to be the culmination of my graduate research into the history of European witchcraft and folklore. In its finest, most realized form, I imagined the dissertation to be a staid, serious, possibly even modestly significant work that I would eventually publish with a distinguished university press, and which would cement my place in academia. In contrast, this manuscript—the one you are about to read—was originally intended to be no more than a personal journal, a catalogue of my findings, a space to muse, reflect, and interpret. It has grown into something quite different, and altogether more sinister. As you shall see, the events recorded in this manuscript have rendered any attempts at securing my PhD—much less a normal life—wretchedly moot. But we shall get to all that in time.

At the outset of my dissertation, I wasn't in the best state of mind. My dog, Kant, had just died, and my boyfriend had just dumped me. He politely asked me to leave the Red Hook apartment we shared, complaining that I was "monomaniacal." Try putting that one on your Tinder profile. The trouble was, he wasn't wrong. I had become a little fixated on a recent betrayal, but we'll get to that in a minute as well. So, finished with my coursework, but still needing to complete my dissertation, and now also in need of a place to live, I found myself at a crossroads. In a stroke of luck, my dear cousin, Paloma, suggested the two of us move into her rich father's rent-controlled East Village townhouse, and I jumped at the chance. He was away in Europe for the year and had given her the run of the place. Paloma would take the year off to paint, and I would quit my part-time job at ABC Carpet, knock out a few hundred pages of brilliant text, defend the dissertation, and get on the job market. Easy-peasy, right? But the universe had different plans.

First a bit about me, or rather, about the person I thought I was before my "dark night of the soul," as we are calling it on the internet these days. I was born in Vancouver, Washington, the child of a single mother. No close relatives aside from my uncle and cousin Paloma. I would describe my temperament as bookishly pugnacious, and perhaps not unrelated, I've never had a relationship that lasted more than a few months. A therapist once told me that my father's abrupt departure when I was five was to blame for my inability to form healthy romantic attachments. That could be true, but I would also argue that most people are super difficult and prone to calling you "monomaniacal," and who wants to deal with that shit?

Living at my uncle's was pretty idyllic at first. Paloma and I fell into a schedule of evening walks through the city, days spent painting and researching, respectively, and quiet nights reading by the stone fireplace.

Dissertations aren't typically the most enjoyable undertakings, but mine had been especially onerous. I had perhaps been too ambitious at the outset, dead set as I was on delving into a theory called the witch-cult hypothesis. Proposed in the 1920s by anthropologist Margaret Murray, the theory is built around the idea that the Inquisition and European witch hunts in general, instead of just being a misogynistic frenzy, were in fact a concerted effort by the church to eradicate the remains of an ancient fertility cult, most likely centered around the goddess Diana and the god Janus. Either way, innocent women were killed, but Murray's theory posits that they were killed for practicing an actual organized religion, which, while not witchcraft, was systematized and goddess-focused. Murray's work was later squarely rejected, and her methods denounced as unscientific. Having examined her work closely, I'd initially found myself in agreement with her detractors, but I'd always held out a distant flicker of hope that there might be something to it—perhaps an academic's puckish desire to upend my contemporaries' research, or possibly it was something more primal. The notion of a powerful cabal of women working in concert to undermine the establishment was perhaps a girlhood fantasy of which I'd yet to let go.

And then I hit on something—a correspondence between

Joan of Arc and Gilles de Rais that had the potential to prove that Murray's work was worth reconsidering. Suddenly my dissertation went from run-of-the-mill to potentially ground-breaking. This was around the time a student a year ahead of me named Charles Danforth began inviting me out for drinks. It wasn't long before we were lurching around the city, freshly minted best friends getting along like a house on fire. That time spent at the epicenter of our friendship was perhaps the happiest of my life. I can still see him now, wearing that stupid burgundy knit cap of his, laughing like a hyena as we drank tequila in unmarked bars and searched for used vinyl in hole-in-the-wall shops. I was so stupidly trusting and confident in that friendship that when he eventually suggested collaborating on an article, I showed him everything I'd found—and I mean everything. The next thing I knew, that research (which he willfully mis-construed to bolster his own lackluster argument) had gone directly into his dissertation (which he passed with distinction). We had a horrendous fight, stopped speaking, and before you could say *fool me once*, he'd already placed his manuscript with a prestigious academic press and been offered a tenure-track job at a top-tier university. Meanwhile, my career seemed to be over before it even began.

An obsessed sort of depression followed (which certain parties may have unjustifiably referred to as *monomaniacal*) during which I considered quitting academia altogether in favor of something less soul-sucking, like cleaning up murder scenes or inserting rusty nails under my fingernails. Thankfully, a woman in my de-partment named Danica Felton pulled me out of it. We weren't particularly close, but she was smart and funny and drank anti-quated cocktails with names like *sidecar* and *lime rickey*. When she suggested we drink some together at an oak-paneled bar near campus (Dylan Thomas is rumored to have puked there!), I finally got out of my pajamas and left the apartment.

"I'm not saying it doesn't suck, Robin," she said after her fourth gin fizz, leaning an unstable elbow on the table. "I'm saying don't let it *define* you."

"I just don't understand why he did it." The tears that now hovered perpetually on the surface of my eyes threatened to spring forth. "I thought we were friends."

"Well, you were wrong," she said with a flourish of her wrist, her charm bracelet tinkling. "Academics are evil. Don't let it ruin your career. Get out there and write a better fucking book and make him piss himself with jealousy."

"But how?" I grumbled into my beer.

"It was *your* research that he stole. That should show you that you're better at this than he is. Do it again. Find what you need, and write a book that will absolutely destroy him."

Something delicious rippled through my brain. Of course! Vengeance! Why hadn't I thought of that?

And thus my revenge dissertation was born. Buoyed as it was by rage and a desire to humiliate a freshly minted enemy, the research went quite well until I came up against a loggerhead. The infamous Joan of Arc–Gilles de Rais letter referenced a recipe for a witch's ointment that contained an herb called *sangdhuppe*, which I had thus far been unable to locate in any herbal encyclopedia. I suspected that I needed access to a set of pharmacopoeias that I couldn't seem to locate digitally or through interlibrary loan. Separately, I also needed to find confirmation of deaths by execution in fifteenth-century Rouen, and was having trouble on that front as well. One of the foundations of the witch-cult theory hinged on Murray's contention that witch executions tended to take place in sets of thirteen, which just happened to be the number necessary for a coven. I had been able to locate some of that raw data, but not enough, and I needed to confirm that Murray's accounting was accurate.

Until I could find those particulars, I wasn't able to fully explore that section of the dissertation, but I was still able to make some headway in other areas. Recently I'd been turning my attention to modern ripples of ancient witch hysteria. This was a tough one because it meant keeping up with the news, and it seemed that in recent times, the world had become increasingly violent and unhinged. Murders, brutality, horrifying examples of nearly inhuman depravity—they were everywhere I looked. A few years ago, I could expect to encounter maybe one or two such stories, but now it seemed like every single headline was designed to give me a panic attack. Was the world really getting that much more intolerable?

Mostly these forays into modernity left me empty-handed and exhausted, but now and then I would stumble onto some gold. Every once in a while, some incredibly antiquated-sounding accusation of witchcraft would crop up somewhere. Often it would be in areas that had suffered from witch-hunt troubles in the days of yore—Scotland was a big one—but sometimes it was somewhere closer.

The day everything changed, I was doing some research on recent animal attacks that were attributed to witch-adjacent mythical creatures—vampires, werewolves, and the like—when I'd stumbled onto a recent case in a tiny mountain village in the Rockies. It concerned a young woman named Sabine Étienne who had been mauled beyond recognition by a wild animal—most likely a bear—but whom locals were convinced was the victim of a werewolf attack.

"They're everywhere here," a man in the article was quoted as saying. "They breed them up there." Something about the case intrigued me. Perhaps it was the mention of an ominous *they* and the unspecified *up there* that drew my attention. A very grainy photograph of the young woman accompanied the article. I couldn't make out much of her face, but with her chic glasses and long blond tresses, she didn't exactly look like someone who might be attacked by a werewolf, though I suppose even lycanthropy can be modernized. Intrigued, I flagged the incident as something to circle back to, and for some reason, I mentioned the case to Paloma. I even showed her the photo while she was knitting.

Paloma had seemed uninterested at the time, but later that night, she started acting strange. I was reading in the living room when I saw her slowly shuffling toward the front door. There was something off about it, her movements jerky and erratic. I set my book down, stood up, and called out to her. It sounds like an exaggeration to say the hairs on the back of my neck stood on end, but that's exactly what happened. Why, I wondered, would my body react with utter terror to seeing my cousin walk toward the front door?

I called out again, but she didn't respond.

When I caught up to her, I grabbed her arm and she whipped around, the fury in her eyes almost blistering. If you'd asked me before that moment if I'd be able to identify hatred in someone's eyes, I would have said no, but that day, gazing into Paloma's absorbingly dark irises, I was certain there was no other emotion it could have been.

I took a step back without even meaning to. "Paloma, are you okay?"

Her eyes bored into me. "I know what you are."

Because I am conflict avoidant and hadn't the slightest clue what to do, I laughed and tried to play it off.

"You know what I am?" I joked with forced laughter. "You mean a lazy academic with a bit of a drinking problem?"

She smiled, but it was wrong, somehow not her smile. "Good luck with your research," was all she said, and then she turned, opened the door, and stepped out into the bustling city. I ate dinner alone that night, and when Paloma returned well after dark, she shut herself up in her room.

I awoke the next morning with a bee in my bonnet about Sabine Étienne. I poured myself a cup of coffee and settled in to work as an especially blistering sun rose over the city. After reading through my notes from the previous day, I then searched through several databases for anything I could find about the case. It wasn't long before I stumbled onto a piece in a small local paper that mentioned her. It was about the disappearance of another woman, Dr. Isabelle Casimir, who had vanished about fifteen miles from where Sabine was found dead. There was no accompanying photo, but the article referred to Casimir as a research scientist who worked at Hildegard College in Colorado. She vanished without a trace exactly three weeks after Sabine was mauled, but the article didn't mention any biographical information, not even Casimir's field of research.

The internet didn't turn up much, but I was able to find an interview with Dr. Casimir on a blog, and that was when things got interesting. She talked about a recent overseas excavation she'd been on and mentioned a discovery she'd made near Cressing Temple in Essex, describing it as "an interesting artifact. It's a sculpture that seems to show thirteen female figures in a circle, and at the center is a representation of a human with two faces." She went on to say that she had brought the relic back with her to Colorado for further study.

Could it possibly be? Thirteen female figures—the number Murray claimed was representative of a coven—and at the center, Janus, the two-faced god a sect of fertility cults was supposed to have worshiped. If I could get my hands on that statue, I could reclaim the throughline of my dissertation and potentially undermine Charles's entire argument. That could completely destroy him (and also help my career, though that was honestly secondary to me by that point). Maybe I was reading too much into it, but I suddenly felt very certain that this sculpture Dr. Casimir so casually mentioned could be the key to proving the veracity of Murray's hypothesis. My heart stilled for a moment when I remembered the fact that Casimir was missing and that another young woman was dead. Was it insensitive to think about my research when this woman might be in danger? Probably, I determined. Yes, it most definitely was.

I bit my lip and pushed my chair back from the desk. Needing some fresh air, I headed out onto the spacious balcony, stopping in the kitchen to refill my coffee. Outside, the redwood patio slats, massaged by the rays of the late-morning sun, gave off a pungent, pleasing aroma. Gripping my mug, I stared out at the city, my eyes trailing from steaming vents and jaded pigeons up to what I could make out of the glorious New York skyline. It was always possible that nothing untoward had happened to Isabelle Casimir. It wasn't wrong of me to be interested in the artifact, not if it could help fill in a missing piece of the historical record. Charles wouldn't think twice about pursuing this lead if he saw it. A sudden panic seized me. What if he already had?

After pouring myself yet another cup of bitter coffee, I settled in at my desk and pulled up Hildegard College's website. Could I just cold-call the archaeology department and ask to examine Dr. Casimir's research? Inserting myself into an active missing person case didn't seem incredibly smart, but I was feeling desperate. The joke was on me, though, because it turned out the college didn't even have an archaeology department. A quick perusal of the site made it clear that it was one of those weird colleges that decide they don't need to have typical majors (think Evergreen State and its Earth Dynamics track, or College of the Atlantic and their single human ecology major). At Hildegard, the only course of study was Anthropocene Systematics, whatever the fuck that was. Although there were several impressive photos of recognizable tech moguls standing with faculty in front of architecturally important arches, there was very little in terms of actual information about the school. The website did, however, have a good deal about their library, the offerings of which struck me as surprisingly impressive. Located in what had once been a monastery, Hildegard's library boasted extensive archives of ancient manuscripts—codices, bestiaries, and pharmacopoeias.

Further exploration of the site led me to information about a residency for academics, artists, scientists, and "thinkers" to come to Hildegard College and work on a project using their facilities. It couldn't have been more perfect. I had a feeling that what Dr. Casimir had stumbled onto was possibly the linchpin of not only my research but perhaps my entire career. I just needed to get access to it. Without missing a beat, I emailed the head librarian (a Dorian Dubois) and outlined my situation: I was working on an examination of the intersection of medical herbology and historical accusations of witchcraft (which was of course true), and access to their archives would prove invaluable to my research (which it probably would, especially if they had any rare herbology books that would help me understand the nature of *sangdhuppe*), and could I have an application for their residency, please? I just left out the creepy part about how I was actually stalking an artifact that belonged to one of their professors, who just happened to have disappeared under mysterious circumstances. Thirty minutes later, I received a reply and a link to the application, which I completed and submitted with more efficiency than I'd probably ever done anything in my life.

Meanwhile, I was walking on eggshells around Paloma. Her behavior was just so off. It was only little things at first—superstitious attachments, an uncharacteristic focus on the macabre. She seemed consumed by a pervasive, endless sense of dread. And then there were her eyes. It was like a film had been removed from them, rendering them clearer, yes, but almost violently so. A manic aura began to surround her, and without any indication as to her motives, she started adhering to increasingly bizarre rituals—taking the screens off windows and hanging strange things out of them like Coke bottles and compact mirrors. Removing screens from windows was especially upsetting: I am allergic to bee venom and was pretty sure some neighbor was operating a rooftop apiary because I kept finding dead bees inside. But when I tried to talk to Paloma about this, she denied having done anything. And then there was the night she spread coffee grounds all over the kitchen counter and used them to draw what looked like a map.

I should have done something, but I just ignored the situation. Paloma kept to herself, and I spent my days immersed in research. One afternoon when Paloma was out, I went into her room to see if she had any safety pins in her drawer. That's when I noticed her computer open with an email drafted, but not addressed to anyone in particular.

I know I shouldn't have snooped, but it wasn't so much snooping as seeing. It was hard to miss: *Help!* the missive began. And from there, it got increasingly deranged. She wrote about being kidnapped. She wrote about what sounded like monsters—she called them Terrible Ones—and was convinced that people were following her and stealing her memories. That was the day I decided to get her some medical attention. I set up an appointment with a psychiatrist in Midtown for the following week, but as it turned out, we wouldn't make it that long. The next morning she was gone. There was a note sitting on the kitchen counter.

Went to California.

That was all it said. I tried to text her, but I got no reply. When a day passed and I didn't hear from her, I thought about calling and reporting it, but who the hell would I call? She hadn't actually done anything except act a little batty and go to California without a plan. That had to describe at least 50 percent of the people currently in California. I decided to be chill about it and wait for her to return.

The days that followed—my time alone in the apartment—were to serve as my introduction to one of the strangest, most unsettling episodes in my life. Time alone shouldn't have bothered me, but there was something about the way the wind seemed to moan as it swept through the balcony railings that set my nerves on end. That first night without Paloma, I was plagued all evening by a sense of a presence.

Now, what do I mean when I say "a presence"? In woo-woo new age circles, we mean a ghost or a spirit, but I am neither woo-woo nor new age. I am persnickety, contrarian, and old beyond my years. When I say I felt a presence, I mean that I felt like someone was watching me, or like there was an actual person inside the apartment with me, something I knew to be impossible. And yet that eerie, creeping sensation of being watched persisted.

When I went to bed that night, I fell asleep easily enough, but was tormented by nightmares. The next day I still couldn't shake that horrible feeling that I wasn't alone. And then just before bed, I was working at the desk in the living room when I began, yet again, to feel uneasy. I had a bunch of papers spread out before me and was sipping orange juice to keep myself awake—I wasn't to the point of drafting, where I would drink coffee all night, but I was getting close. I was reading about a werewolf sighting in Bavaria that took place in the summer of 1816. I won't bore you with an exhaustive account of my research, but in this instance, it's worth unpacking a little. You will understand why later.

So, Bavaria, 1816, we have a peasant who swore she saw a creature attacking her lambs. Terrified, she locked herself and her children in her home and didn't dare come out until morning, at which point, she discovered that the poor lambs had been drained of blood. She didn't call it a vampire, although that's what most superstitious people would call it today. Instead, she called it a werewolf. I was tempted to categorize it as a vampire for the purposes of my research; after all, our current conception of the vampire wasn't as much in the public consciousness back then. Although the idea of the vampire was an old one, it didn't take on a life of its own until John William Polidori published his short story "The Vampyre" in 1819. Famously, in 1816—the same year the lambs in question were exsanguinated in a far-flung Bavarian province—Polidori and his much more famous friends Percy Shelley, Mary Shelley, and Lord Byron were holed up in a villa on Lake Geneva writing their ghost stories, one of which would become the "The Vampyre," and one of which would become *Frankenstein*. Eighteen-sixteen was known as the Year Without Summer because of the aberrant, dreadfully cold weather, with dark skies and black rain all caused, it would seem, by the eruption of a volcano in Indonesia disrupting weather patterns. Without that eruption, we might never have had the modern incarnation of vampires or Frankenstein's monster, or . . . or . . . whatever Byron and Percy Shelley wrote during that fateful trip.

I found it curious that this case of the Bavarian lamb-slaughtering vampire occurred in the same year that the weather patterns had been so disrupted, and I wondered if this might have anything to do with a change in the hunting habits of predator populations in the region. I was making a note of it when suddenly—I swear to you—I heard someone whispering right behind me.

With a jolt, I turned my head, but the hall was empty.

"Hello?" I called.

I turned back around and picked up my pen, but my hand was shaking so badly that I couldn't even pretend to write. All at once, the hairs on the back of my neck stood on end again. Please excuse the reuse of this cliché, but it's a genuine response to fear called piloerection, and there's just no other way to describe what happened to me.

Once again, I distinctly heard someone say:

This isn't real.

It was so loud and clear that I jumped up from my desk, knocking over my glass of orange juice, which was lapped up by the eager piles of the shag carpet. I was so terrified, though, that I didn't care. I just stared in horror.

The hallway was empty. And then I heard someone whisper:

Hell . . .

I'm embarrassed to say I screamed. I picked up my pen as if to use it as a weapon, like a girl walking alone at night.

"Who's there?" I demanded, my voice reaching octaves I didn't know were within my power.

But there was no reply. I mean . . . obviously there was no reply. The hallway was always empty.

When I looked back down at my desk, I saw that there were four symbols now in my notes—symbols I had no memory of drawing.

The next morning, I received an email from Hildegard College. I'd been accepted for their library residency. They said they could welcome me as early as the following week. That message couldn't have come a moment too soon.

1.2

DEMONOLOGY

The devil sometimes made them fall suddenly asleep; they fell to the ground and became so heavy that the strongest man had great trouble in even moving their heads.

—The History of the Devils of Loudun:
The Alleged Possession of the Ursuline Nuns,
Des Niau, translated by Edmund Goldsmid

I'd all but insisted on renting a car, but the college arranged for a driver to pick me up at the airport in Denver. He was tall and lanky with longish gray hair pulled back in a ponytail. He told me that his name was Jim and that he worked at Hildegard as a handyman. I tried to seem cheerful, but stepping out into the midday sun, I felt almost exactly as if someone had splashed hot tea in my face.

As Jim was stowing my luggage in the trunk of the big black Mercedes, I stumbled, bracing myself against the car.

"Are you all right?"

"Yeah," I said, righting myself, "just dizzy."

"You're feeling the elevation?"

"Maybe. How high up are we?"

"They don't call it the mile-high city for nothing. We'll be going up a lot higher. Close to seven thousand feet." He grew very serious. "Are you sure you want to go?"

I thought that was an odd question. I was here, wasn't I?

"Yes?" I said, slightly confused.

I could have sworn my answer upset him, but he looked away too quickly for me to be sure.

"It's important to drink plenty of water and eat lots of greens." His accent was difficult to place.

"French?" I asked.

"Yes," he said. "Many of us are French in the area around the college. It is an enclave."

That also struck me as odd. I'd heard of French-speaking areas near the Canadian border and definitely down in Louisiana, but in the middle of Colorado?

Jim got in the driver's seat and started the ignition. When I climbed into the back, I was relieved to find that the car was air-conditioned. Through the rearview mirror, I could just make out Jim's eyes. They were deep-set and hinted at a good sense of humor.

The car had a plush leather interior and smelled like the morning after a rainstorm. I noticed some bottled water in the seat back, and grabbing it, I unscrewed the top. It was too warm and slightly bitter, but I drank it enthusiastically. My lack of sleep beginning to catch up with me, I balled up my jacket and leaned against the window. I was out in no time, dreaming of Charles.

We're sitting together at a picnic table beneath a blazing orange sun, eating sweet sandwiches as bees begin to swarm. He's angry with me for leaving.

"You took everything." He scowls. "All the research."

He motions to a box that sits in front of us on the picnic table. A bee lands on my arm. I swat it away. I lift the top off the box, expecting to find pages, but instead, there are test tubes and syringes inside.

"I was just looking for my bluebird," I say, swatting away another bee.

The sound of the swarm grows louder. Angry. Soon the box is filled with bees. One lands on my neck and stings me.

"I'm allergic." I cry out in pain, looking to Charles for help, but he just laughs.

I awoke with a start and was astonished to find that in the time I'd been asleep, the landscape had changed dramatically. As we'd driven up into the mountains, the foliage had grown lush and green, and the air, though thin, was crisp and invigorating. My head was spinning from tiredness, and even the car itself seemed vaguely different, unfamiliar. I rubbed my temples and rolled down the window. A burst of fresh mountain air filled my lungs.

"You are awake," Jim said with a smile. "You slept quite a while. We are in the mountains now. Near Hildegard. We will be there soon."

Outside, rich, late-spring greenery blanketed the land. We were on a narrow road, and I had the feeling of being somewhere unknown, somewhere secret. It wasn't long before the college gates came into view. They were wrought-iron monstrosities, looping and intricate, and at their center was what appeared to be a giant heart.

"What does the heart mean?"

"What heart?" he asked.

"Right there on the gate. It's a heart, isn't it?"

"My apologies, but I don't see a heart."

Jim brought the car to a halt in front of the gates. Leaving the motor running, he dashed out and opened them with the ease of a man who had done this a hundred times. He returned to the car, smiling broadly.

He settled himself back into the driver's seat and started up a long, narrow drive, lined on both sides by magisterial quaking aspens. I wanted to ask again about the heart, but my attention was drawn to an ornate sign posted near a large oak. It read: CELUI QUI NE COMPREND PAS DEVRAIT APPRENDRE OU SE TAIRE.

"*Who does not understand should learn or be silent,*" I read. That seemed vaguely familiar, but I was still groggy and couldn't place it.

"You speak French," Jim said, obviously pleased.

"I read French, and not very well. Just enough to get by for my research. It's a strange message, isn't it? Not very welcoming."

He shrugged. "It's just one of their sayings. They have a lot. I pretend to understand them, but I am more like you. I think, let them have their sayings."

As we emerged from the long drive, the campus rose up before us. The style was Collegiate Gothic, but with a slight flair of Romanesque Revival. We drove past a redbrick bell tower with ornate windows followed by an even older-looking building. Sunk into the ivy and hellebore, it stretched out in dark stone, covered in parts by a patina of vibrant green moss.

"Is that the monastery?"

"Yes. It's a library now. Magnificent. People come from all over the world to use the books in there."

Finally we came to a stately manor.

"The chancellor's house," he said. "You'll be staying here, I believe."

Almost Mediterranean in style, it was enormous, with a creamy exterior and dark blue shutters. From the upstairs center window a balcony with a curving wrought-iron railing jutted out. It looked like the photo on a postcard of a villa on some magical isle. As the car pulled into the rounded driveway and parked, a figure emerged from the front door. He was hand-some, probably in his mid-thirties.

"Ms. Quain, it's so nice to have you." His dark hair was pushed up and out of his eyes. He gave me a winning smile. Dressed somewhat extravagantly in a dark burgundy blazer and expensive-looking slacks, he looked like he would be more at home in a club in Soho than in a library in the middle of the Rocky Mountains. "I'm Dorian Dubois, the head librarian. We corresponded through email, but of course it is a pleasure to meet you finally in person."

"It's great to meet you as well," I said, trying to get my bear-ings. The grounds were gorgeous, but the altitude was definitely a concern. The air was so thin I could barely breathe. "It's quiet," was the most cogent thing I could think to say.

Dorian lifted my luggage and led me inside. "Hildegard is a very small school. We cap enrollment at three hundred."

"Only three hundred students?" I stopped in the foyer of what was proving to be an obscenely gorgeous house.

"Small is the way we like it at Hildegard. We like to think of ourselves as offering a one-of-a-kind educational experience, and one of a kind by its very nature isn't for everyone. And now everyone has gone home for the summer."

"Everyone?"

"There is a skeleton crew, of course. We're glad to have you here," he continued. "It will be good to have some new blood around." He lowered his voice, creating an air of unearned inti-macy between us. "We've recently had a faculty member leave, and none of us is very happy about it. So if people seem a little squirrelly, that will explain it."

My heart beat a violent tarantella against my rib cage. This was my chance. "The professor who left, may I ask their field of expertise?"

"Cognitive neuro-programming," he said.

So not archaeology after all. Interesting. Dorian led me into a large central room. From the ceiling hung an ancient-looking chandelier, but it wasn't lit. To my right, affixed to the wall, was a large bronze heart embossed with the image of a face, and to my left was a marble table on top of which sat a vase of wildflowers. As we made small talk, I followed Dorian along the baked red tile that lined the floor and up an enormously wide staircase.

At the top of the stairs, Dorian paused and pointed down the hall to his left. "I'm just down there if you need anything. And if you'll follow me this way," he said, stopping outside a door at the end of the hall. "Your room."

When he opened the door, I was nearly blinded. All the windows were open, and the room was flooded with sunlight. I could hear birdsong lilting up from the eaves beyond the window casements. The room was large and lavishly decorated with purples and blues. An intricate flower pattern adorned the walls, and the sitting area was comprised of a puffy chair and love seat in a matching print. In the far corner there was a writing desk that looked out on a large vaulted window. I set my bag down on a gorgeous four-poster bed made of dark wood and piled high with fluffy white bedding before wandering over to the window.

Outside, the grounds stretched through a series of intricate gardens and twisting paths down to a crystal-blue lake from which arose a small island, brilliant green and exploding with plant life. Beyond the lake lay a majestic pine forest.

"I didn't realize there was a lake."

"If you enjoy swimming, there is a pool on campus, but I'm afraid the lake is much too cold to swim in."

I nodded and then stared back out at the expansive grounds. It was a breathtaking view, but I was struck by the noticeable lack of activity. I wondered how different it might feel during the school year.

"Well, you must be eager to get to your work," Dorian said, snapping me out of my reverie. "The archives are located in the nave of the old monastery. The entire building has been converted into a library, with the scriptorium belowground. I expect you'll be spending most of your time down there. There is also a small herbal library attached to the apothecary garden, which I'm sure you'll want to make use of."

"There's a physick garden here?" That could prove promising.

"Yes, of course. It's a replica of a famous one. We call it the apothecary garden, though. Would you like to get refreshed, or if you're keen, I can show you the library."

"Rest is for the dead."

His smile was broad. "A girl after my own heart. The library it is, then."

Dorian led me downstairs and through the house, and soon we were wending our way along a dark passage and then out and through a covered walkway, speckled with moss the color of a ripe avocado, and into the entrance to the old monastery. Inside that ancient structure, the atmosphere felt starkly different. What had once been the nave had been converted into a library, with books stretching up and across as far as the eye could see. Dorian continued on through toward a stairwell, but I stayed put, staring in awe at that magnificent space. A door high up between the shelves caught my eye. For just a second, I could barely breathe. That door—I'd seen it somewhere before, I was almost sure of it. In a childhood dream, perhaps.

"Where does that door lead?"

"That's an old wing. It's closed off now," he said, continuing on.

"The monks' quarters?"

"At one point, but not anymore. Come, I want to show you the scriptorium."

Together we started down a dark, circular stairwell. As we descended, our way lit by wall sconces, the air grew frigid.

"It's important to keep the manuscripts cold," Dorian explained. "But I'm sure you know that."

At the bottom of the stairwell, we passed through a stone arch, but almost as soon as we did, I backtracked and pointed up at a carving at the apex of the arch. At first it appeared to be a crude rendering of a heart, but on closer inspection, it wasn't a heart at all. It was a snake eating its own tail.

"Is that an ouroboros?"

"Hm?" He seemed distracted. "I think so."

Throughout history, a variety of different meanings have been ascribed to the ouroboros, everything from the cyclical nature of time to fertility to immortality. It was even said that our understanding of the structure of benzene sprang from the ouroboros. German organic chemist August Kekulé dreamed of an ouroboros and woke up with the knowledge that the carbon atoms that composed benzene were structured in a ring formation mirroring the structure of the ouroboros. It was a universal symbol, to be sure, but it was gnostic and alchemical, not something that would typically appear in a monastery.

"Why is it in a church?"

He shrugged. "This place is old. I don't know everything about it."

"But it's not a Christian symbol."

It wasn't clear if he hadn't heard me or if he chose to ignore me, but he left my observation unacknowledged and continued on, leading me into a scriptorium filled with old oak tables. The vaulted ceilings and cold stone walls gave the impression of a catacomb, and when I breathed in the cool air, a sweet tangle of scents swept over me. Through the space, I scanned the area, looking for Dr. Casimir's relic, even though I knew it was unlikely I would find it down here.

"Are you okay?" Dorian asked.

"Fine," I said, crossing my arms over my chest and indicating a narrow corridor with my chin. "What's through there?"

"Most of what you're looking for. Come on."

I followed him through to a back room and was astonished to see row after row of shelves filled with leather-bound manuscripts—mostly what looked like religious tracts, but also a good deal of what had to be pharmacopoeia, bestiaries, and the like. It was an absolute gold mine.

I pulled out an herbal text. "There is an herb I've been trying to locate information on. You wouldn't happen to know anything about rare herbs, would you?"

He shook his head. "Not my area, I'm afraid, but you're welcome to comb through anything in our collection. I'll give you a key and you can work down here as much as you like," he said, noticing my enthusiasm. However, my excitement turned to dizziness, and I thought I might even faint. I steadied myself on the edge of a desk. He gently took my arm.

"Are you all right?"

"Just dizzy, I think I might need to lie down for a bit."

"Of course," he said. "Altitude sickness is fairly common up here."

"Is that what this is?"

My temples throbbed, and my heart beat so loudly in my head that it was hard to hear much else. I'd read about altitude sickness, but had never experienced it—something to do with the body not getting enough oxygen as it attempts to adjust to the lower levels available at extreme heights.

"It should pass if you rest and hydrate. Let's get you to your room."

When we arrived back at my quarters, he gave me a gentle pat on the back. "I'll have your dinner brought up to you—we've a marvelous cook, and all our produce is grown right here at Hildegard—and if your symptoms worsen, we will have you examined."

"I don't want to be any trouble."

"You're no trouble at all. Eat, rest, and you can get started with your work as soon as you're feeling up to it."

After Dorian left, I made my way over to the window and opened it, letting the fresh mountain air wash over me. In the distance, the tops of large pine trees swayed like fragile dancers. An array of brightly colored birds flitted through the garden, darting between hedgerows and fountains. Leaning farther out, I inhaled deeply. The air was amazing, fresh and fragrant, riven through with a hint of floral spice I couldn't quite identify. From my perch high above the rest of campus, I felt like a cartographer staring down at her map, tracing lines from building to building, from garden to garden.

After showering, I felt a little better, so I set my computer up on the rustic oak desk and streamed some shows, mostly old episodes of *The Twilight Zone*, including my favorite, the one about a mannequin who gets lost in a department store. Later that evening, Dorian arrived at my door bearing an enormous tray filled with delicacies: cassoulet, fresh salad, rolls, and even crème brûlée. After he set it down, he pulled a bottle of Advil from his pocket.

"Thank Christ," I said, immediately downing a couple.

"You look like you're feeling better."

"I think I am."

"Eating will help. I can sit with you, if you like."

I dragged a wingback chair over and we sat together, talking while I ate.

"The land is gorgeous here," I said. "And the air is something else."

"This entire area is breathtaking. And there's a village a few miles down the mountain. It's an interesting spot, settled by a small group of French immigrants in the nineteenth century. They still speak the language in the village. Hardly any English."

I set my water down and chose my words carefully. "I read about the town. Petit Rouen, isn't it? A young woman was killed there recently, right? An animal attack?"

There was a long pause, and immediately I regretted speaking too soon. He cleared his throat.

"Excuse me," he said, his tone heavy. "You must forgive me. I didn't want to burden you with our recent troubles, but yes, a young woman was killed down in the village, and as you know, our dear friend Professor Casimir left not long after. The trouble, you see, is that no one has heard from her since. There is no logical reason to connect the two incidents, but they happened such a short time apart that one fears . . ."

"I'm sorry about your friend," I said, the enormity of the situation really hitting home. Isabelle Casimir wasn't just some cardboard cutout representing the apotheosis of my research pursuits; she was an actual person with friends and loved ones who were obviously worried about her. I felt a squalid emptiness inside my chest that slowly began to fill with guilt. "Can I ask about the circumstances? Do you have reason to believe she was . . . that something bad happened to her? Could she maybe have just left without telling anyone where she was going?"

"That is what the authorities think. She did take a bag with her, and her ID and her phone were missing. But it was so unlike her. She gave no indication that she was going to do anything strange. She was working on a big project at the time. I'm sure she would have wanted to see it through."

"But if she took her ID, at least you know it was planned to some degree."

"Yes," he said, but his tone made it clear he didn't actually believe what he was saying. "But my fear is that she went into the woods. The woods here are very dangerous. You must never go off the marked trails. Never. There's a history, you see. And she disappeared at night. If she went into the woods at night and came across . . . You know, bears take the bodies back to their dens. We might never find her."

"But why would you think she would go into the woods in the middle of the night?"

"We just don't know what happened. One moment she was here, the next she was gone. To understand Isabelle, you'd really have to understand this place. It's more than just a college; it's a community, and during the summers, those of us that stay on campus form bonds that go beyond just being colleagues. In some ways, Isabelle was the epicenter of those bonds."

He went on for some time, describing the card games, the soirees, the shared meals. To hear him tell it, it was hard to imagine how any of them ever got any work done. It sounded like carousing with Jazz Age artists and intellectuals. One could practically hear Zelda Fitzgerald throwing a jealous fit on some champagne-soaked terrace.

At one point, he disappeared down the hall and returned holding a single photo. In it, Dorian stood smiling between a man and woman, both in their late twenties. They looked positively joyous—bright smiles and outstretched arms. You could almost hear the echoes of distant laughter, the festive music that must have filled the air, and immediately I was gripped by an uncanny ache for a life I'd never had.

"That's Finn Jeon," Dorian said, pointing to the man in the photo. Asian, with attractively tousled hair and a chin line like cut glass, he was smoking a cigarette with so much aplomb that I found myself momentarily wishing the habit would come back in style. "He's in systems science. And that's Aspen Thomas, our director of horticulture. If you're interested in herbology, you will want to talk to her."

Aspen was Black with a nose piercing and Clara Bow lips, and she seemed to be in the midst of a flapper dance, her right leg kicked out to the side to reveal knee-high boots and sparkling tights. The general air was one of very glamorous, fun people cutting loose with wild abandon. They were a lot cooler and looked like a lot more fun than the academics in my department, and I felt a twinge of jealousy, or perhaps it was a vestigial longing for acceptance. I suddenly wondered if they might be hiring a historian anytime soon.

Taking a closer look at the photo, I noticed a blond woman standing a few feet behind the others, her face just out of the frame.

"Who's that? It's not Professor Casimir, is it?"

"No, Isabelle was taking the photo, if I remember correctly. That's Lexi Duarte. She's our behavioral psychologist. She's actually a distant cousin of mine. I think you'll like her."

"Is she here this summer?"

"Yes. Aspen and Finn are as well."

Conversation wound down after that, and once my dinner was finished, he took the tray and bid me good night. After pulling on my obscenely soft pajamas, I turned out the lights and sat on the spacious windowsill a while, staring out at the purple sky. My attention was drawn down to the woods momentarily when I thought I saw a flash of a brilliant white light issuing from the tree line. Focusing in on the area, I waited to see if it happened again, but it didn't, so I opened the window, took a deep breath, and once again was lost in the ache that rose up when I was alone. I was better now, but when things went south with Charles, I was truly an abject mess. My mom used to say that usually when I thought I was mad, I was actually just hurt. And I was hurt—deeply hurt—but when it came to Charles, couldn't I be both?

We used to go to this Russian bar on the Lower East Side that served flavored vodka in little crystal decanters. We'd sit inside for hours, the lighting soft and warm on winter nights, and we'd talk. On those glorious evenings, time seemed to expand, as if the world around us had stopped and there was nothing but laughter and a deeply joyous calm. In the aftermath of the rupture, I was sick with the loss of that friendship. It sounds cliché, but it genuinely felt like losing a part of myself. You read about heartache, when people say they can't sleep or eat, and I always thought, *Yeah yeah yeah, but you still eat, like, breakfast and snacks and stuff, right? You still sleep, like, at least five hours, right?* But it turns out clichés are clichés for a reason. Food repulsed me. I cried so much and so fiercely that I didn't have the energy to get out of bed some days. And the nights were somehow even worse. When I closed my eyes, all I saw were the happy times, the person I used to know, the sense of being whatever the opposite of alone is. But here I was again, alone. Perhaps that was just my fate.

As I sat in the windowsill, I poked at those emotional wounds like a tongue running over an aching tooth, and no doubt I would have gone on like that for hours, but then I saw that light again. Out in the woods, it flashed unmistakably, a series of beats. Morse code? I was just leaning out to get a closer look when a single terrible howl rose up, a monstrous pained growl that drifted out over the trees and up toward the pale moon. I pulled away from the window, stunned.

My mind immediately went to werewolves, though I knew that was ridiculous. My research was getting to me. It was a dog, that was all, and I had gotten way too used to the city. I closed the window and drew the curtains. Climbing into bed, I turned out the light, and before I could even take in a breath, it was as though the room suddenly dimmed. Confused, I tried to reach for the light, but to my utter horror, I could no longer move my limbs. Inside my body, I stretched and strained, but outwardly, I remained totally immobile. I couldn't move a muscle. Trying not to panic, I did my best to take deep, steady breaths. I'd read about this state—sleep paralysis. It was a common phenomenon, no more than a parasomnia in which waking states and REM states overlapped, resulting in the cognizance of wakefulness with the normal muscle paralysis associated with deep sleep. It would pass eventually. I just needed to ride it out.

However, as I lay there, unable to control any part of my body—except for my eyelids, which, curiously, I was able to open and close at will—it soon became clear that understanding the science behind the disorder did nothing to relieve the visceral terror of actually experiencing it. No wonder people throughout history equated it with demon possession. It really felt like there was some demonic force holding sway over me. It truly was unnerving. I didn't believe in witches or demons, but if I had grown up in a culture that gave credence to such things, I would have been close to losing my mind with fear. The truth was, there was something about the experience that simply felt *wrong*. It felt malevolent.

I was doing my best to stay calm when once again that terrible howl rose up. It was deafening and I closed my eyes against it.

When I opened them again, I was outside.

Cool evening air brushed against my cheek as I stared around in horror. With a cold shock I realized I had no idea where I was or how I'd gotten there. Just a moment before, I had been in bed dreaming, but now I was fully awake, standing outside on a garden path in the dead of night. Trying to get my bearings, I realized I was on a brick walkway on Hildegard's grounds, not far from the main house. How I had gotten down here, though, was anyone's guess. In front of me stood a blue-and-white cabana, the blues turned to shadow by the waxing gibbous moon. The sign above the door read: DR. ISABELLE CASIMIR.

Around me the night seemed to beat, a thick blackness that throbbed despite the clarity of the starlit sky above. I stared straight ahead at that door, feeling a terrible compulsion to go toward it. My heart raced and my brow was sprinkled with sweat. As if moved by some unseen force, I walked toward it and turned the handle, but it jarred, the door firmly locked.

Somewhere far off, an owl screeched and terror shot through

me. I knew with every fiber of my being that I had to get out of there. I bolted up the path back toward the house, where I found a set of French doors standing wide open. Apparently this was how I'd gotten outside, but I couldn't for the life of me remember opening them. I hurried inside, careful to lock up behind me, and then crept upstairs as quietly as I could.

Once inside my room, I locked the door and got back in bed. Had I seriously started sleepwalking? How was that possible? To sleepwalk, one must fall asleep, and I was absolutely certain I hadn't fallen asleep. The room had seemed to dim, but I'd never lost consciousness. I'd been awake the whole time. Hadn't I?

I'm not sure when I drifted off, and although I must have dreamed, it seemed instead that I was consumed by a velvety darkness. From within that darkness, I was aware of an onslaught of strange noises as if something large were moving just beneath my window—heavy legs, labored grunts—but when I awoke just after dawn, I found the terrace completely empty, save for a pair of blue swallowtail butterflies that landed on the balustrade momentarily before flitting away again.

1.3

LYCANTHROPY

The Were-Wolf is a fearsome beast. He lurks within the thick forest, mad and horrible to see. All the evil that he may, he does. He goeth to and fro about the solitary place, seeking man, in order to devour him.

—MARIE DE FRANCE, TWELFTH CENTURY

I didn't want to disturb anyone, so I spent my first morning at Hildegard up in my room doing some light reading and feeling generally positive about life. It was true that my uncharacteristic bout of sleepwalking had left me uneasy when I'd first awakened, but as dawn bled into a heavenly morning, I began to feel alive with possibility. I couldn't stop thinking about Casimir's relic. Thirteen figures and a two-faced god—it seemed very likely that this could reverse popular opinion of Murray's work and vindicate my own. Of course it would need to be authenticated, but I had a feeling deep down that we were dealing with the real thing here. I just had to get my hands on it.

The possibility of the relic meant that my dissertation had taken on a decidedly more exciting tenor. Suddenly my lot in life had gone from pitiful to potentially important within the span of a few months. It was a reminder, I supposed, that the wheel of life is always turning. Apexes swiftly plummet to nadirs, but nadirs never need trap us for long.

Once I heard stirring downstairs, I wrapped up my work and

began readying myself for the day. After brushing my teeth, I tried to make myself look presentable (academic presentable, which isn't saying much), slipped on some shoes, and headed out into the hallway. Downstairs, I stood mesmerized by the daylight view out the grand French doors that opened onto the terrace. The sky was the color of a tropical sea, and nasturtiums and bougainvillea dripped from trellises just outside.

Finding myself alone, I took the opportunity to poke around. Until I knew more about Casimir, I had to assume that the artifact could be anywhere. As quietly as I could, I started down a narrow hallway. When I came upon a room with a piano in it, I slipped inside and looked around, scanning shelves, looking on every surface. Satisfied it wasn't in there, I returned to the hall and walked until I reached what appeared to be an old-fashioned flower room. There was a large counter, a deep sink, and a surplus of glass cabinets filled with vases, but nothing else of note.

"Feeling better?" Dorian's voice came from behind me, and I whipped around to see his smiling face.

"Yes. Thankfully."

"Come in to breakfast, and once you have eaten, you can get to work in the archives."

I followed him down the hall and into a formal dining room, its walls painted a vibrant blue. A silver coffeepot sat atop a long, intricately carved oak table. Cups made of delicate porcelain were set near a basket of fresh pastries. I poured myself some coffee, grabbed a croissant, and sank into a high-backed wooden chair with a deliciously soft blue cushion. The croissant was warm and fluffy, with a wonderfully buttery lightness.

"Professor Duarte may join us. She's finishing up some work, but she's eager to meet you. Everyone is," he said, sliding into a chair kitty-corner to mine.

"So you live here alone?"

He looked slightly embarrassed. "My father is the chancellor. I've lived here since I was a boy."

"Nice if you can get it." I gazed out the window at the bright blue sky beyond. "And the campus looks amazing. I'd love to get out and explore."

"I'll make sure you have a tour of the grounds this morning, and then we'll have lunch with the others."

I knew by *the others* that he meant the attractive pair from the photograph. Just looking at them had made me feel like a tumble-dried cat. In academic circles, everyone always wants to test your accomplishments—What have you published? Where did you study? etc.—and I knew how to play that game even though I hated it, but I wasn't sure about the rules here. I had a vague fear that someone might try to measure my waist or judge the intellectual merit of my work based on my lack of facial symmetry.

"In the meantime," he continued, "is there anything I can help you with?"

The relic was on the tip of my tongue, but it didn't seem like the right moment to ask about it. I didn't want to risk seeming too eager and arouse suspicion. "No," I said. "Not right now, thanks."

"Well, if you need anything, I'll be in my office. It's right down the hall from here and to your left. Next to the music room."

"Just out of curiosity"—I cleared my throat and tried to sound casual—"where is Professor Casimir's office?"

For a second, I thought I caught a glimmer of suspicion in his eye, but it quickly faded. "Funny you should ask. It's actually just off from the scriptorium."

That seemed odd to me. Why would a neuroscientist have her office down there? I didn't press it, though. I just took another bite of my croissant and nodded.

When breakfast was over, I headed down to the archives to work, but as I passed through that glorious library, the door on the upper landing caught my eye once again. It couldn't hurt to have a look, could it? Setting my things down on one of the wooden tables, I started up the unstable stairs, grasping the railings for balance. When I reached the door at the top, the handle turned with a creak and the door opened onto a long, thin corridor, illuminated by a stained-glass window at the far end that depicted Virgin Mary cradling an olive branch in her lap like one might hold a baby. On the left side of the corridor was a single imposing ornately carved oak door. I tried the handle, but unfortunately it was locked. So much for secret passages leading me directly to the artifact. I climbed back down the rickety stairwell and readied myself for work.

Down in the scriptorium, I set my bags on one of the tables and went to investigate. I found Casimir's office in the back of the scriptorium, but it was fairly underwhelming. Windowless, it didn't contain much more than a metal desk and a wooden chair. It gave the impression that she hadn't spent much time there, and it seemed like someone had made quick work of clearing it out after she left. There was a closet filled with office supplies, but little else. I'd been hoping her computer might have still been there and that she might at least have photos of the relic on it, but there was nothing. Still, I would keep an eye out. There were some people who still insisted on keeping hard copies of their work. Charles was one; mistrustful of relying solely on technology, he always printed his work out and kept it in binders. I often teased him about being a Luddite, but he was the one with the tenure-track job, so the joke was on me.

I closed up the office, intent on looking through some herbal texts. My first day, I had noticed what I thought might be a fairly old translation of the *Shennong Bencaojing*—one of the earliest pharmacopoeias. Although Western and Chinese herbalism were very different practices, I thought it couldn't hurt to diversify my existing, albeit scant, herbal knowledge. My time in academia had taught me to never discount the role of serendipity in research, and while I had such an impressive collection of herbal texts at my disposal, I might as well widen my scope.

However, before I reached the herbal section, I found myself drawn to the many shelves lined with bestiaries. The monstrous, that was what had originally catalyzed my interest in folklore. In my dissertation, I had quite a bit about modern accounts of monsters, but it was the ancient ones that truly fascinated me. In the Western world, the origin of the bestiary was a text called *Physiologus*. Of unknown authorship, it appeared in the second century BCE, and was one of the first to discuss the unicorn and the phoenix. However, it was hardly the first text to mention monsters. In Asia, the *Physiologus* was predated by two centuries by the *Shan Hai Jing*. Also of unknown authorship, it was one of the first texts to describe dragons and sea monsters. A century prior to that, Herodotus gave us a collection of monsters in his *Histories*, upon which Pliny the Elder extrapolated in *The Natural History*. However, the bestiary as we know it developed directly from the *Physiologus*.

I selected three codices from the shelves and brought each over, laying them out on the table. In movies, people always put gloves on when examining a rare book, but in reality, it's best to handle them with bare hands. The oils in our hands are actually beneficial for them. If only people were inherently less damaging to each other than we are to books.

The first, composed in Latin, was a fairly standard bestiary. My guess was it was probably written somewhere between the twelfth and fourteenth centuries. It contained many of the usual contents—unicorns, sea serpents, griffins—but the craftsmanship was extraordinary. The second was similar, though perhaps not much to write home about.

The final book, though, was absolutely extraordinary. It was gorgeous, with exceptionally supple pages, the softest parchment I'd ever touched. Inside were the most glorious drawings of plants, rendered in vibrant, almost succulent color. And the edges! Marked with curlicued filigree, they were works of art in and of themselves. I'd perused rare manuscripts plenty of times before, but there was something altogether different about this—it bordered on a religious experience.

Paging through it, I was surprised to find that while it was mostly composed in Latin, there were also elements of a different, much older-seeming language as well. Interspersed in the text of what appeared to be a bestiary was a mixture of curious diagrams, illustrations, and maps. I was reminded momentarily of the Voynich manuscript, that inscrutable fifteenth-century codex, the mysterious contents of which served as a perennial topic of debate in academic as well as occult circles, but this wasn't the Voynich or any manuscript of which I was aware. I wanted to linger over the text, but herbology called. With a heavy heart, I returned the book to the shelf, but I told myself I would revisit it when I had the time.

In the Joan of Arc–Gilles de Rais letter, a blurry screenshot of which I had on my phone (retrieved from a digital archive), Gilles de Rais wrote about an arcane magical text that he believed contained an alchemical recipe for immortality. It wasn't clear what that recipe was, but he did note three ingredients: petales d'aconit, racine d'angélique, and sangdhuppe—aconite, angelica, and a third, unknown substance. Despite my best efforts, I'd been unable to uncover anything about this rare text, but if sangdhuppe was in any of the pharmacopoeia, then I might be one step closer to proving that Joan of Arc and Gilles de Rais were actually members of a witch cult, potentially proving that witch cults were real. Take that, Charles.

After searching around in the back, I selected a stack of herbal texts, spread them out on the desk around me, and got to work. None of them contained any mention of sangdhuppe, but where the other herbs were concerned, they were definitely illuminating. For instance, I knew that angelica had been used in traditional medicine as a "woman's tonic" for centuries and that it treated a variety of symptoms associated with painful and irregular menstruation. It was still considered an effective medicinal, most likely due to the phenols, terpenoids, and phytoestrogens it contained, but what I found in the first few herbal compendiums I consulted was altogether unexpected. They focused on angelica's magical properties as opposed to its healing properties. For instance, one text, *Isak's Language of Hermetic Plants,* noted that it was the herb of choice for hexing gossiping women, and another claimed it was used primarily to break curses.

I encountered similar results when I looked into aconite, which though highly toxic was used in trace amounts as an analgesic in various traditional medicines. In these texts, though, it was considered a sacred herb and was mostly used to communicate with the inhabitants of the underworld. It was looking like my residency was going to be much more useful than I'd expected.

No sangdhuppe so far, but then a thought occurred to me. Might this be another name for some kind of metal? Nothing about Gilles de Rais made me think he could be an alchemist, and the process of mixing aconite and angelica was pretty far removed from turning metal into gold, but he had used the term *alchemical* when describing the recipe, so perhaps it was more of a substance than a plant. Referring to non-plant matter as herbs wasn't unheard of. Traditional Chinese medicine practitioners, for instance, had long used oyster shells as part of formulas to "calm the spirit," and in small doses, the velvet from discarded deer antlers was used as a yang tonic. But that got me thinking. Maybe I was going about this all wrong. Maybe I needed to consult a book of herbal formulas instead of combing through single herbs.

I was just about to get up and go in search of such a text when I noticed an elegantly dressed woman standing in the doorway to the scriptorium.

"Find something interesting?"

She was fashionably tall, and she wore a blue suede pencil skirt with high leather boots. Her purple blouse was sleeveless and silk with a ruffled collar, and she wore her medium-length golden hair in waves that gave her an unexpected innocence. She was hands down the most gorgeous woman I had ever seen.

"I'm Lexi Duarte," she said with a charming smile as she strode over and offered her hand.

Awestruck, I stood and shook it. Staring up at her, I was reminded of the one time I'd been around an actual model, feeling minuscule and insignificant in comparison.

"I'm so glad you've come to use our library." She had just a hint of an accent, and her dark eyes held my gaze an uncomfortably long time, almost as if searching for something in particular.

Those eyes were odd, seemingly filled with emotion, though the precise emotion I would be hard-pressed to name.

"It's wonderful you were able to join us for the summer."

She was staring at me intently as if searching for something very important. Her breath was even a little ragged, as if she had just exerted herself.

"Dorian tells me you'd like a tour of the grounds," she said with a tense smile.

"That would be fantastic." I started to pack up my things, but an elegant flick of her wrist seemed to communicate that there was no need. I could leave my things here. It was that kind of a place.

I followed her up the stairs to the main library, and as we walked, I couldn't help but notice a tension between us, as if an alarming degree of electrical energy was circulating between us, repelling us almost like magnets.

The grounds were even more lavish than I had been able to discern from my bedroom window, and the air was so fresh and crisp it made me feel newly alive. We strolled along the paths, through the full color wheel of flowers: the arching birds-of-paradise, the fluttering lantana, the wisteria-heavy trellises. It was like a bejeweled wonderland, a monumental garden fit for royalty.

After leading me down a flight of stone steps, Lexi walked me along a gravel path that led to the lake, that little island sitting at the center of it like a lonely beauty. The water was a brilliant blue with an opaqueness to it that struck me as odd. A short pier jutted out over the water and toward the island on jagged-looking wood pilings, a section of which had been worn away as if something had been repeatedly tied to it, but there was no boat in sight.

"You're welcome to come down here as much as you like—we find it's a good spot for meditation—but I'm afraid . . ."

"Right, no swimming. Dorian told me. Too cold."

"Actually, it's environmental," she said with a tilt of her head. "There are several species of endangered fish, and of course you can see by the color that the ecosystem is quite delicate. So we ask that you don't put so much as a toe in. And the island is off-limits."

"That's why you removed the boat?"

She nodded gravely. "We had an incident." She clapped her hands, her mood shifting abruptly. "Now let me show you the apothecary garden."

As I followed Lexi down a side path that led to the same brick walkway I'd traversed the previous night, anxiety rose in my belly. I hadn't wanted to mention my night excursion to anyone. I'd never experienced sleep paralysis or sleepwalking before, and it wasn't like it was going to happen again, so I didn't want to call attention to it, but now that we were here, I suddenly felt like an interloper. I didn't know much about how sleepwalking worked, but I'd read that people could do all kinds of things during an episode, even drive a car. Some part of me must have been conscious enough to leave the house and find Casimir's cabana, but why?

Was I so desperate to find the relic that my subconscious had begun acting as a free agent? I'd read some about somnambulism and knew that people were actually capable of committing crimes while asleep. There had even been cases of sleepwalkers being acquitted of crimes because they were afflicted with what was called non-insane automatism due to somnambulism. But the question remained: Even if a person's conscious mind had no desire to commit that crime, was it possible that they were spurred into action by a subconscious drive so strong that although it could be repressed during waking hours, it couldn't be contained during sleep? Not that I had committed any kind of crime, I told myself as I stood there, beads of guilty sweat nonetheless beginning to form on my brow.

In the light of day, the cabanas lined up alongside the path had a bright Caribbean feel to them, the blue of their wooden shutters bringing to mind pineapples and tropical breezes. As we passed one, I could hear laughter trickling out from between the blue shutters, and for a moment I thought I recognized one of the voices.

"Some of the faculty housing is down here. Hildegard College is unique in that . . ."

Lexi stopped suddenly and stared at the front door of what I now realized was Dr. Casimir's cottage.

"That's strange."

She strode up the flagstone path to what I now saw was an open door. Panic surged through my body. Had I misremembered the night before? Had the door actually been unlocked when I tried it? Cautiously Lexi opened it and stepped inside.

"I'm just going to check that nothing is amiss," she called over her shoulder. "I'm sure it's fine, but I really should check. You're welcome to come inside."

I did so with some trepidation. Luckily, I hadn't scrawled *Robin wuz here* on the wall or anything. The cabana was lovely, decorated in rosewood and teak with island prints. A plush bed took up the majority of the space, but there was also an alcove with an elegant sitting area and a mid-century writing desk. In the back was a bathroom and a kitchenette. The walls were dotted with tasteful artwork, and French doors led out into a small back garden.

Quickly I scanned the room. I didn't really think Casimir would keep an ancient artifact in her own living quarters, but I knew so little about the woman that I didn't want to rule anything out. I still didn't understand what a neuroscientist would be doing on an archaeological dig, or for that matter, why she would have been allowed to take the piece back to her own institution. There had to be something more to the story, but it was hard to make any assumptions without knowing anything about the woman.

Something about one of the paintings caught my eye, and I moved to take a closer look. It was a nature scene that showed a pair of cardinals perched on the edge of a fountain. As I stared at their crimson plumage, I was reminded of the dream I'd had on the way to Hildegard, of that odd compulsion to find my bluebird. I had no idea what it could mean, but it suddenly felt terribly urgent.

"Everything okay?" Lexi asked.

"Yes," I said, startled. "It's a lovely painting."

"It was one of Dr. Casimir's favorites."

"Dorian told me about her," I said, trying to seem casual. "She sounds like a fascinating woman."

"Oh, she was—our most promising researcher," she said, and again I sensed she was on the precipice of some intense emotion that she was trying very hard to suppress. "I'm sorry she'll not be continuing on. And even more sorry that she felt a need to leave without giving notice or the decency to let us know what she was thinking."

I craned my neck to get a better view of the garden patio. "I peeked in her office this morning and I noticed there isn't much in there. I was wondering where her things are."

"Why?" Lexi asked, blinking slowly.

"I was just thinking she might have left something behind in there, something that might give you a clue where she went."

"Hmm, that's a thought," she said somewhat absently, but if I was hoping for an invitation to go search it, it seemed none was forthcoming.

We started to leave, but when Lexi reached the door, she stopped and looked at me, raising her eyebrows as if surprised by her own idea. "You know, you're welcome to take over this bungalow if you like. There's no reason you should be trapped up at the house when this is standing empty. Would that interest you?"

I tried to seem nonchalant, but I was already imagining prying up floorboards and digging in the garden for the artifact.

"That might be nice," I said. "If it's no trouble for you, that is."

"Of course not. I'll have your things brought down this afternoon."

With the air of a petulant queen, Lexi started back down the brick path, and I followed, nodding enthusiastically as she pointed out several greenhouses, a hothouse, and a seemingly endless succession of fountains. At one point I noticed a forest path marked with an ancient-looking sign that read TO OBSERVATORY, and I made a note to ask about it later. The brick path eventually gave way to dirt as we wound through the grounds, the surrounding foliage growing denser and thicker. As we were passing a stone statue of a peacock, something caught my eye. In the distance, I could just make out a magisterial-looking building with a slate roof.

"What's that over there?"

"Academic buildings. Classrooms mostly, though Dr. Jeon

and I have our offices in there. You'll meet him at lunch. We eat most of our meals together here. It's the Hildegard way."

We continued on until finally we descended a flight of flagstone steps into a beautiful garden area partially enclosed by a rustic wooden fence. From an old-fashioned mint copper roof hung a hand-carved wooden sign that read APOTHECARY GARDEN. Where the other gardens had been spaces of elaborate, even uninhibited beauty, this space spoke of structure and simplicity, of regimentation and precision, but most of all, it was a peaceful place, the kind of place where time tends to disappear. Herbs grew plentifully in mathematically organized patches, and tools hung evenly spaced from trellises.

Almost immediately, we were greeted by the Black woman with the nose ring from Dorian's photo—the one doing the flapper kick. Diminutive, with an ebullient kind of beauty, she wore work clothes that still managed to make her look cool, like a celebrity dressing down in an effort to disguise herself. Clipboard in hand, she stood over a row of tall plants topped with vibrant yellow flowers. When she saw us, she set the clipboard down and approached with a transfixing smile.

"You must be Robin Quain." She shook my hand. "Welcome."

"Dr. Thomas is the director of horticulture here at the college."

"Call me Aspen," she said with a genial flick of her wrist. I noticed her charm bracelet jingle when she moved.

"I like your bracelet," I said. "My friend has one just like it."

"Thanks," she said, toying absently with it. "Would you like a cup of tea? I can brew some up in the garden house." She tilted her chin toward a charming wooden structure that stood a hundred feet or so from the entrance to the garden. Beyond that, the plants continued to stretch out in what seemed like infinite rows of greenness.

"Not right now, but I'd love to take you up on it sometime."

"Well, welcome to Hildegard. If there's anything in the way of botany or herbalism I can help you with, just let me know."

"You don't happen to know what sangdhuppe is, do you?"

Quick eyes darted around the garden as if she were performing an inventory of her realm. "I'm afraid I've never heard of it. Is it a plant?"

"I'm not sure, actually."

She pursed her lips. "Nothing's ringing a bell. Are you an herbalist?"

"No. I just have a section in my dissertation on folk remedies."

"Interesting," she said. "Feel free to come poke around down here whenever you need."

Surveying the garden, I was immediately caught by the calculated delicacy with which the plants were laid out, the vibrant colors, and the fronds of green fanning like outstretched hands. "I've read quite a bit about medical botany, but only as a historian, focusing mostly on the role it played for wisewomen and healers as it relates to the stigma of witchcraft. Do you just grow them, or do you use them?"

"Oh, we use them," Aspen said. "We study the science behind their efficacy, or inefficacy if that proves to be the case. We're particularly interested in antimicrobial properties of certain plants, especially when used in combination with other herbs. And of course we're focusing quite a bit of research on plants that boost immune function and pulmonary health. At the institute we use them both medicinally and culinarily. The first line of defense against disease is the food that you put in your body every day. I always say, if you listen to your body, your cravings will tell you what it needs."

I thought about my fondness for cheap beer and fried pickles and wondered what my body was trying to tell me with that combination.

"Come on, there are a few specimens in particular I want to show you."

The three of us wandered through the apothecary garden, Aspen pointing out plants like turmeric for inflammation, veronica for respiratory problems, and chrysanthemum, which she said could do wonders for a simple head cold and congestion. We were starting toward a section filled with vibrant red blooms that reminded me of pineapples when a male voice called out for Lexi.

I turned to see the handsome Asian man from the photo—Finn apparently. He stood at the entrance to the garden, his posture stiff, almost as if he didn't want to set foot inside the area. Although he was talking to Lexi, his gaze was fixed on me, and it wasn't exactly friendly.

"Lexi, we're setting up lunch in the glade now," he called. "Did you want wine or cocktails?"

That struck me as odd. It was only eleven-thirty.

"Would you excuse me a moment," Lexi said before clacking off toward the entrance in her high boots.

When she'd gone, a particularly beautiful bloom of purple flowers drew my attention.

"Aconite?" I asked.

"Hyacinth," Aspen corrected. "But I have some aconite just over here."

I followed her to a bed of similar-looking flowers, though they were a darker hue than the hyacinths.

"I'm actually researching aconite right now. That and angelica."

"Interesting. I'm sure you know aconite's other names, right? Monkshood and wolfsbane?"

I nodded. "So called because werewolves were said to use it to turn themselves back into human form."

"Exactly. I prefer to call it monkshood, though, considering we're on monastery land."

"I never understood that. Why monkshood?"

"See the petals here," she said, delicately holding them between her gloved finger and her thumb. "How this one droops down like that? They used to think that looked like a monk's hood."

"It's an analgesic, right?"

"And a cardiac depressant, but in very small doses, and I'm talking infinitesimal. It also contains an array of cardiotoxins and neurotoxins that can be absolutely lethal. A strong dose of the alkaloids in it, especially from the root, could stop a person's heart. Every part of it is poisonous, in fact. People don't realize, and they grow it all over the place. It's in gardens everywhere because, I mean, look at it. It's gorgeous." She crossed her arms, and for some reason, even though we were completely alone, she lowered her voice. "So you really study witches and werewolves?"

I nodded, confused by the need for secrecy. She almost seemed to be acting like what I did was somehow secret or taboo.

"What on earth led you to specialize in that?"

"It's just where I ended up. Almost by accident, really. I thought I wanted to study the agricultural economics of early modern England, but once I started digging into the discipline, I ended up with a passion for folklore and for where folk beliefs intersect with historical fact. And it led me here."

Aspen held my gaze a moment. "There are no accidents, Robin," she said, and then turned and continued on through the garden.

1.4

SPECTRAL VISITATIONS

The belief pattern that has been created around the UFO abductions is reminiscent of medieval theories of abduction by demons, pacts with Satan, and flights of the Sabbat, complete with the Mark of the Devil on the body of the witch.

—JACQUES VALLEE, CONFRONTATIONS

We had lunch at twelve-thirty sharp—a feast laid out on a blanket atop a soft patch of grass. Everyone from the photo was there, eating magnificent food and partaking liberally of crisp white Spanish wine. The food was spectacular, with the standouts being a salad of bright green leaves glistening with oil and vinegar and bursting with an intense flavor of onion, and a chicken dish served with aromatic yellow rice.

The group had a vibrancy to it that I wasn't really used to. They seemed comfortable with one another, quick to laugh and tease. Dorian was an exceptionally generous host, constantly smiling over at me as if we were old friends. Finn, who had so unnerved me with his cold gaze in the garden, turned out to be warm and friendly. I couldn't think why my initial take on him had been so off. In fact, he was the life of the party, making sure everyone had wine before drinking from the bottle with unbridled enthusiasm. Handsome almost beyond measure, he had a Byronic celebrity feel to him, and I found it strange that he'd chosen to go into academia instead of into the performing arts.

The others were equally elegant. Dorian gave off young Cary Grant vibes. Lexi had changed into linen palazzo pants and wore her hair in a low chignon that seemed to catch the sun every time she turned her head. Aspen, now sporting scarlet lipstick and movie-star sunglasses, had covered her overalls with a man's dress shirt that hung on her small frame in exactly the right way. In their presence, I felt my own lack of style quite keenly.

"Enjoying the chicken?" asked Dorian, placing a cool hand on my shoulder.

"It's delicious." I took a sip of water to try to even out some of the wine I'd drunk.

"Poule au riz," Lexi said. "A classic French dish."

"So Lexi tells me you're moving into one of the bungalows?" said Dorian.

"Yes, into Dr. Casimir's old place," I said, seeing a green light to press on some of the questions I'd been so desperately wanting to ask. But as soon as the words left my mouth, an obvious pall settled over the group and everyone stared at me blankly except for Finn, who looked off toward the woods.

"Into Isabelle's cabana?" Aspen asked uneasily. She shot a glance at Lexi.

"That's okay, right? I know she left just a while ago. If you think she might return, then I don't want to invade her space."

There was a silence that lasted too long for my comfort.

"I'm sure it's fine," said Aspen, giving me a dimpled smile.

"What exactly did she do here? Dorian, you said cognitive neuro-programming?"

"Yes," said Finn. "Incredibly gifted. She was at the precipice of an important discovery when she left. It's a shame she didn't get to share her research with us."

"How can you be sure she won't be back?"

Again, there was a silence filled with uncomfortable eye contact.

"She's not coming back," Lexi said finally. "She did leave some of her things, but we stored them. They won't be in your way in the cabana."

"Aren't you . . . aren't you worried something might have happened to her?" I knew Dorian was, but the rest of them didn't seem especially bothered.

Finn let out a peal of melodious laughter. "Worried? About Isabelle?"

"What he means is Isabelle could take care of herself," Lexi said quickly.

We ate heartily after that, and as we began to fall into a natural rhythm, I started to feel comfortable with them, laughing easily at their jokes, enjoying the beauty of the natural world and the healing balm of good company.

"So, Robin," said Finn during a lull in the conversation, "tell us about your research!" Crouching in a floppy sun hat, swinging the bottle of wine he held between his knees, he had the curious talent of making you feel as if you were at the center of some important arts movement. The group grew quiet, the sudden cessation of their raucous laughter leaving only the sounds of birdcalls whipping through the trees.

I did a fast mental calculation and quickly saw the path forward. I would tell them about my research, then later that day, I would pretend to look Casimir up and find the post about the statue. Then I could ask to see it, and having laid the groundwork, they would probably be pretty willing to help.

"Are you familiar with the work of Margaret Murray?"

"The anthropologist?" asked Aspen.

"Yes. So if you know her work, you know that it's been dismissed many times over."

"Who is this?" Lexi asked absently. "I've never heard of her."

"She was an early twentieth-century anthropologist who studied the history of witchcraft," Aspen explained. "Didn't she argue that witches were real?"

"Not quite. She proposed a theory that witchcraft as we know it is actually the vestiges of an ancient organized religion that was driven underground by the church, but which has never fully died out."

"I thought she argued that the Inquisition was actually hunting real witches," said Aspen, her brow furrowed. "Which is obviously ludicrous."

"Not real witches—real covens that grew out of Dianic cults. She argued that instead of just randomly killing old women, the church was making a concerted effort to find these covens and execute their members in an effort to drive a competing religion out of existence. I mean, of course there were also people who were persecuted as witches for all the classic reasons—misogyny, ageism, fear of losing power, and so forth. Of course there was widespread belief in folk magic, a largely innocuous belief in things like goblins and sprites, and a whole sort of morally ambiguous realm that existed side by side with our own. 'Appease the house brownie and have good luck,' etc. But that folk magic wasn't what Murray was interested in. She was convinced that alongside that, there also existed an actual, organized religion that the church claimed to be witchcraft."

"Skip to the good part," Aspen said. "You found something that you think backs up her claim, didn't you?"

For a split second, I thought she might know the real reason I was here, but then the fleeting suspicion vanished.

"I did," I said, swirling the wine in my glass.

"You have to tell us now. You know that, right?" She was sitting up on her knees, her eyes lit up with a childlike excitement. "We won't breathe a word, and it's not like any of us are in competing fields."

I took another swig and nodded. "Okay, do any of you know who Gilles de Rais was?" When I was met with blank stares, I continued on. "He's most famously known as a notoriously evil serial killer, but there is a theory that these crimes might have been falsely attributed to him in an effort to smear his name."

"Oh, right," said Dorian. "Wasn't he that man who claimed to be a werewolf but was actually a cannibal?"

"Couldn't he be both?" asked Finn with a grin. "Whitman said we all contain multitudes."

"Shush, you," said Aspen, with a drunken swipe of a finger, as if she were administering a spell. "Let Robin finish."

"You're thinking of Gilles Garnier. Different Gilles, and that one probably wasn't framed. He was just a psychopath. But our Gilles—Gilles de Rais—he wasn't your typical serial killer. See, his other main claim to fame is that he was basically Joan of Arc's right-hand man."

"Joan of Arc?" Lexi said, arching her brow. "I didn't see that coming. Oh, but Joan of Arc was burned as a witch, right?"

"I'm intrigued," said Dorian.

"Actually, she was burned for heresy," I said, "but this is where Margaret Murray's theories come into play. You see, Joan of Arc chose Gilles de Rais as her escort during the Hundred Years' War. He was marshal of France then, and by all accounts fiercely devoted to her. And yet when it came down to the wire, he let her burn. Why?"

"Maybe because he was a werewolf serial killer?" Finn said, pouring more wine into my glass.

"Sure. That's one way of looking at it. But Murray had a different idea. She argued that Joan and Gilles de Rais were actually practitioners of an ancient religion and that Joan was designated as a sacrifice. Murray claims that because Joan was the chosen sacrificial victim, that Gilles couldn't do anything other than stand by and let it happen. He was bound by a religious oath to uphold the sacrifice, even though he was supposed to be her friend and protector. But Joan most likely had accepted the sacrificial position. When you read the accounts, she seemed almost acquiescent to her own death. She was given several opportunities to receive a more lenient punishment, but she seemed almost resigned to dying."

"So you found something that makes you think Murray's theory might actually be correct?" Aspen asked.

"I did. A correspondence between the two that references, among other things, a magical recipe. Why would the marshal of France and a Christian prophet be discussing the specific ingredients in a witch's ointment? Especially in the way that he seems to be doing. It's as if he's giving her instructions. It doesn't make a lot of sense as it stands, but if we assume they were linked to this older religion, then the picture begins to grow clearer. But I need to understand more about that last ingredient before I can claim that it really is what I think it is."

"You think this will prove that there were actual witches?" Lexi asked with a hint of sarcasm.

"No, but it would prove that there was an ancient religion that we have been suppressing and ignoring for a century."

"Interesting," Dorian said, tapping the rim of his glass. "And this cult, you said they worshiped Diana?"

"Murray argued that it was an outgrowth of an ancient cult that worshiped Diana and Janus, but their ultimate deity was a horned god."

"Like . . . Pan?" asked Finn, suddenly serious.

"Yes, exactly. And this is where Murray's complete conversion theory comes into play."

"Complete conversion? I don't know what that is," said Finn, raising the now-empty bottle and pointing it at me like a gavel. "Explain yourself."

"You see, there are countless records from the Middle Ages that show people all over Europe engaged in a religion that worshiped a horned god. There is no indication that the deity was malevolent, but as the church took over, they saw this worship as a threat that needed to be eradicated, so the horned god of the old religion became the ultimate enemy of the Christian church."

"The devil," whispered Lexi.

"Exactly. They cast Gilles de Rais as a monster, turned this god into the devil, and eventually claimed Joan of Arc as one of their saints."

Silence hung over the group as if no one knew how to respond. And then with a twinkle in his eye, Finn raised his glass.

"To the great horned god!" he declared, and then he turned to me and winked. "If you can't beat 'em, join 'em."

Finn and Dorian moved me into the cabana when the sun was just starting to sag heavily in the cloud-thick sky. I really could have done the whole thing myself, but I got the sense they were jockeying to out-masculine each other. If I had been a different sort of person, I would have suspected they were competing for my attention. But typically I am not the kind of person for whom people compete. I'm more of a "steal her research and pass it off as your own" kind of person. So whatever was going on between them was squarely their own issue, but it was interesting to observe.

Once inside, they both lingered as if waiting for me to invite them to stay or to offer them drinks, but I didn't have anything to offer, least of all hostess skills. I practically had to shoo them away, but once I did, I heaved a sigh of relief and got to work. Lexi had mentioned that they had moved Dr. Casimir's things into a storage space, but honestly, it didn't seem like it. The place looked as if she'd only just stepped out to run to the store.

Quickly I got to work searching for the relic, pulling out drawers stuffed with silk scarves and lacy lingerie, looking through armoires filled with elegant outfits and strappy heels. Whoever this person was, it was hard for me to believe she was a scientist. Was I so prejudiced against *the beautiful people* that I assumed they were all inherently dumb? I blew hair out of my eyes and wiped sweat from my brow. Yeah, if I could have pulled off that lingerie, I probably would have occupied myself with something much more fabulous than slogging through archives and writing revenge dissertations.

As a last-ditch effort, I got down on my hands and knees and looked under the bed, but there was nothing there, not even a dust bunny. Standing, I wiped my hands on my jeans and then headed out into the little patio garden. It was lovely out there, all mossy stone and creeping vines. Around the side of the garden, I noticed a flight of stone steps leading down into the dark. A basement would be the perfect place to hide the relic. With a hint of cautious excitement, I took the steps gingerly, careful not to slip on the moss, and when I reached the bottom, I found a metal gate. When I tried the handle, though, I found it was locked. Typically, I wouldn't violate someone else's locked door, but these were special circumstances. It might be inside. I reached through the bars and tried the handle from the inside and the door gave way. I wasn't sure why I'd tried that, but it did the trick.

I reached for the light switch and flipped it, illuminating a sight that took my breath away. Colored glass bottles hung from nearly every square inch of the ceiling. At first I thought they were strung haphazardly, but then I realized they were arranged in a series of concentric circles.

"What the hell?" I whispered to myself.

There had to be hundreds of them. It looked almost mathematical, calculated, as if a necessary step in a science experiment that, when viewed out of context, resembled pure madness. Deeply unsettled, I headed back out the door and up the stairs. I had no idea what I'd just found, but it was vaguely unnerving. I went back inside and tried to call Paloma, but again there was no answer.

Contacting Paloma was something I tried to do every few days, but she never called me back. This silence from her was going on too long. Lately I had been reconsidering her strange behavior before she left for California. It had seemed so over-the-top that I was beginning to wonder if it had actually been a prank of sorts. Perhaps she was punishing me for something, trying to make me worry about her. And I *was* concerned about her. I couldn't fathom what I might have done to upset her so much that she would completely ignore me. I just hoped she was okay.

Later that afternoon when I went down to the scriptorium, I retrieved the large codex that had so enchanted me earlier and sat down at the table to examine it. This time, I moved quickly through the sumptuous illustrations and meticulous diagrams that comprised the bestiary section and spent some time with the rest of the contents. I turned the pages slowly, examining each rendering, each figure, until I came upon something I must have missed on my first pass. It was a triptych that took up an entire page. The first image depicted a woman dressed in blue, with a red cape and an indigo veil. She stood outside among rolling green hills, and she pointed to a strange tableau. To her left stood a pot from which smoke billowed. This smoke seemed to rise up before splitting in two. It encircled a cluster of yellow flowers before entering a second chalice. Or was it the other way around? Was the smoke pouring out of the top chalice? And for that matter, was it smoke? Or could it be steam?

The next panel showed this same woman drinking from a chalice, and the final one showed her sitting blindfolded on a pillar. Taken together, they called to mind the Oracle of Delphi, but something seemed off about it, unsettling.

In ancient Greece, female prophets called sibyls or oracles were thought to have the ability to speak directly with the gods or goddesses of whatever temple they oversaw. The Oracle of Delphi was called the Pythia, and she was considered to be the most potent of all the oracles. Encountering a depiction of her in an ancient manuscript wasn't that odd in itself, but something wasn't quite right about it. Something stirred in my subconscious, some memory of who this was, but it was just out of reach. I closed the book and pushed it aside. It was time to focus.

That evening when I got to dinner, Dorian was already seated, and small plates of food had been set out. The others weren't there yet, though their places had been set.

"How was your afternoon?" Dorian asked genially.

"Good. My work gave me an appetite."

"Here," he said, passing a plate. "This will do the trick."

I took a portion and examined it. A piquant olive spread, languishing over a piece of crusty bread. I bit into it and the salty treat seemed to revive me almost immediately. In the center of the table sat an array of succulent fruits. I selected a few grapes and set them on my plate.

Aspen and Finn straggled in a moment later, looking charmingly bedraggled from their day's work.

"God, I need a cocktail," Aspen sighed.

"Boulevardier?" offered Dorian, getting up.

"That would be divine."

"I'll have one, too, if you don't mind," Finn said, a finger raised in the air like he was summoning a garçon in a quaint Parisian café. He turned his attention to Aspen. "Plants giving you a hard time today?"

"You have no idea." She slumped into the seat across from me.

Lexi sauntered in, wearing an elegant slip dress, her hair done up in a messy bun.

"Lex, you want a drink?"

She shook her head at Dorian as she took her seat at the table. "Good Lord, don't you all look haggard. Robin, did you have a good day?"

She reached out and grabbed an apple from the bowl, daintily taking a bite.

"Yeah. I'm still getting the hang of the archives, but there are some amazing things down there."

"You want a cocktail, Robin?" Dorian called from the bar, where he was clinking things about.

"Not tonight, thanks," I said. "I really can't get over how massive this place is. How many acres is it?"

"Once you factor in the woods, it's several thousand," said Aspen.

"When Lexi took me on the tour today, I noticed a sign for an observatory. Do many of your students take an interest in astronomy?"

Lexi stared at me as if I'd taken them by surprise. "Oh, the observatory. That old thing was torn down ages ago. How is the cabana working out for you?"

"Great," I said. "But I noticed that Dr. Casimir left a lot of her personal belongings in the cabana. Do you want me to pack those up?"

"We'll deal with them at some point. For now, just ignore them unless they're bothering you," said Dorian.

"They're not bothering me, but they seem very expensive."

He shook his head. "Don't give it another thought."

I took a breath and tried to steady myself. *Here we go.*

"I did some googling and came across a blog post about Professor Casimir and her recent trip to Essex. She talked about a statue they found, and she mentioned that she brought it back to Hildegard. Is that right?"

No one spoke for a moment, and I couldn't tell if they were confused or considering. Finn sat down and tented his fingers. He looked over at Lexi, who looked at Dorian, who shrugged and continued making cocktails.

"This is the first I'm hearing of it," said Lexi at last.

"It said she brought it back with her?"

"I don't think she would have been able to bring something back from an excavation site," said Lexi. "I don't know much about archaeology, but I doubt it's just finders keepers. Wouldn't she have had to leave it with the rest of the finds?"

This was something I had considered, and the whole thing did seem unusual, but I didn't know what kind of facilities they might have here. It seemed possible that they would have been able to conduct further research on campus. It still didn't explain why Isabelle was there in the first place, though. Something was off about the entire thing, though I couldn't place my finger on what.

"I saw her office. It seemed very empty."

"Yes, I packed up her things," Dorian said.

"Why pack up her office so soon? It doesn't seem like the space was needed."

"Well, it was," Dorian said, setting gleaming ruby cocktails before Aspen and Finn.

"And where are her things now?"

"Storage," Dorian said quickly.

"Would I be able to look through them just to see about the relic? I mean, if there is an important artifact on campus, surely you don't want it shoved into some box in a storage space."

He frowned. "I don't think we could authorize that."

Heat rose up in my cheeks and I could feel myself gearing up for a fight. I'd always had a problem with authority, but especially when it felt unearned. What right did the librarian have to hold dominion over Dr. Casimir's things? But I knew arguing would get me nowhere, so I tried to be civil about it.

"Then could one of you look through and make sure you didn't miss the statue? She described it as representing thirteen female figures in a circle, with a two-faced being at the center of the circle. You can probably understand why that would be important to me."

"Your coven," said Aspen.

"Exactly. Depending on when it dates from, it could be pretty important."

"I think it would be fine for you to look through her things," said Aspen brightly, "but the storage space is in Denver. We can try to arrange for you to get down there in a few weeks if you want, though."

"Denver?" I said, the wind swiftly leaving my sails as I realized the space was hours away. "Sure. That would be great."

Lexi set her napkin on the table and excused herself. I half wondered if she was going to go scold a cook somewhere.

Dorian turned to me and smiled. "How is your new living space? Everything to your liking?"

"Actually," I said, setting down my glass, "I found the strangest thing today. Down in the basement."

Dorian froze, his fork nearly to his mouth. "Seriously?"

"Yeah. There were these stairs down to it and—"

"The gate wasn't locked?"

"It was open," I lied. "And inside was the weirdest thing I've ever seen. All these glass bottles hanging from the ceiling. Is that like an art thing? Or an experiment?"

Finn and Aspen exchanged confused looks.

"No," Dorian said, "not an experiment."

His attention drifted, and I got the sense that these bottles had some other meaning to him. Just then there was a commotion in the kitchen and Lexi emerged with a tray of salads.

"Hope you're hungry," she said brightly.

"Lexi," he said, hesitation in his eyes, "Isabelle had witch bottles in her basement."

Her hand shaking, she set the tray of plates clattering down on the table. "No." She locked eyes with Dorian, aghast and amused all at once.

"Yes," he said with a broad smile.

I looked on, completely confused, and then as if finally noticing me, she snapped out of it, smoothed down her skirt, and sat.

I tried to get a sense of where Aspen and Finn stood on witch bottles, but they both seemed preoccupied with their salads.

"How curious," Lexi said, taking a sip of her wine before nodding to me. "Please, Robin. Eat up!"

I stared down at the salad. The vegetables were crisp and glistening with a dressing I knew I could expect to be the perfect combination of savory and sweet. Laid across the top were thinly sliced pieces of some kind of meat.

"It is jambon de Bayonne," said Dorian. "Very delicious. You will love it."

"Dorian was telling me about your . . ." said Lexi. "What was his name—oh yes, Charles?"

A spasm in my larynx, and I nearly choked on my food. Why would Lexi ask about Charles? I had barely mentioned him to Dorian.

"Yes." Slowly I set my fork down. "Charles."

I'd practiced this moment so many times, and yet it never seemed to go as planned. Act normal. Adults don't cry when they get their feelings hurt, do they? They don't cry when it turns out the person they thought was their best friend was actually just using them. And yet here I was again, fighting back tears because someone mentioned his name.

"And where is he now, this Charles?"

The table was silent, everyone seemingly set to hang on my next word. Why should they care where Charles was?

"I'm not sure," I said. "I think he took a job somewhere. Nevada, maybe?"

"Don't you know?"

"No, I don't know. We had a falling-out, and I honestly don't know the first thing about him anymore. Since that day, I've just tried not to think about him."

"What day?" Dorian asked.

I stared down at my fork, at the light from the chandelier glinting off the tines, and it was like I was back there again—swept back into that memory I wanted nothing more than to forget.

The last time I had seen Charles was in Washington Square Park. It was night—a full moon—and snow was falling, gathering along the upturned edges of his burgundy cap. By then I knew what he had done. By then he'd accused me of being overly sensitive, irascible—anything to avoid looking at his own behavior. And this meeting was our final act.

As I stood there that night, the pain in my chest, that monster that tore through me was unlike anything I'd ever experienced. I'd been through breakups, I'd lost loved ones. I'd been abandoned by my own father, for Christ's sake. But those losses had made sense; there had been clear reasons, something to point to. This made no sense to me. And I never saw it coming. He was the brother I'd never had. I had trusted him completely. And yet he stared at me with utter cruelty.

"Just talk to me," I pleaded. The words were so simple, much too simple for the expansive crevasse in my heart they represented. "Tell me why you did this."

He turned and looked away, his gaze fixed on a nearby sundial growing slick with snow.

"Please, it's me. Talk to me like you know me. Look into my eyes."

He shook his head. "You want more from this friendship than I can offer."

A cannonball straight through my chest.

"What the fuck does that mean? You think I want to sleep with you? Please. Get over yourself. You stole my research, Charles. I trusted you and you betrayed me."

"You're acting hysterical. It wasn't your research. It was our research."

"That's not true. You know it's not true. Charles, it's me."

"Don't contact me again," he said, and as he turned to leave, I saw it there for just a second, a flicker of the old him, and every piece of me wanted to reach for it, to pull him back to that timeline where he had been softness and warmth. And then that light in him was gone, the goodness in him turned to stone. Turned to rot. And a terrible guilt welled up inside me.

"Are you not feeling well?" asked Finn.

I blinked and was back in the dining room at Hildegard, the light glaring off the fork. Looking down at my salad, I now found something unsettling about the meat, sliced so thin that muscle striations were visible in the tender pink flesh. Suddenly I became queasy just looking at it.

"I'm afraid I'm not. Would you mind terribly if I went back to my bungalow?"

"Of course not," Lexi said, though I could detect not only disappointment in her voice, but something else as well. Disapproval, perhaps?

I tried to keep it together as much as I could as I hurried down the path to my cabana. I could still hear voices and laughter drifting down from the main path. They sounded so joyful that I briefly considered turning around and joining them again, but instead I went inside, and without even pulling down the covers or turning off the lights, I collapsed into gut-churning sobs and cried myself to sleep.

The next morning, I awoke with swollen eyes and a promise to myself that I wasn't going to think about Charles ever again. We'd see how long that would last. I made myself coffee in a

French press I found in the kitchenette and took it and my computer out into the patio garden to breathe in the fresh morning breeze. It really was spectacularly lovely out there.

I was reading an article about the use of defensive magic in early modern England when it came to me. The bottles—I knew what they were! Throughout history, people have believed in supernatural forces as a way to make sense of that which they couldn't explain. When their loved one suddenly grew feverish and died, it was perhaps easier to attribute that misfortune to the work of evil spirits. They of course had no knowledge of viruses and bacteria, so the horrors of the bubonic plague must have felt like the wrath of an angry god or the work of a hungry demon. By displacing their fear of disease and mortality onto an external visible source they could use folk magic to try to protect themselves against, people could at least recapture some semblance of agency. This sense of agency, real or imagined, often involved the use of what were called apotropaics, physical objects believed to be endowed with the ability to protect against bad magic and evil spirits.

A quick internet search of *apotropaic bottles* reminded me that they had been used by many cultures, mostly by benevolent folk healers specifically to protect against attack from entities and spirits. As I continued to search, I found a reference to the left-hand path. I knew this term. If I wasn't mistaken, it first appeared in the works of Madame Helena Blavatsky, a nineteenth-century mystic and founder of Theosophy.

According to Blavatsky, there were two kinds of magicians. The first were those who followed the right-hand path that she recommended, operating within the confines of strict ethical rules, avoiding taboos, and believing that any bad magic practiced would come back threefold to the practitioner. Alternatively, adepts of the left-hand path broke taboos, had little consideration for human suffering, and summoned demons in an attempt to harness their power. Their own selfish ends always justified the means. Apparently the bottles were often used to protect against these diabolical practitioners of the left-hand path.

But why did Isabelle have witch bottles in her basement? Was Isabelle really trying to protect herself from evil spirits? She was a scientist. She should have known better. Shouldn't she?

Just then I heard a cough coming from over the garden wall and a magnificent cloud of pot smoke bloomed into the air. I started laughing, and a few moments later, I heard an embarrassed *sorry*, followed by another series of coughs.

I closed my computer and went over toward the wall. Stepping up on a rock, I peered over the wall to find Finn sitting there in board shorts and flip-flops, his hair tied into a messy bun atop his head. He looked incredibly sexy, but I tried to pretend I didn't think so. He gave me a moderately embarrassed shrug, but didn't say anything more. I waved and he nodded, and then, feeling awkward, I climbed down and went about the rest of my decidedly non-sexy day.

I spent the better part of the afternoon in the scriptorium, drifting from pharmacopoeia to pharmacopoeia, eventually landing on another series of ancient bestiaries. I was lingering over some of the images—dragons with tiger faces, snakes with multiple heads—when I looked up to see Dorian.

"How's your research going?" he asked.

"Good. Just perusing some of your marvelous bestiaries."

"Oh, good. I'm glad you found those. I would have pointed them out myself, but I was taught that one should never show his bestiary to a woman on the first date."

"An outdated custom," I said, leaning back in my chair.

Grinning, he took a seat opposite me and leaned forward,

rested his chin on his hand like a girl with a crush. "So let me ask you. I know you study witchcraft and monsters and such, but you don't believe in all that, do you?"

"Do I believe in witches and monsters?" I laughed. "Like real witches and monsters? No, of course not. When it comes to the supernatural, I'm a firm skeptic."

He raised his eyebrows. "So you don't believe in the supernatural, but what about biblical entities like angels and demons? Do you believe in those?"

"Hmm. Do I believe in demons?" I considered for a moment. "Not actual demons, of course. But every time I look at the news, I see something horrifying—brutality, inhumanity, seemingly ordinary people committing unspeakable acts. Part of me wants to believe in demons if only to point to their influence in such cases. I would rather believe that than the truth—that humans are inherently bad, and for some reason, getting worse."

"That's a cheery thought."

"What about you?" I asked. "Do you believe in demons?"

"Yes, absolutely."

"Really?" I said, laughing in a way that I realized was rude only after the fact.

"Yeah. But I haven't really thought about it much. I believe in angels, though, and if you believe in angels, you must believe in demons."

"Angels, huh?" I winced.

"You don't believe in angels?"

"God knows we could use some, but no. I don't believe in angels."

His eyebrows shot so far up on his forehead it was almost comical. "But there have been sightings. People have seen angels."

"Have you seen an angel?"

He froze, a pained expression crossing his brow. "Isabelle. She was an angel in human form."

I tried to ignore the obvious cringiness of that statement. "That's very sweet, but I'm being serious. Have you seen an actual angel? A holy spiritual being?"

"No, but people have. It has been documented."

I set my pen down and leaned back in my chair. "That's absolute bullshit. I'm sorry to be the one to break it to you, but angels don't exist."

"How can you prove something *doesn't* exist?"

I groaned. "You're not a conspiracy person, are you?"

He rolled his eyes. "We're all conspiracy people. It just depends which one you believe in."

"Listen, I don't want to criticize your beliefs," I said, holding up a hand. "I really don't. But I'm an atheist. I don't believe in God. I don't believe in the devil or demons or angels or any of it. But I do believe that people think they've seen angels. Just like in the nineties when everyone was seeing aliens around every corner. I think those people believed in what they thought they were seeing."

"I'm sorry, but what the hell are you talking about? Aliens?"

"Yeah. In olden times people read their holy books and then they saw angels or djinn or whatever supernatural beings were prominent in the texts they were consuming. Then in the nineties everyone was watching *The X-Files* and they all started seeing aliens. Really, if I'm being honest, I think these sightings are all part and parcel of the same thing."

He balked. "Did you just compare the Bible to *The X-Files*?"

"Yeah, that was rude. Sorry. I just mean popular media influences the collective unconscious."

"You think that angels and aliens are the same thing?"

"Yes, but only in the sense that I believe that krakens and

leviathans are the same thing. None of it is real, of course, but when someone sees something that's not there, you can't say for sure exactly what it is that they're not seeing."

He smiled. "One can't argue with that, I suppose."

"But I do think that they might think they see the same thing as someone else because of other shared external cultural influences. I think they're having hallucinations that follow a pattern dictated by the era."

"No." He shook his head. "I'm sorry, but that sounds crazy to me."

"It's not crazy. It's not even my theory. But it makes sense. Sometimes people get lost. Who can blame them? They get lost and they look for answers. They long for transcendence, and that transcendence shows up in the form of an angel or an alien— some external force that's going to show them that there's more to this life than what we've got in front of us. So they hallucinate these otherworldly beings out of a very human desire for deliverance and hope."

"You really think that the angel that appeared to the Virgin Mary and the little green men who abduct people and probe them on their spaceships are the same thing?"

"Yeah. That's my best guess. It's a shit thing to say to someone who's religious, though, so feel free to tell me to piss off if you want. I get it."

He looked down at his pencil. "So what about now?"

"What about it?"

"Like you say, we live in uncertain times, frightening times. Why aren't people seeing angels and demons and aliens around every corner?"

I bit my lip. "Because I think there's something much more dangerous going on."

"What's that?"

"I mean, the conspiracy theory thing you mentioned. There's something weird going on with it, right? They started popping up like mad the last few years. And it's not just from one walk of life. You have people on every possible side of the political aisle, from all walks of life, people who normally would never agree on anything, and suddenly tons of them are convinced of these conspiracy theories. I mean, don't you think that's weird?"

He shifted in his chair, and from the change in his body language, I got the sense that the conversation was making him uncomfortable. "Yeah. What do you think it all means?"

"I don't know. It's just that the world seems especially chaotic and violent to me lately, like basic human decency has gone out the window. Most days I think I'm imagining it, but some nights I wake up with this certainty that it's real, almost like there's this slow leak of evil drifting out into the world tainting everything it touches."

An easy lupine grin spread across his lips, and suddenly I felt a little flushed. "Lucky we're in the middle of nowhere, then, isn't it?"

Vaguely unnerved, I changed the topic after that. Soon we found ourselves discussing recent novels we'd enjoyed. He asked me a lot about my time in New York, and I told him everything about my grad school friends, my terrible ex-boyfriend, and my favorite professors at NYU.

I was careful, though, not to tell him too much about myself. I was never making that mistake again.

1.5

THE HORNED GOD

The first recorded instance of the continuance of the worship of the Horned God in Britain is in 1303, when the Bishop of Coventry was accused before the Pope of doing homage to the Devil in the form of a sheep. The fact that a man in so high a position as a bishop could be accused of practicing the Old Religion shows that the cult of the Horned God was far from being dead, and that it was in all probability still the chief worship of the bulk of the people.

—Margaret Murray, The God of the Witches

The next morning, after my coffee, I wandered down to the apothecary garden and found Aspen at work in the culinary section, the fresh woody scents of rosemary and mint rising on the breeze.

"Good morning, you," she said with a bright smile. She wiped her hands on her overalls. "Would you like a cup of tea? I was just about to make one."

I took her up on the offer, following her over to the garden house. We went through a little wooden door into what must at one time have been a storeroom but was now a comfy sitting area. Bookshelves lined the entirety of the back walls—mostly medical and botany books with a few Latin books here and there as well. I took a seat in a plush green chair as she put a kettle on over in the kitchenette.

"It's nice back here. Cozy."

"This is where I spend most of my time," she said. "You're welcome to join me whenever you like."

My gaze shifted to a thick metal door at the back of the room. "What's through there?"

"Nothing. Just some sleeping quarters for when we have visiting scholars. Also, there are times when it just makes sense to crash out down here."

A moment later, she brought over two mugs of steeping tea, followed by a smattering of cookies artistically arranged on a yellow plate. I took one as she settled into the couch.

"Did Professor Casimir spend much time here in the garden?"

"Isabelle?" she laughed. "No. She wasn't a plant person by any means."

"Were you two friends?" I adjusted my position and sank farther down into the soft fabric of the chair.

She gazed over her mug, her eyes growing distant. "I thought we were," she finally said.

"What was she like?" I asked. "I find everything about her to be somewhat contradictory. It's like I can never get a complete picture of her. Like, do you know what she was doing on an archaeological dig?"

Aspen sighed and looked down at her hands. "Can I give you some free advice?"

"Sure," I said cautiously.

"I would stop worrying about that relic or artifact or whatever it is."

"Why?"

Aspen shook her head. "It's a waste of your time."

"It definitely isn't. I'm convinced that it's the key to everything I've been working on."

"Look, Robin, this blog post you're talking about—this is the first I'm hearing of it. And if she really went on some kind of expedition to Egypt—"

"Essex," I corrected.

"Wherever. If she went to Essex, she did it somehow without any of us knowing."

"I don't think I understand what you're trying to tell me."

"Robin, as far as I know, before her big departure, Isabelle hadn't left the college in more than five years."

I sat staring at her in silence, completely dumbfounded. Five years? She really hadn't left the campus for five years? That made no sense to me, but I also didn't know how much I could trust Aspen or why she would necessarily have been privy to every-thing that Casimir did. Clearly she wanted to throw me off track, but I hadn't the slightest idea why. I decided to change the subject, hoping that it might ease some of the tension that had been building in the room. Getting up, I wandered over to the bookshelves. She came to stand beside me, looking over them with a mother's approval.

"Do you have a favorite book?" I asked.

"It's quaint of me, I know, but I still love Culpeper." Stand-ing on her tiptoes, she reached and grabbed a recent print of the seminal seventeenth-century herbal text and handed it to me. "It's what first got me interested in botany."

"I can understand that," I said, turning it over in my hands. "What about fiction?"

"I don't read novels." She grimaced.

"Seriously? Why not?"

"I don't like things that aren't real. They make me nervous."

"To each her own, I guess."

"What about you?"

"I don't have a favorite book, but if hard-pressed, I would have to say that Jorge Luis Borges is my favorite author."

"Ah yes," she said with a giggle that spoke of familiarity. "He was Isabelle's as well."

"Really?"

"She made me read some of his stories. I didn't mind them because they're basically philosophy, aren't they?"

I shrugged, not wanting to enter into a literary debate. "Is philosophy more your cup of tea than fiction?"

"It certainly is." She met my eyes. "I don't like being lied to."

Conversation turned to other topics as we finished our tea, but I felt a discernible shift in Aspen's demeanor. It was ridiculous to think, but for a moment, I sensed something ominous from her—something like fear.

That night I went to bed early, drifting off with a sense that I needed to remember something very important. I tossed and turned, aware of my head against the pillow, a breeze on my cheek, but never fully awake.

I'm dreaming of Charles. We're in Washington Square Park again, standing by a sundial. Whirls of snow glisten in the light cast by the streetlamps.

"Why did you leave me?" I ask.

I'm angry, yet I'm the one filled with guilt. I feel that I've done something horrible, something irreparable. I push him and he stumbles back. He falls against the sundial but catches himself, stands upright. I stare up at the now-blazing orange sun.

"I didn't leave," he says. "You left me. Don't you remember?"

He's himself again, all warmth and charm and little-boy innocence. There isn't even a shadow of the monster he would become.

"There is so much I need to tell you," I say.

He takes my hands. "There's no time. You need to find the blue-bird."

"My bluebird?" I whisper, and a rush of longing sweeps over me. He's right. I need to find my bluebird. I need to find it more than anything I've ever needed. Even more than I need Charles back.

There's a noise like a screech owl, and he jolts, turns, holds out his arms as if to shield me from something.

"It's coming," he says, and then he turns and holds my face in his hands. "You have to wake up."

And then I'm in the cabana, sleeping, but also staring at a very tall person standing at the foot of my bed. No, not a person. The dimensions are all wrong. It's more of an animal, isn't it? An enormous doglike creature, but bipedal, with antlers. No, horns, twisted horns. I can't see its eyes, but I know it's staring at me. It lets out a terrible, earth-shattering howl.

I close my eyes and it's gone.

I surged out of sleep, the fear stretching so tightly across my chest that I felt like my ribs might break. Sweating and shaking, I was reaching over to turn on the light when I realized the sound—that howl—had followed me into the waking world.

That's when I noticed my patio doors were standing wide open. Somewhere in the distance, a siren was going off. I could hear voices, movement, and people outside. Bounding out of bed, I grabbed my robe from the back of a chair and rushed to the door, but before I could open it, Aspen and Lexi burst inside. Pushing past me, Lexi rushed to the French doors and closed them. Aspen grabbed me by the shoulders.

"Listen to me," she said, staring me squarely in the eyes. "We've had a problem and we need you to stay inside. Do you understand?"

Outside, the siren seemed to move through time and space as if spreading out into a canyon of echoes and then retracting into a shadowy whisper. I'd never heard anything quite like it. It was like a tornado siren or a tsunami warning, but somehow different, carrying with it an ominous sense of ever-increasing danger.

The sound of hurried footsteps pounding down the brick path drew my attention, and I saw a shock of gray hair flash by. Jim, the handyman?

"What's happening?" I asked, trying to see around Aspen, but she was blocking my view.

"It's fine," she said quickly, "but we need you to stay in here."

I looked over to where Lexi now sat. She'd pulled a chair over to the French doors and was watching the garden intently. I tried to focus. Whatever was happening, I didn't have any cultural reference for it.

"Are we . . . in danger?"

Aspen shook her head quickly. "Everything's fine. We just need you to stay in here. Do you understand?" I looked over at Lexi and suddenly understood that she was staying with me. I nodded. "Great. I'll be back in a bit," Aspen said, and then hurried out the door. "Lock it behind me," she called from the other side.

My hand shook as I turned the bolt. I stood there in my robe, alarmed and confused. I looked over at Lexi, but she just sat in the chair, staring outside. When I walked over toward her, she pointed abruptly at the bed.

"Stay away from the windows. Just . . . just sit on the bed and . . . and read or something. Don't talk to me."

I wanted to tell her about my open doors, about what I thought I'd seen, but it couldn't have been real, and if I was going to confide in someone, it wasn't going to be Lexi. So I did as instructed, trying to make sense of the odd noises that trick-led through the walls. There seemed to be more voices, more footsteps than made sense. And that siren, swelling up and then receding in an irregular rhythm, chilled me. I don't know how long I sat there, but when it ended, it ended suddenly, and I noticed Lexi's shoulders immediately relax.

"Is everything okay now?" I asked. "What does that mean?"

But she ignored me. A few minutes later, a heavy pounding sounded against the door and I startled, jumping off the bed.

"What's that? Should I get it?"

Again, Lexi didn't answer, but she stood, walked to the door, and opened it. No one was there. This surprised me, but it was clear Lexi hadn't expected there to be.

"You're free now" was all she said, and then she stepped outside and closed the door behind her, leaving me alone and confused, with a sick feeling rising in my chest.

I wasn't able to get back to sleep for hours, and when I did, it was fitful, and I had a sense that someone I didn't trust was nearby, too close. In the morning, I woke with a start, so frightened by something I couldn't explain that I jumped out of bed. Now standing in my room, wincing at the light of the early-morning sun, I understood what it was that had alarmed me. The French doors to the garden stood wide open again.

"Hello?" I called, trying to sound menacing. When no one answered, I slipped into my robe and stepped out into the garden. "Who's here?"

My heart thudded uncomfortably in my chest. The garden was empty, but when the steps down to the basement came into view, I knew I had to check down there.

"Hello?" I called as I started down the stairs, my voice echoing around me.

As I stepped into the dank space, it took a moment for me to process what I was seeing. Or rather, what I wasn't seeing. The bottles were gone, completely gone. The basement was empty.

Shocked, I backed away and darted back up the stairs and into the garden patio. Movement I caught out of the corner of my eye sent a scream bursting from me, and I turned to see Finn poking his head over the wall.

"Are you okay?"

Standing there in my robe, half crazed with exhaustion and paranoia, I probably looked an absolute mess.

"I'm just . . . I think someone might have been here last night."

"That racket. I know. I'm sorry you had to go through that. One of the dogs escaped and it was a whole thing."

"No, it was before that. Initially I thought it was a dream, but now I'm convinced someone was in my room last night. I thought I saw someone, and then my French doors were open. And they were open a second time this morning. Now someone has been in the basement."

Finn's smile wavered, his expression shifting to a pinched sort of fear before finally settling on blank uncertainty. Did he know more than he was letting on?

"I'll come check it out," he said.

I let him in a moment later and was pleased to find he was once again wearing board shorts and flip-flops.

"Show me the basement," he said, following me out into the garden. Together, we headed down the steps and into the dark, empty space.

"There were bottles hanging from the ceiling. Hundreds of them. And now they're just gone."

Finn shook his head. "Weird. Housekeeping probably cleaned them up."

"Housekeeping? There's a housekeeping staff? I thought everyone but you all went home ages ago."

"There's a small staff," he said, shoving his hands in his pockets. "Probably responsible for the French doors being open, too. I bet they came in, wanted to air the place out, removed the bottles, and left again. There's nothing to worry about."

Together, we climbed back up the steps and into the garden.

"The cleaning staff, eh? And the sirens last night—was that the milkman?"

"I already explained that. It was one of the dogs."

"A siren like that for a dog? Is this like a hellhound, Cerberus-type dog? It all seemed a little extreme for a dog. And my doors were open last night, too, not just this morning. Was that the cleaning staff, too? In the middle of the night?"

Whatever uncertainty he'd been feeling now gone, he smiled, a comfortable, brilliant smile, and shoved his hands deeper into his pockets.

"I have no idea. Maybe keep your doors locked. A year ago, that would have been a ridiculous thing to say, but since Isabelle disappeared, this place hasn't felt the same."

"What do you think really happened to her?" After last night, her disappearance had taken on a decidedly more ominous tone.

He shrugged. "Fuck if I know."

I sat on the stone bench at the center of the garden and stared up at him. "You don't seem especially bothered by it."

"I'm not."

"You're not worried about her?"

"Not in the slightest."

"But everyone else is despondent. Dorian called her an angel. Everyone else keeps talking about what a genius she was and how much you needed her work."

He shook his head. "They've all got it wrong. Look, she was gifted or whatever, but the work she was doing, it wasn't good. It wasn't ethical. I'm glad she's gone."

"You're *glad*?"

"Okay, fine," he said, sighing deeply and gazing skyward. "Someone will probably tell you, so why not me? I couldn't stand Isabelle. Despised her, even. And it was mutual. Most likely she disliked me because I knew what a terrible person she was. She was pissed she didn't have me fooled. We were enemies, in fact. Sounds silly to say, but it was true."

"You're not answering my question, though. What do you think happened to her?"

"I told you already," he said, patting me on the head. "Fuck if I know." And with that, he left the cabana.

1.6

WITCHCRAFT

That there is a Devil, is a thing doubted by none but such as are under the influences of the Devil.

—COTTON MATHER, ON WITCHCRAFT

I intended to get dressed and head up to the house to see what the others had to say about the previous night, but I found myself sitting on the couch staring into space for quite some time. I began to wonder where exactly I was. I'd been so determined to best Charles that I'd jumped at this opportunity without a modicum of the research I might have given to, say, buying a new pair of sneakers. Sure, it had seemed like this place was respected and historic (there was a photo of Winston Churchill on the website!), but there was precious little to lead the casual reader to think there might be night sirens and threats of uncontained hellhounds.

And what was it exactly that I'd imagined I'd seen standing at the foot of my bed? There was no way it could have been real, and yet it *felt* real. Its head had seemed vaguely canine, but I'd seen horns atop its head, not to mention the fact that it stood upright. The most obvious explanation was that I had experienced some kind of waking dream in which I'd hallucinated a manifestation of Margaret Murray's horned god. My research was simply bleeding into my subconscious.

And yet the idea of upright-walking canids was a fantasy that mankind had inexplicably clung to for millennia. Maybe my subconscious was trying to communicate with me. Taking a deep breath, I ran through what associations it brought up. There was, of course, Anubis, the ancient Egyptian god of death who sported the body of a man and the head of a jackal. Saint Christopher was said to be one of the cynocephali, or dogheaded men, some of whom were thought to eat human flesh. Indeed, Saint Christopher is often pictured sporting a canine head in religious iconography. Some fringe academics even linked the cynocephali to the famous sixteenth-century Piri Reis map. Discovered in 1923, it showed a fairly accurate rendering of South America and featured depictions of various animals, including what appear to be dancing dog-headed men.

And then there was the werewolf. Unlike its dog-headed cousins, the werewolf had proven singular in its capacity to provoke a deep, primal fear. Was it simply the fact that wolves were more dangerous than dogs, or was there something that inherently made the idea of a werewolf more plausible?

Almost without thinking, I grabbed my laptop and opened it. My most recent association with werewolves was Sabine Étienne. Her mauling—her supposed werewolf attack—had been the catalyst for my initial interest in Hildegard. And now here I was hearing mysterious howls in the middle of the night and seeing monsters at the foot of my bed.

Quickly I reminded myself of the details of the case. Sabine Étienne had worked at a local tavern called La Tanière de Loup. A well-liked young woman, she'd lived at home with her parents and her younger brother, Guillaume Étienne. On an unseasonably temperate evening five months ago, she'd left the tavern and had started home. On the way, she'd met up with some friends and had told them she'd come over to their cottage for a bottle of wine after stopping by her house to change. Unfortunately, she never made it.

When she didn't arrive at her friends' cottage, they assumed she'd gone to bed. Likewise, her parents assumed she'd spent the evening with friends. It wasn't until the next afternoon, when she missed a shift at work, that anyone realized there was something wrong. Her brother, who also worked at the tavern, was the first to raise the alarm. It wasn't long before her body was found, just off a path that led through an area of the woods locally known as *le bosquet de la sorcière*. Her death was written up as an animal attack, but a local veterinarian weighed in that the bite marks didn't match those of any known local predators. In the end, though, it was decided to have been an animal, most likely a bear. The only problem was that according to my research, black bears almost never attack humans, and there were no brown bears in Colorado. And then there were those quotes from the locals, the whispers of something more malevolent stalking the woods. The term *werewolf*, or more precisely, *loup-garou*, was thrown around. And then the stranger's testimony—that phrase that, upon a second reading, struck a note of fear into me:

They breed them up there.

Shaking my head as if to cast off my fear, I pulled away from my computer. I needed to get myself together and head up to breakfast.

Up at the house, I found Lexi, Dorian, and Aspen sitting at the dining table. They all were looking very serious, but as soon as they noticed me, they broke into smiles.

"You're up!" Dorian bellowed, standing to greet me.

"We didn't want to wake you," said Lexi with a sweet smile.

"We must apologize for last night. We have dogs we keep on the far side of campus, and unfortunately one got loose."

"Yeah," I said, "I heard about the dog. Must have been *some* dog."

"Dogs are responsible for more human fatalities per year than almost any other animal," Lexi said like a child proudly reciting facts. "They have the capacity to be incredibly dangerous creatures."

"That's true," said Dorian, nodding serenely. "Second only to snakes. And mosquitoes of course, if you factor in malaria."

"I always try to factor in malaria. But let me just get this straight. Is there some kind of danger I should know about? That siren made it sound like we were going to get hit by a tsunami or like there was some kind of breach in a power plant. A toxic chemical leak or something."

They looked at me blankly, and then Dorian shook his head. "You have nothing to worry about," he said. "There was a problem, but the problem was solved."

"Right. So I can just wander the grounds and that's fine?" I said almost by way of a dare, but as soon as I said it, I began to consider that the possibility of a day spent walking in the woods might be rather pleasant. I could use the opportunity to clear my head. Plus, it couldn't hurt to have more of a look around.

"Of course," said Dorian, but Aspen was quick to jump in.

"Just make sure to stay on the trails," she said. "Don't go deep into the woods."

"Why? What's deep in the woods?"

"It's an environmental thing," said Dorian. "The ecosystem is fragile."

"I'll be sure to stay on the forest path. And if I see a witch's cottage or a big bad wolf, I'll go in the opposite direction." I took a croissant from a basket and left.

After stopping by my cabana to pull on some sturdy boots, I set out. I did exactly as I was told not to do: Pretty much as soon as I was in the woods, I went off the path. After trudging through some underbrush, I found a game trail that led me down a ravine and into a hollow, at the center of which rested an expansive, old-growth yew. The sight of it stopped me in my tracks.

With roots creeping like a massive tentacled beast, the ancient tree took up a large portion of the hollow. Around its base a thick, etheric fog had settled. The hollow felt enchanted down there, hidden from the world, with the scent of pine needles slipping past on the morning breeze, but there was also something vaguely unsettling about the area. *Unquiet* is the word that came to mind. The idea that the earth was somehow disturbed in certain places was by no means a new concept. It came up repeatedly in folklore the world over. I'd read many an account of villagers convinced that a certain part of the woods was haunted, infused with an otherworldly evil presence, but I'd never actually understood what that might feel like until now. Was it really possible for land to somehow be malevolent, even deranged?

Carefully I walked toward the ancient tree, but as I came near it, I noticed a chain-link fence stretching up on the other side of it. When I walked over and peered through one of the gaps, I was struck by the uncanny image of a large red X painted on the trunk of an alder tree. I knew that sometimes the Forest Service painted symbols on trees for their removal, but something in my bones told me that this X had a different meaning. Taking a step back, I peered up at the fence, which was extremely tall and had barbed wire around the top.

Nervous, not wanting to linger, I turned back and started up the side of the ravine until I hit a proper trail, and then followed it along a ridge before dipping down and across a shady land bridge flanked by two quaking aspens. I stopped there to admire them. A twig cracked and I startled. Catching my breath, I stared into the dense thicket. Was there someone—or something—there? That creature at the foot of my bed had been a hallucination left over from sleep. It had to have been. And yet in that moment, standing there alone in the middle of the forest, it felt like almost anything could be real.

"Hello?" I called, but was met with silence.

Picking up the pace, I started up a steep slope that led to a ridge. Once I was out of the thickest part of the woods, I felt decidedly more myself again—less affected by the sublime paranoia that only nature can evoke.

After I hooked up with the main path to campus, I crested a hill and came upon a curious sight. Fields of switch grass, horseweed, and silver grass were growing shoulder height, sprinkled with lovely blue flowers I couldn't identify. Curving paths cut through this sun-drenched field full of insect life, each one lined with paper lanterns. It was an extraordinary sight that made me feel immediately that I'd been transported to somewhere distant and fictional—a fairy tale of sorts. I set off along one of the paths. It led me down and around a small hill and then up along a slope that led to something in the distance I couldn't quite make sense of. A jagged oak loomed against the backdrop of the woods, and around it stood what looked like colorful little houses. I'd never seen anything quite like it and hadn't the slightest idea what to make of it.

I headed toward it, and as I approached, I saw that indeed

the tableau was composed of twelve brightly colored miniature houses. Lifted off the ground a few inches, they resembled elevated beach cottages. Each intricately carved house had a slanted roof and was painted a different brilliant color. A figure was moving among them wearing what appeared to be some kind of veil. As I neared, I began to understand. The figure was Finn, and the veil was protective headgear. I'd wandered out to what must be the apiary.

My curiosity satisfied, I decided to head back, but Finn had already spotted me and was waving me over. He met me just outside the marked-off area.

"We meet again," I said.

"Are you stalking me?" he asked with a cocky laugh.

"Nice bees," I said because I lacked the requisite nomenclature to compliment an apiary.

"You can come have a look, if you want." He pointed to a small shed. "We can suit you up."

"I'm allergic."

He raised his eyebrows. "Really? Then maybe you should think twice before barging into an apiary."

"I'm not barging."

"Sorry. Force of habit. Isabelle used to steal my honey," he said almost wistfully.

"Why?"

"I think just to mess with me," he said, shrugging.

"Hey," I said, pointing toward the woods, "I noticed a tree out there with a red X on it. What does that mean?"

He held my gaze, and for an instant, I thought he was going to challenge me. By mentioning the tree, I'd just given myself away. I could tell from the look in his eye that there were no such trees visible from the trails. But if he knew this, he didn't press the matter.

"Root rot," he said. "It's tagged for removal."

"Ah. I see," I said, shoving my hands into my pockets. "Well, I'll leave you to it. I'm gonna head back."

He tilted his head. "I'll walk you back. Give me a minute."

I didn't agree to an escort, but as I watched him jog back to drop off his gear, I found that I wasn't moving, either. He returned, and together we started toward the main part of campus.

"Do apiaries always look like that, like little houses?"

"No," he said with a sheepish grin. "That's all me. I thought it would be cute. They remind me of the colored houses on the shores of Greenland."

"Are you an entomologist? I thought you said you did something with systems."

"Yeah, I do systems science. The bees are just my hobby. My one true love, if you will."

"I'm embarrassed to say I don't really know much about systems science."

"It's basically the study of the relationship between structure and behavior," he said as we walked back along the lantern-lined path through the switch grass. "If we can understand that relationship, we can understand why a system might function poorly or well, and if we can identify a place of weakness, we can step in and intervene to improve it. Like, for instance, do you know what a feedback loop is?"

"Like homeostasis?"

"That's a great example. It's the mechanism that allows us to change the relationship between, say, the inflow and outflow of a system. In the case of homeostasis, if a biological process in the body gets out of whack, we have feedback loops that help us return to normal."

We shifted onto a trail I hadn't been on yet, a slightly overgrown one, but I could tell we were getting close to campus.

"A major mistake humans make," he continued, pushing aside a branch, "is that when we deal with a complex system, we tend to take out balancing feedback loops that only really kick into gear in emergency situations. These feedback loops might be expensive or difficult to maintain, so the tendency is to think that because they are rarely used, they aren't important. But this couldn't be further from the truth. Sometimes these feedback loops are so key to the functioning of the system that if you remove them, and something goes wrong that should trigger the loops to kick into gear and they're not there, the entire system will collapse. It's like a fire extinguisher. It might be annoying to keep. It's unwieldy, it takes up space, and we almost never use it. But when we do need it . . . we really need it. In my opinion, people don't think enough about complex systems. We like to think things are simple, but for the most part, they aren't. Yes and no, black and white, these tend to be oversimplifications, because in reality, everything is bound up with and affects a plethora of other things."

"This sounds more like philosophy than science."

"In some ways the two fields are related, but then often the way we make distinctions between fields of study can feel arbitrary. Even in the biological sciences the way we categorize things is essentially just an agreed-upon taxonomy. Take entomology, for instance. There are many insects that we have yet to fully understand, and we will put them into one category, only to decide later that they fit better into another. But it doesn't make that earlier categorization untrue exactly. It's just a reflection of the way our understanding of the natural world evolves."

"Do you have a specialty within your field?"

He nodded. "Game theory, mathematical models, that kind of thing."

As we neared campus, we diverged onto an arterial path—a shorter one that led us back toward the lake. As we passed an ornate wrought-iron bench flanked by juvenile orange trees, I stopped suddenly.

"I've seen this before," I said.

"It's in some of the promotional materials."

"No . . . it's the strangest feeling. Déjà vu, I guess."

We continued down a stone path and through a garden alive with the fluttering of gossamer-winged insects. Suddenly the path opened directly onto the shore of that magnificently cornflower-blue lake. The lake almost seemed to glow. The surface appeared incredibly still, and yet it lapped gently against the shore. In that moment, I thought the sound of lake water breaking against smooth stone must be the most beautiful sound in the world. I walked closer to the water, breathing in its clean, crisp scent. Staring out at the island, I felt oddly at peace, almost sedated.

"There's a scientific explanation for déjà vu, you know," he said.

"I think I read something about that. Something with neurotransmitters and synapses."

He winced. "Yeah, kind of. But you could say that about almost anything even remotely related to the process of perception."

"Jesus, has anyone ever told you that you can be a know-it-all?"

"No, but I imagine you probably get that a lot, long-winded, witch-cult-hypothesis lady."

"I am not long-winded."

"Oh, trust me. You are. Anyway, most people experience déjà vu, but what's really weird is jamais vu. Do you know what that is?"

"'Never saw'?" I said, translating.

"Yeah. Never seen. It's when you look at something you should recognize, but don't."

Behind us, someone cleared her throat, and when I turned around, I saw Lexi standing there, appearing somewhat edgy.

"What are you guys doing down here?"

"Talking about feedback loops and déjà vu," Finn said.

"Oh." She shrugged. "Boring. Finn, Dorian sent me to find you. He wants to talk to you about the harvest."

Arms crossed and head held high like an ancient queen, Lexi turned back toward the path and disappeared between the trees. Finn followed her, and suddenly I was left alone, staring out across the lake.

Something about Lexi's choice of words had hit me wrong, had made me uneasy. Maybe it was the sense of isolation, maybe it was the campus itself—so ancient-feeling—or maybe it was something else I couldn't quite put my finger on. Maybe there was just something vaguely sinister about the way she had talked about a harvest, but there shouldn't be, should there? Harvests weren't innately sinister. So why, I wondered as I stared out at the island, was I shivering?

Trying to shake off the feeling, I let my mind flow to the

island. It really was extraordinarily beautiful. Although I doubted it could have anything to do with the relic, I had a gnawing compulsion to go investigate it. My gaze drifted to the pier, to the phantom rope marks. At one time there had been a boat. Someone used to go to that island, so why had they stopped?

———

The next morning, I awoke suddenly just before dawn. After a few failed attempts to get back to sleep, I gave up and started making coffee. I still couldn't shake the feeling I'd had in the clearing with the yew tree, the feeling that the earth there was somehow unquiet. Grabbing my computer, I started researching locations that were said to be cursed.

I read about Poveglia in Italy, Angkor Wat in Cambodia, and Satan's Synagogue in the South of France. There were locations around the globe said to be filled with malevolence, and despite my die-hard skepticism, I had a fleeting notion that I was in such a place. Of course none of this was too far from the historical claims of witches cursing their neighbors' fields. That was something that came up repeatedly in my research. A harsh winter destroys the crops and someone must pay. It must be someone's fault. Bad things can't just happen. The human mind must always find someone to blame.

There was an infamous, fairly recent case in England, one that Margaret Murray pointed to as an instance of proof of modern witchcraft. In Gloucestershire in 1945, a man named Charles Walton was found with a pitchfork driven through his neck, his chest sliced open in a cross formation, and his blood draining into the ground, a practice known as bleeding, which was meant to feed the crops. Notably, he was killed on a day known in Druidic traditions as an auspicious one for performing a blood sacrifice. Walton was something of a witchy fellow. Hermitic and rumored to be clairvoyant, he was reported to have once witnessed a mysterious black dog roaming the hillside in the days leading up to a loved one's death. He was also suspected of having cursed his neighbor's fields, leading to an exceptionally bad harvest. Despite Scotland Yard's best efforts, his murder was still unsolved.

My coffee cold now, I was reading more closely about Poveglia, the so-called Island of Death, when I heard a distant howl. Startled, I set my cup down, put on some clothes, and opened the door to the cabana. Outside it was still dark, but there was a cyanotic quality to the atmosphere, as if the sky were holding its breath trying to maintain its grasp on the night.

I strained to hear something, anything, but there was only silence. It must have just been a dog. Except something told me that it wasn't. I closed the door and went back inside, but about half an hour later, I could have sworn I heard ragged breathing and movement pass by right outside my window. When I opened the door, again I found nothing, but as I stared into the woods, I saw a flash of light like I'd seen on my first night at Hildegard. The sun was just beginning to rise, but I didn't think this was a reflection. I grabbed my jacket and phone and set out, intent on finding the source. I wasn't sure what the hell was happening at Hildegard, but something didn't sit right with me about the sirens and the bizarre animal sounds. The shadow of animal testing had been slowly creeping over me, and if something like that was going on here, I needed to know about it. If there was one thing I couldn't handle, it was an animal being harmed, especially needlessly for human profit.

Outside on the brick path, the scent of honeysuckle and

lilac rose up and calmed me almost immediately. The morning light was dim, the sun still just barely a sliver rising in the east as I started down the path to the woods. I only walked a short way before I saw the flash of light again. I followed it, and then a sudden burst of sound stopped me. The bushes seemed to tremble as what sounded like countless woodland creatures suddenly took flight.

I stood completely still. Something was in the woods with me.

"Hello?" The only reply was a flutter of animals skittering through the underbrush and a birdcall I didn't recognize. I continued walking deeper into the woods, trying to follow the path, but as I went, I began to notice the hairs on the back of my neck standing on end. Maybe this wasn't such a good idea.

"Who's there?" I tried again.

This time the silence that followed was punctuated by the sound of something large moving through the trees. I could hear it clearly now, something large coming through the woods directly toward me. Suddenly I realized how incredibly dumb it was to come out into the woods at dawn. Holding my breath, I took a step back, and then from between the ivory bark of a pair of birch trees, I caught a flicker of amber eyes shining through the foliage staring directly at me. I was frozen with terror, afraid that if I moved, whatever it was would suddenly lurch forward and go for my throat. Because I could see it now, the dark gray fur, the solid lupine body—a wolf. It took a step toward me and let out a low, menacing growl.

I didn't think. Before I knew what I was doing, I'd stepped forward and clapped loudly.

"Git!" I snapped at the creature, but it didn't move. Instead, it seemed to simply consider me. "I said get out of here!" I yelled again.

Lunging forward, I waved my arms over my head, trying to seem larger than I was, but still the creature didn't react. It stared at me as if deciding my fate, and then calmly, stoically, it turned and retreated into the darkness of the wood beyond.

It was only once the creature had gone that I noticed what it had been standing in front of. In that space between the trunks of two white birch trees, I could make out a stone rising up like a jagged tooth. My heart raced as I strained to focus my eyes.

A gravestone.

My legs shaking, I approached the headstone, telling myself it was probably just a grave for an animal, part of a pet cemetery. Not that entering a pet cemetery has ever turned out especially good for anyone. I'd read my King.

But when I reached it, I saw that although it was definitely a headstone, the side facing me was blank. Slowly I walked around to the other side, and when I saw the name on the stone, my head began to throb.

"No," I said, pulling away. "No, this isn't right."

It read ISABELLE CASIMIR.

In shock, I stared at the gravestone. Taking a step closer, I knelt down to examine it more closely. That's when I noticed the Latin inscription: EXURGE ANTIQUA ET JUDICA CAUSAM TUAM—the motto of the Spanish Inquisition. Above it was an inverted crescent resting atop a full moon. My blood ran cold and a silent scream caught in my throat. I knew this image all too well.

It was the symbol of the horned god.

MONSTERS AND LEGENDS

2.1

THE UNDEAD

The curiously ambivalent allure of the vampire herself lingers in the memory . . . haunted by the dual images of "beautiful girl" and "writhing fiend."
—Fred Botting, Gothic

As I stood in those eerily silent woods, staring at that gravestone marked by seemingly contradictory symbols, I felt vaguely like I might be losing my mind. Setting the fact of the grave aside for the moment, why, I wondered, would anyone ever want to memorialize the Spanish Inquisition? Most people are familiar with the trials in Salem, and in Scotland before that, and perhaps with the bloodshed enacted during the seventeenth century by Matthew Hopkins, England's monstrous Witchfinder General, but nowhere were the horrors of the witchcraft massacres more evident than with the Spanish Inquisition. It was the very incarnation of evil, and its motto wasn't the kind of thing I want to run into in the middle of the woods.

But then I noticed what I'd missed on first inspection. It was almost the Inquisition's motto, but not quite. One key word had been changed. Whereas the original motto, *Exurge Domine et Judica Causam Tuam*, translated to *Arise, O Lord, and Judge Your Own Cause*, what was written here was *Exurge Antiqua et Judica Causam Tuam*: *Arise, Ancient One, and Judge Your Own Cause*. Ancient One? Who was this Ancient One? Suddenly the phrase took on an entirely different meaning. This wasn't some bizarre tribute to the Inquisition; it was an invocation of an ancient god.

As I started toward the campus, my stomach soured and I felt increasingly paranoid. When I emerged from under the tree cover and onto the path, I turned and stared back into the woods in disbelief. I had no clue what to make of the situation. Wrapping my jacket around my torso, I hurried back to the cabana and locked the door behind me.

I don't know how long I sat there, and I can barely tell you what I did in that time. I think I must have been in shock, just staring straight ahead at my wall. Eventually I showered and had breakfast, and when enough time had passed, I decided to go up to the house and tell Dorian what I'd found.

He and Lexi were in his office on the first floor, their heads bent over what appeared to be a balance sheet. I couldn't help but notice that Dorian seemed pleased to see me, but Lexi avoided my gaze.

"Robin, is something wrong?" Dorian asked.

"Yeah. I think so. I went for a walk in the woods this morning. And I found . . . Well, I think I found a grave."

They stared at me blankly.

"I'm sorry," said Lexi, tilting her head, "but did you just say you found a grave in the woods?"

I nodded. "At first, I thought maybe it was a grave for an animal, but the inscription on the stone was 'Isabelle Casimir.'"

They just stared at me.

"Doesn't this concern you? Aren't you all under the impression that she left?"

Lexi pursed her pretty lips and nodded. "She did."

"Then why is there a grave with her name on it out there in the woods?"

"There isn't."

"Yes there is," I said as politely as I could manage. "And it has some weird inscriptions on it, too."

Lexi looked away, and I could have sworn she grew markedly paler. Dorian cleared his throat. Tapping her manicured nails against the leather desk blotter in front of her, Lexi nodded, finally meeting my eyes. She looked angry and almost like she'd been put on the spot.

"Can you take us to it?" she asked.

The three of us headed out almost immediately, and when we reached the mouth of the woods, I noticed with some interest that Lexi seemed to hesitate. Her expression grew grave, almost fearful, but the moment passed quickly. She led the way once we were under the cover of the trees, but when we reached the spot where the grave should have been, I was shocked to see that it was gone. There was nothing there.

"No," I said in disbelief. "It was right here."

I could barely speak as I stared openmouthed at the spot where the grave should have been. Lexi and Dorian glanced furtively at each other. I could tell they thought I was crazy.

"Right here," I insisted, pointing at the spot where the marker had been. "You have to believe me."

Lexi shook her head while Dorian slowly walked the area, a careful eye trained on the ground.

"What are you looking for?" I asked.

"I'm trying to see where the ground may have been disturbed, but I'm not finding anything."

"I don't understand," I said, my voice shaking. "How could it just disappear?"

"You must have imagined it," said Lexi. "Have you been getting enough sleep? Perhaps you are working too hard."

"I'm not sleep-deprived, and I didn't imagine it. I know what I saw."

"Well," she said with a sigh, "there is nothing here now, so we should be heading back."

"No. It was here. We need to dig."

Lexi shook her head. "We should head back. There is no grave. You were seeing things, I'm afraid."

I held up an authoritative hand, and when I did, I was surprised to see them both flinch, as if I somehow held the power in the situation—which perhaps I did. Probably even places like Hildegard didn't want a social media controversy on their hands. "Everyone keeps telling me these woods are dangerous, but no one has told me why exactly. I saw a wolf here earlier—right here like it was guarding the grave. Is that what everyone is so afraid of? Wolves?"

"No. There are no wolves here."

"But I saw one."

"It must have been a dog."

"There's no way in hell that thing was a dog."

"A coyote, then," Lexi said definitively, and then she turned and started walking back through the woods toward campus.

"Lexi is right," said Dorian. "We shouldn't linger."

As he spoke, I noticed some fallen leaves begin to pick up and dance lightly along the ground. A strange wind blew through the trees, and there was a shift to the energy in the air. Above us, shadows drifted across the sky, and although I knew all this probably was an indication of an approaching storm, in my bones I felt something else, something ancient and malevolent breathing down my neck.

"Look," I said, running my hand through my hair in frustration, "you have to see this from my point of view. I've been told that this woman left recently and no one has seen or heard from her since. Now I find a grave with her name on it in the woods. You can understand how I might be alarmed?"

"But there is no grave here," said Dorian as if he were talking to a confused child.

"I can see that now, but there was. And it wasn't just a grave. It had weird inscriptions, something about an Ancient One, and a symbol associated with the horned god. Why would I make something like this up?"

"I'm not saying you are," he said. "But it must be some kind of prank."

"A prank? Who would think this is funny?"

But he had nothing to say to that.

I held his gaze. "So Dr. Casimir isn't dead?"

He shook his head.

"Swear to me on whatever it is you hold most holy—swear to me she isn't dead."

Gracefully he slipped a hand over his heart. "I swear to you on the breath of the Mother, Isabelle is not dead."

A cold wind flitted across my brow.

"The Mother?" I whispered. "Who the hell is the Mother?"

A noise came from behind us, something I couldn't identify—a strange grunt, a low growl.

Gently he grasped my forearm. "We should go."

Later, I would kick myself for giving in to the flight impulse that consumed me in those woods, but in the moment, I was so gripped by otherworldly terror that getting back to the cabana suddenly became the only thing that mattered to me. We hurried along the path—never running, but walking very quickly.

When we reached the opening, I turned and stared back into the recesses of the forest, but all I saw were lush green ferns and creeping lianas.

"Dorian," I said, never taking my eyes from the woods, "what the hell is in there?"

"I told you." He touched me gently on the shoulder. "Bears. Coyotes. It's not safe."

I pulled away. "I know what I saw in there. It was a grave. Now give me an explanation or I'm going to alert the authorities."

He rolled his eyes. "Do what you want, but there is no grave. Call the police. Call the FBI. There is no grave in those woods. Isabelle Casimir did not die."

"How can you be sure of that?"

"You're shaking. Let's get you inside. Make you some tea."

Frustrated, I started walking toward the cabana, my mind racing. Something was wrong. Something was deeply wrong, and I needed some space to think. As I walked, Dorian followed along behind me with the practiced repentance of a reluctant boyfriend. When I reached my door, though, I had a sudden thought.

"That young woman from the village, Sabine Étienne?" I said. "Did she ever come up here?"

He looked at me blankly. "Sabine Étienne?"

"The one who was mauled by the bear."

Recognition flashed in his eyes. "Oh, no, I don't think so. Why?"

"Why?" I balked. "Because it's possible that Isabelle's disappearance and Sabine's death might be connected. You said as much yourself, remember?"

He looked away and I observed what I thought was a flicker of fear in his eyes.

"What is it you're so afraid of?"

"Don't be ridiculous," he said, but his face contorted into a pained expression. "I'm not afraid."

"I realized what those bottles in my basement were. People use them as protective magic. They're supposed to deflect spiritual attacks. Why would Dr. Casimir think she was under spiritual attack? Is there something I should know about her?"

"I can't speak for Isabelle, but I can tell you that belief in witchcraft and belief in science are not mutually exclusive."

"I'm pretty sure they are. And I think we should all be a lot more concerned about what might have happened to Casimir, especially after what happened to Sabine Étienne."

Annoyed now, he put a hand on his hip. "You're being ridiculous. And I'm not sure what you would like me to do here. Do you want me to find the bottles and hang them back up in your basement?"

"Of course not. I just want people to stay out of my space."

"That can be arranged," he said rather too abruptly. And then he started toward the main house.

When I headed back into the cabana, I was so annoyed, I had to keep myself from kicking something. I hadn't imagined the grave, and it wasn't ridiculous to think that Isabelle and Sabine might be connected.

Huffing to myself, I put the kettle on for tea and grabbed my laptop. Maybe Sabine Étienne's death was worth revisiting. Of course the details were horrific, but there was more to it than that. There was something mysterious about it. I could sense it.

When the water boiled, I made myself a cup of tea and sat down on the couch, laptop on my knees. The heady scent of raspberry and mint lifted my spirits as I read over my notes on Sabine. Once again, I shivered when I read those haunting words: *They breed them up there.*

I stared at the screen, biting my lip. Was I deluding myself, seeing connections that didn't exist, or was there a potential link between Isabelle and Sabine? They say there are no coincidences, but in this case, I wasn't sure if the bigger coincidence would be if the two cases were connected or if they *weren't*.

Determined, I tracked down the phone number for the pub where Sabine had worked. An older man answered, and after trying to get past my terrible French, he put me on with her brother, Guillaume, who was working that day. He slipped nervously between English and French. I spoke to him only briefly, but he seemed anxious and was quick to suggest that we talk in private. Something seemed a little off about him, so when he asked to meet in person, every bone in my body told me to come up with an alternative.

"What about Zoom?" I suggested. "That might be easier."

He grunted his assent, and I gave him my email so he could send me a link.

I tried to work after that, but I found myself growing increasingly aggravated. It wasn't just effectively being gaslit by Lexi and Dorian. There was more to it, and if I was honest with myself, it all went back to the relic. I'd searched Casimir's office and the cabana, but had found nothing. I tried to tell myself I had time. I was here all summer, and academic research was often slow and plodding, more about methodically paging through archives than chasing exciting leads, but the desire to find it had moved beyond professional curiosity. After the past few days, I was fairly certain I didn't want to stay at Hildegard all summer. Something wasn't right. I just wanted to find it and get out of this place as quickly as possible.

A violent frustration building in my chest, I walked out into the garden, and before I even knew what I was doing, I found myself digging through soil, searching inside planters, looking for the relic in places I knew it couldn't possibly be. My desire to find it felt nearly biological, and I had to admit that on some level, that drive was actually starting to frighten me. But my frantic search came to naught. After about fifteen minutes, it was clear that it wasn't hidden in the garden, and then I had to spend the next thirty trying to make the overturned space look presentable again.

Covered in dirt and feeling like a fool, I went back inside, cleaned up, and tried to think. Whatever was going on with that grave, there was no way I could just leave it be. I knew what I'd seen, and I knew that although it might be quick work to re- move a headstone, moving whatever was underneath it wouldn't be so easy. If it really was Casimir, then she was still there, and if someone was hiding her body out in those woods, then I had a much bigger problem on my hands than a missing artifact. It was very possible a woman had been murdered, and I wasn't going to sit idly by and let it be covered up. What I needed was a shovel.

After closing up the cabana, I headed down to the apothe- cary garden, where I found Aspen with her hands also buried in soil.

"Oh!" she said when she saw me. "I've been thinking about your sangdhuppe. Are you sure it's one word?"

My mind was in such a different place that initially I was startled by her question. "What? Oh, yes. That's what is in the letter."

"But what if it's not?" She removed her hands from the soil and began wiping them off. "What if it's a misspelling or a typo?"

"What are you thinking?" I asked.

"What if it's supposed to be *sang d'huppe*?" She pulled out her phone.

"What's that?"

"Well, nothing, but *sang de la huppe* would mean blood of the hoopoe."

"What's a hoopoe?"

Aspen was typing on her phone. She looked up at me with a sparkling smile and flashing eyes, even her diamond nose stud glinting in the early-morning sun. "It seems to be a bird."

"Blood of the hoopoe? The formula calls for bird's blood?"

"Seems like it." She was busy typing on her phone with the infectious enthusiasm of an academic faced with a mystery in her field. "But you didn't come here to discuss bird blood, did you? What's up?"

"I was wondering if I could borrow a shovel."

Her eyes widened. "You're never going to believe this, but I can't find any."

"What?"

"Yeah, all of mine are inexplicably missing today. I'm about to go yell at someone, but I'm not sure at whom I should yell."

"Are there shovels anywhere else on campus?"

"Probably in one of the toolsheds," she said distantly, still focused on her phone.

"Thanks," I said, but she didn't respond.

When I left the apothecary garden, she was still distracted. I climbed the low steps and set off in search of a toolshed. I wended through formal garden after formal garden, taking a detour through a Japanese garden and a moon garden (so named because it is intended for nocturnal viewing), and then back to an English garden—all regrettably shed-less. Finally, I took an arterial path that emerged onto a grassy clearing, on the edge of which stood (thank god) a wooden shed. As I stared at the structure, a cold, curious feeling washed over me. I supposed toolsheds in general were never particularly sunny places, but there was something about this specific one that gave me the creeps. Squarely built and composed of old dark mangled-looking slats of wood, it resembled more of a remote torture chamber than a building for storing helpful implements.

I strode toward it, and finding the door ajar, I yanked at the handle. It lurched open and I stepped in, closing the door behind me. Inside, the shed was extremely orderly, though dank smelling. The tools hung neatly on hooks, and a thoroughly modern chest of drawers stood in the corner. It was uncommonly clean, without a spider in sight, though I could still feel them there with their ten billion eyes, secretly watching me from their hidden lairs. I picked up one of the three shovels, and turning to head out, I noticed a shadow filtering through the slats in the wooden door. Startling, I dropped the shovel on my foot.

"Fucking hell," I yelped, wincing from the pain.

Jim towered in the doorway, framed by the midday sun, evincing none of the buoyant charm he'd displayed on the ride up to the college. Rather, he now seemed straight out of a vampire novel, giving off serious Renfield vibes.

"Hey, Jim," I said, trying to sound casual. "I was just wondering if I could borrow some tools."

"What for?" he muttered.

"A project."

"What kind of a project?" he asked like he was trying to catch me in a lie.

"A gardening project."

"What kind of gardening project?" He stepped closer. My heart was beating too quickly.

"Birdhouse," I said without thinking.

Jesus, Robin. A birdhouse? This is what you come up with? I was so nervous that the word just escaped before I had a chance to assess its plausibility.

He eyed the shovel in my hand. "You want to build a birdhouse with a shovel?"

I stared down at it. "No. The shovel is for a hole I need to dig."

He took a step closer. "Why do you need to dig a hole?"

I took a step back, edging ever nearer to the back wall where those billions of spider eyes were waiting.

"For the birdhouse."

"If you need tools, there are plenty in the apothecary garden. There's no reason to invade my shed." He glared down at me, the tips of his canines showing, and I suddenly became very aware of the size difference between us. Cautiously I started toward the door, still gripping the shovel tightly.

"I'll bring this right back, I promise." Quickly I pushed past him and barged out the door. When I had made it safely outside, I turned around and saw that Jim was still staring at me, and if I wasn't mistaken, suspicion burned deep in those eyes. The pure intensity of it actually made me shiver.

"Latecomers dig," he said ominously.

"Excuse me?" I asked, taken aback by his odd turn of phrase.

But as if not hearing me, he turned and went inside the shed. When he closed the door, I noticed a hint of gold on his wrist peeking out from under his sleeve—an expensive-looking watch.

My run-in with Jim the Impaler had left me deeply unsettled. I even checked over my shoulder when I reached the path to make sure he wasn't following me. I had no idea what was going on with him or what could have led to such an abrupt change in demeanor, but Jim was now on my list of people to stay the hell away from.

Moving as fast as I could, I hurried to the mouth of the woods. The shovel felt heavy in my hand as I entered the forest, and once under the cover of the trees, I raced along the path until I reached the small clearing where I'd found the grave. Locating the two birch trees, I walked between them until I was exactly lined up and then began digging. It didn't take long.

When my shovel struck something solid, I cleared off the top layer of dirt until a length of burlap shone clearly through. I set down the shovel and swept off the top until I could see the whole of it. It was at most a foot in length and maybe seven inches across. Whatever it was, it wasn't a person, thank God. I thought it would be difficult to pry the package from the ground, but the task was remarkably easy. Hesitating only slightly, I lifted it up and set it before me. My hands moved quickly through the material, unfurling what lay hidden within. When I stripped back the final layer, I saw two glassy blue eyes staring back at me.

I screamed and stumbled back, horror rippling through my body. I don't know how long I stood there convinced that I'd unearthed a dead child, but then I studied what I'd found more carefully. It was just a doll, an old-fashioned baby doll.

"Jesus," I gasped, laughing now as I held a hand over my heart.

Gingerly I lifted the doll and examined it. It was a ratty old thing, with scraggly orange hair missing in patches as if it had been haphazardly cut by a child. It was also missing an arm, and half of its face had been sun-bleached. Yet there was something about it that looked almost human in the way that dolls can look only when they have been poorly treated—as if the pain of being loved and then abandoned is the only thing that can infuse them with the necessary dose of humanity. What, after all, was more human than suffering?

When I turned it over, I thought I heard something shift inside. Listening closely, I jiggled it again, and indeed, something rattled just below the doll's head. There was definitely something in there. Carefully, I twisted off the head and peered inside the hollow cavity. Something metal glinted there. Turning the doll upside down, I shook it, and the treasure wedged itself within finger's reach, just inside the opening. Fishing it out, I saw that it was an ornate brass key with a bow at the top that resembled a peacock feather. A piece of paper was rolled up and slipped through a space in the filigree.

I pulled out the tiny scroll and read:

Dear Robin,
Welcome to the threshold. What you seek is here on the grounds.
I left it for you. But you must be careful. Ceci n'est pas triVial.
Good luck and safe passage.

Isabelle

What the hell was this? I looked around, suddenly worried someone might be watching. Was it some kind of sick joke? For a while I stood completely still, in shocked silence, and in that silence, the forest seemed to come to life around me. Birdsong sounded especially beautiful, the colors were more vibrant, and I was unexpectedly shocked by the brightness of light shafts cutting through breaks in the trees, illuminating passing dust particles like fairy dust.

I began to understand. I had stepped through a veil of sorts. Hildegard wasn't like other places. There were rules here I didn't understand. There were puzzles and clues and mysteries, and even though I felt an almost immediate and palpable sense of danger, some part of me was excited. I'd spent my entire life waiting for something to feel real, to feel important. I'd always wanted to feel at the center of something truly grand. And though I couldn't say definitively that what was happening to me was necessarily grand, at least it was something. And moreover, I no longer needed to call the police. Isabelle Casimir's disappearance had transformed from being a thing of horror to being a stark and haunting mystery.

I slipped the note and the key into my pocket, picked up the shovel, and then headed out of the woods.

WHISPERS FROM BEYOND: SCRYING, DIVINATION, AND CARTOMANCY

In ancient Ireland, the choosing of a new king involved the sacrifice of a sacred bull, on which a Druid gorged until he fell asleep. During sleep, incantations were recited over him, and he would receive "revelation" of the rightful claimant to the throne.

—COLIN WILSON, THE OCCULT

As I made my way back to the cabana, I toyed with the key in my pocket. I wasn't sure what was going on, whether this was some kind of game or what, but I didn't want to waste any time. If Casimir wanted to communicate with me, however indirectly, if she wanted to give me the relic, I was going to listen. I would have preferred that she simply hand over the artifact, but if she wanted to play games, then I would oblige.

A disturbing sensation stopped me on the path just outside my door. Looking around, I tried to understand why I felt so unsettled. Again, that uncanny sense of being watched was upon me, giving me pause as I considered a previously unexamined possibility. If Casimir knew my name, could it mean she was somewhere nearby? Perhaps even somewhere on campus. A brief image flashed before my mind's eye: wild woman of the forest, leaves in her flowing tresses. I gazed toward the darkness of the woods. Could she be out there somewhere even now? Watching me? And if so, could she be dangerous? The sirens the other night, what if it wasn't about a dog? What if the danger we were dealing with was actually Casimir?

Back in my cabana, I spread the little scroll before me on the desk and considered it. I couldn't help but note the different level of attention the author had given to the word *trivial*. *Ceci n'est pas triVial*, it had said, meaning *this is not trivial*, and indeed it wasn't, but with the V capitalized and the word underlined, it was clearly meant to draw focus. My first thought was that it might be an anagram. If one wants to hide meaning in plain sight, it was easy enough to do so by disguising it within another word. It was, in fact, a favorite trick of mine.

With a pad of paper and a pen, I started rearranging the letters, beginning with words that began with V. Vitrial—not a word. Valirit—not a word. Vitrail—wait a minute. I tapped my pen against my bottom lip. That was a word in French, wasn't it? Something architectural, though I couldn't quite place it. I looked it up, but before I'd even hit Enter, I knew what it was. *Vitrail* meant *stained-glass window*. The corridor on the second floor of the library.

Without hesitation, I headed up to the main house. After a quick hello to Finn and Dorian, who were having coffee in the dining room, I made my way to the library as if I meant to work as usual, but instead of descending to the scriptorium, I stopped in the main room of the library and climbed the creaky staircase to the second floor.

It was quiet up in that hidden corridor, and as I slipped the key into the old oak door, it eased its way in and then, with a satisfying *thunk*, it turned. Eureka! The door opened onto a simple storeroom filled with neatly stacked boxes and metal filing cabinets, and at the back of the room was another ornate wooden door. I made my way through the stacks to the door and tried the handle, but it was locked, and when I tried the key, it didn't work. Swearing under my breath, I turned my attention back to the room and started searching.

I couldn't be sure these were Isabelle's things, but it seemed fairly likely that this room was where Dorian was storing her belongings. Methodically I began sifting through the boxes, but they seemed to be mostly filled with receipts and work orders. Nothing jumped out at me as particularly useful, and the relic was nowhere to be found. After about forty-five minutes, I slumped down and sat with my back to a box and glared at the door at the back of the room. Why would my key open only the antechamber? Shouldn't it open both? And what was so secret that it needed to be closed up behind two locked doors? Would I need to find yet another key to open that? But just because something was locked didn't necessarily mean it could only be opened with a key. Weren't there whole YouTube channels about how to pick locks? There was nothing stopping me from watching a few DIY lockpicking videos. I didn't necessarily need an ornate key.

A short googling stint led me to believe that I was most likely dealing with something called a warded lock. This was a fairly old kind of lock, one that was commonly used in monasteries. Unfortunately, such locks were among the most difficult to pick. I had to accept that as a novice with no specialized tools, I was unlikely to make much headway.

I was about to leave when I noticed something that had escaped me when I'd first entered the room. The square decorations along the baseboard looked strange yet familiar. The indentations around the square were especially deep. I moved over to one and bent down to press the square, and it sprang open to reveal a small hiding space or cupboard. I reached inside but found nothing. Then I moved on to another and yet another. In the third I found the box.

It was medium-sized and made of dark wood, with a carving of a bee on its top. It opened easily, and inside I found a deck of cards and a velvet bag filled with metal tiles. I didn't know what it could mean, but I knew I wanted to examine it more closely. As I closed the cupboard and stood up, box in hand, I had a vaguely uneasy feeling that there was something else, and that I was missing it. But more than that, I was overcome by the need to be out of the room before someone caught me.

As I made my way downstairs, excitement began to build in my chest. I suspected I was on the verge of something extraordinary. I just didn't know what.

Back in my cabana, I drew the curtains and climbed onto the bed, tucking my feet underneath me, a delicious excitement building. I opened the box and examined the contents more closely. First, I inspected the deck of cards. They were bound by a plain green rubber band that seemed at odds with the gorgeous design on the back of the cards. Almost like a web of fractals, it spun out from a central point, cascading toward the edges, where it disappeared yet seemed to go on forever. I turned over the first card and was greeted by the image of a peasant planting crops in a field. Another card showed an angel descending from above. A third showed an owl-woman sitting on a pillar, a curtain of ivy behind her. I got a bad feeling when I looked at that one.

I shuffled through a few more cards, the art on each more bizarre and sinister than the last (a rotting corpse, a wasteland of smoldering rubble, a small girl missing both eyes—scarlet caverns where these ought to have been), and then put the deck aside. Next I pulled out the velvet bag and dumped the metal tiles onto the bed. There were images on the tiles, almost like runes.

There were only nine tiles in all, which I organized into sets of three. One set showed three phases of the moon: a bright crescent, a waxing moon, and a dark crescent. The second set depicted a series of curving lines: one that resembled a stylized S, an image that looked like ocean waves, and then two curved lines intertwined and turned on their side. The third set showed a square divided into four parts, eight parts, and finally, a square divided into multiple parts that seemed to be fracturing to the point of disintegration.

The cards and tiles were clearly implements of divination, but ones with which I was unfamiliar. And I must say, this in itself was odd. My academic research often intersected with prophecy and fortune-telling, and as such, I was very familiar with most systems of divination. I knew how to cast runes and read tarot, and how to throw yarrow stalks for the *I Ching* and read tea leaves. I even knew about the general process one would use to divine the future by reading bird entrails (haruspicy, as opposed to anthropomancy—don't look that one up on a full stomach). But even though there was something vaguely familiar about them, I'd never seen these specific systems before. The cards seemed related to tarot, but they weren't tarot. Nor were they any other generally accepted implements of cartomancy—the Lenormands, for example, or oracle cards. Similarly, the tiles nearly resembled runes, but they absolutely were not runes. They bore circular images that were purely pictographic, not runic glyphs. I was definitely intrigued and more than a little unsettled. What was a scientist doing dabbling in the occult?

Startled by a knock on the door, I panicked. "Just a second," I called as I shoved everything under my mattress.

When I opened the door, I found Aspen there, holding a tattered book. "I found your hoopoe's blood," she said with a grin.

"You did?" I was so thrilled I had to stop myself from hugging her. "How did you find it? What is it?"

"Don't get too excited, because I don't have the full picture yet." She held what appeared to be a weather-worn journal.

"What is that?"

"It belonged to a skilled herbalist who studied with Paul Sédir, the French occultist who wrote *Les Plantes Magiques*. His journal was passed down to me. In it, he talks about reading a rare nineteenth-century botany book, and in the footnote of an entry on belladonna, he came across an ancient recipe for witch's ointment."

"Seriously?" Excitement surged through me. If the herb mentioned in the Joan of Arc–Gilles de Rais letter was indisputably an ingredient in a witch's ointment, I was one step closer to proving my theory.

"Here's the fascinating thing, though," she said. "Apparently, it doesn't stand for a single herb. Instead, it seems to have appeared almost exclusively in grimoires and was used as a kind of code or stand-in for various ingredients often too horrific or criminal to write down."

"So it could mean anything?"

"You can read for yourself, but it looks like the only thing it's definitive for is witchcraft."

She let me keep the journal, provided I was careful with it, so

I took it to the scriptorium and spent the next few hours combing through it. It was fascinating as a historical text, but if there
was something else useful in it, it didn't immediately jump out
to me. Eventually my energy started to wane. The weight of an
overly long day upon me, I yawned and let my head rest on the
desk. I told myself I would just close my eyes for a few minutes,
but really, I was edging ever closer to sleep.

I sat at the desk, only now I knew I had to be dreaming, because Isabelle Casimir stood in front of me.

She wore a commedia dell'arte mask with ribbons that trailed
down over her bronze shoulders. Her long black hair was soaking wet, and pondweed clung to her damp dress. A gust of cold
wind swept past as she raised her arm and pointed to the corner
of the room, where instead of the wall that should have been
there, now stood a wooden door shaped like an arch. A curious
buzzing seemed to emanate from it. The door swung open to
reveal a shelf that held a single book that bore a familiar blazing
orange sun on its cover. It was illuminated by a shaft of light
from some unseen source.

I jolted back into consciousness to find myself still at the
desk, alone in the scriptorium with all the walls exactly as they
should be. Struggling to get my bearings, I tried to understand
what I'd just seen.

Deciding I'd had enough of the scriptorium for the day, I
cleaned up, grabbed my things, and headed back to the cabana.
After a quick shower, I retrieved the box of divination tools and
examined it once again. Only this time I saw something that
had previously escaped my notice. Inside the box, affixed to
the inside, was a long, thin object wrapped in a swath of blue
silk fabric. Quickly I unwrapped it to find a scientific drawing
of a plant with a thick dark stalk and a crown of yellow flow-

ers. It brought to mind Linnaeus's botanical illustrations, and it had clearly been cut out from a very old book, but there was something uncanny about it. An eerie feeling came over me as I looked at it. I had the distinct feeling that this drawing was terribly important. I turned it over and was jarred to find what looked like the scrawl of a madman. In jagged letters, someone had written: *The Deep Did Rot!*

What the hell did that mean? Although it seemed vaguely threatening, the more I considered it, the more I thought I recognized it. A quick internet search reminded me that it was from Samuel Taylor Coleridge's poem "The Rime of the Ancient Mariner." I had read the poem as an undergraduate and must have remembered it at least somewhere in the back of my mind. If I recalled correctly, it was about a sailor who killed an albatross and in doing so brought down a curse upon himself and his shipmates. At one point he was forced to wear the dead albatross around his neck as a kind of penance. Could that be what someone was trying to communicate? When I looked more closely at the stanza the line was pulled from, I got a sinking feeling that something darker was going on. It read:

> *The very deep did rot: O Christ!*
> *That ever this should be!*
> *Yea, slimy things did crawl with legs*
> *Upon the slimy sea.*

For some reason, the image of slimy things crawling in the sea repulsed me but also made me feel strangely guilty.

That night I dreamed I was trapped somewhere dark and dank, and somewhere off in the distance, I could hear the squelching and slithering of tremendous tentacles. Somewhere just out of sight.

2.3

MONSTERS

So when the earth, still completely covered with fresh muck from that just receded flood, was heated by the sun's rays, she produced countless species; some were the old ones, restored, and others were monsters, novel in their shapes.

—OVID, METAMORPHOSES

The next morning, I spent some time trying to understand the divination tools I'd found, but made little progress. I knew they had to be important, but I was also keenly aware that I had no idea what to do with them yet. Instead, I turned my attention to the Coleridge poem, but came away with equally little, aside from a certainty that I would have made a terrible sailor. I decided to table it and focus instead on the botanical drawing. I knew it had to be some kind of clue, the first step of which meant identifying it. So I headed to the scriptorium and settled in with a stack of botanical texts. Considering the amount of time I'd spent wading through those tomes in recent days, I would have thought the task might have been quicker, but it took me quite a while before I found a plant that looked remotely like the illustration.

Thapsia garganica, also known as deadly carrot. The similarity to my drawing wasn't exact, but there was a likeness that I couldn't ignore, so I settled in to read about it. A poisonous plant that had proven deadly to grazing animals, especially to camels, *Thapsia garganica* had long been used in traditional medicine as a purgative and analgesic. Apparently, it was also extremely beneficial for the lungs. I tapped my pen against my notebook and sighed deeply. Could this possibly be what someone was trying to communicate with me? Deadly carrot?

My head was spinning and I needed some air, so I decided to walk down to the apothecary garden and see if the plant in question might be growing somewhere in there. The day was lovely, with a light breeze tinged with just a hint of coolness. I experienced a sudden upwelling of optimism and excitement when I saw Aspen, pruning shears in hand, leaning over some shrubs she was tending, appraising them with an intense and quizzical gaze. Surely she would know about deadly carrot. But when I asked her if she had any growing on campus, she looked at me like I was a lunatic.

"In this climate? Never."

"You don't think there is any way it could be hoopoe's blood, do you?"

"No, this wouldn't be an ingredient in any kind of scary witch tonic. It's basically just a carrot, Robin. Carrots aren't scary," she said before returning her attention to her vegetal wards.

Disheartened, I wandered back toward my cabana. It appeared that I was at an impasse. The divination tools were a dead end, the Coleridge poem was a dead end, the deadly carrot was a dead end. It felt like I'd had too much information dumped on me all at once—too many clues and no solutions when really the only thing I knew for sure was that I needed to find the relic. I'd been assuming that the clues would lead me to it, but what if I had it all wrong? What if they were actually a wild-goose chase meant to distract me, to lead me away?

Although I had already searched the cabana, I was constantly tormented by the fear that I had missed something. What if the relic was here, somehow hiding in plain sight? The thought filled me with a compulsion so strong it almost frightened me, and once again, I found myself searching the space, only this time, it was as if something had overtaken me. In a frenzy, I turned the place upside down, pulling out every cushion, searching in every crack and crevice, every cabinet. At one point, I even contemplating prying up the floorboards, but I wasn't quite there yet. That's not to say I didn't spend a good half an hour searching for loose ones.

Once I started looking in earnest, though, I couldn't stop. I spent the rest of the day turning over every stone I could find. I started in Casimir's office, looking through the detritus in the closet, but finding nothing. I bothered Dorian in his office, asking when he might be going to that storage space in Denver, but he deflected. *Soon,* he assured me. In the meantime, he would appreciate my not snooping around the house. He didn't use the word *snooping,* but his meaning couldn't have been clearer.

I walked the grounds for a while, eventually heading over to the main academic buildings. I found my way inside a particularly stately French Norman building. The exterior felt like something out of a fairy tale, but inside it felt like a ghost ship. The classrooms were unlocked, but they had the aspect of having been abandoned suddenly. I went room to room, but all I found were discarded blue books, and in one classroom, a chalkboard onto which someone had once scrawled *Surprise Man!*

I had thought I was alone in the building, but on the third floor, near one of the circular stairwells, I passed an office and saw Lexi bent over a stack of papers with a pen.

She looked up suddenly, surprised to see me. "What are you doing up here?"

"Just exploring," I said, quickly glancing around her office.

"Make yourself at home," she said, and I knew she intended it ironically, but I played dumb.

"Thanks," I said as I took a seat on a puffy pink chair, imagining the poor students who had someone as petulant as Lexi determining their academic fates.

"You're a behavioral psychologist?"

"Mmm," she said, taking a sip from a travel mug on her desk. "Yes. Why?"

"I'm just trying to get a full picture of this place. So your work, does it overlap with Isabelle's?"

"No."

I tried not to be too obvious as I scanned the bookshelves. "And what's your specialization?"

She shook her head quickly. "It's niche. Suffice it to say, if someone would just give me a gaggle of children to raise entirely without environmental influence, I would be a very happy gal. Unfortunately, that's unethical."

"It certainly sounds unethical. So your work really never overlaps with Isabelle's? It seems like the fields of behavioral psychology and cognitive neuroscience might overlap somewhat."

She flashed her brilliant smile like she was the belle of a press junket. "They don't."

"I'm curious, though, I know she was a cognitive scientist, but I can't get a clear picture of her work. Can you tell me anything about it?"

Taking another sip, she smirked. "Not allowed, I'm afraid."

"What, did you, like, sign an NDA or something?"

She looked surprised by that, but remained unflappable.

"Yes" was all she said. "Look, Isabelle was a mystery, and if there's something specific you want to know about her, I'd ask Aspen. Those two were tight—annoying little polymaths always babbling away until the wee hours. If it's insight into Isabelle, honestly, I'm the last person you should ask."

"Did you two not get along?"

"Ha!" She picked up her mug and took an enormous swig. I was beginning to think there was something stronger than coffee in there. "Did no one tell you?"

"Tell me what?"

"We used to date."

"No. I had no idea. You must be worried about her."

"Worried? No. She broke up with me. She's a heartless bitch, it turns out."

We locked eyes, as if each daring the other to speak. There was a palpable tension between us, a sort of violent chemistry that I half suspected might one day end in mutually assured destruction.

"Sounds tough," I said.

She held my gaze an uncomfortably long time, an indiscernible emotion brewing in her crystalline eyes. "There are worse things." She looked at me like I was supposed to understand what that meant, and then she motioned to the door. "I don't mean to be rude, but I have work to do. Can you . . ." She made a shooing motion with her hand, and that was that.

Eventually I called it a day and retreated to my cabana's patio garden. Settling in with a warm cup of Earl Grey tea, sweetened to perfection with milk and sugar, I resumed my *Thapsia garganica* research. After reading a while, I was stunned to come across an image that looked remarkably like the drawing I'd found, and slowly I began to understand why I hadn't been able to locate it in any of the pharmacopoeia I perused.

It turned out that the plant in question was called silphium and had been extinct for thousands of years. Pliny the Elder described it as a wonder drug of sorts. Most likely a member of the *Ferula* genus, it appeared one day after a "black rain." Its resin was said to cure everything from fever to warts. It was also somehow both a fertility booster and a contraceptive, and there was some indication that it had other properties, more mystical ones to which Pliny gave no credence, but to which later occult scholars vaguely alluded. One text described it as "the lifeblood of the Terrible Ones," but I couldn't find an attribution on that, and I came across it in only one source.

Before it went extinct, it grew in an area called Cyrene, located in present-day Libya, resisting cultivation but growing plentiful and wild. It was so beneficial and sought-after that the Romans quickly got in on the action, exploiting the Cyrenes and the plant until it was no more.

Bells were beginning to go off in my head, though I couldn't precisely grasp what I had at my fingertips until a few minutes later when I stumbled across a curious piece of trivia. Apparently the Cyrenes so revered the plant that they stamped the image of its seedpod on their currency. That seedpod, it turned out, looked exactly like the modern-day representation of a heart, and some sources posited that this humble seed was in fact the origin of that symbolism. I thought back to the heart design I'd seen on the front gate when I'd arrived, and possibly even what I'd mistaken for an ouroboros above the entrance to the scriptorium.

My heart raced with excitement, but my mind was getting a little muddled, so I decided to go for a walk to clear my head. The afternoon sun beat down on my shoulders as I headed along the twisting garden paths, around fountains glittering with flowing water, and eventually found myself at a building tucked into a verdant spot in the woods. All heavy beams and stone-work, it resembled a formidable hunting lodge. It seemed like a place where important things might happen, and yet it was dark, with looming windows. Shallow stone steps led to an oak door, but when I tried the handle, I found it was locked. I noticed that there was a slot for a key card nearby.

Standing out there at that building, I was overcome by an eerie, uncanny feeling. I peered through a window, and I'm em-barrassed to say that something about the deserted, darkened hallway gave me the creeps. I couldn't tell if it was a dormitory or a set of classrooms, but I was struck by a profound desire to go inside. If only I could get hold of a key card.

Giving up, I headed back through the garden toward the cabana. When I reached the path, I was surprised to see Finn there, gathering velvety spears of lavender and gently placing them in a wicker basket. The scent rose sharply in the air.

"What are you up to?" I asked.

Around us the lavender plant buzzed with insect activity.

"Picking some lavender for tonight's dessert. Lexi's making chocolate lavender mousse."

"Lavender mousse?" It sounded wretched to me, but I made a noise as if to convey I thought it sounded delicious.

"Yeah. It's disgusting, but we all pretend to like it so Lexi doesn't throw a tantrum."

"Oh, that's right." I'd forgotten we were supposed to have game night soirée tonight—the whole gang. Back in New York, I loathed activities like game nights (I did not play well with others), but I was determined to be polite.

He looked back at the bush, at the flurry of little pollinating wings, and then shook his head. "Pollinators are dying out, you know."

"I've heard. Just one more sign we're staring down the barrel of our own demise. It's pretty bleak."

He looked at me deeply as if trying to figure out the answer to a riddle, and then I detected a strange shift in his demeanor. "You've heard of the Deepwater Horizon oil spill, right?"

"The oil rig that exploded a while back?"

He nodded. "Do you know how much oil spilled into the ocean? Five million barrels. Think of the devastation to marine life that caused, not to mention the workers who were killed in the blast. It was months before they were able to cap the broken well."

"That's awful," I said uneasily. I noticed a particularly large insect that was crawling along the balustrade. "Is that a wasp?"

"Yep. They grow pretty big up here."

I had an uncanny feeling that this had all happened before.

"Do you know the difference between bees and wasps?" he asked.

"Bees make honey and wasps don't," I said. "Bees are pollinators and wasps aren't."

He shook his head. "Wasps are pollinators, too. Very important for our ecosystem. No," he said. "The real difference is that wasps don't die when they sting."

He held my gaze a moment and then cheerfully went back to collecting the lavender.

—————

I spent most of the rest of the day and early evening reading in the cabana before quickly hopping on the Zoom I had scheduled with Guillaume. Thankfully, the connection wasn't too bad.

"You are pretty," he said, and I flinched. He was young, maybe twenty, with floppy reddish-brown hair. Immediately I disliked him. He seemed to be set up in the tavern, because I could see empty barstools lined up behind him. "My manager is afraid of the bad press, but he isn't here now." He scooted forward on his chair, or maybe it was a barstool. "Now, what do you want to know about Sabine?"

"Well," I said, looking down at my notepad, "I've read the newspaper accounts of what happened, but is there anything else you can tell me? Anything that might not have made it into the papers?"

"Like what?" He squinted at me.

"Just in general, is there anything you can tell me about her. What was she like?"

Guillaume seemed to be thinking for a moment. "She was a good girl. Dressed properly. Not like some girls. You know the kind—trashy girls. My sister was not trashy."

I tried not to show the revulsion I was feeling. "Did she have any particular interests?"

"Interests? How should I know? My grandmother, Jeanne, knew her best. You should talk to her probably. Mostly Sabine was, what's the word? . . . stubborn. If Sabine decided something, there was no use trying to tell her something different."

"Stubborn how? Can you give me an example?"

"No. Just stubborn. She did what she wanted, didn't listen to my parents. She was different from most girls. Not looking for romance."

I raised an exhausted eyebrow. "I think a lot of young women are looking for things other than romance."

"Okay, but Sabine, all she cared about was money and power."

I felt a strange chill. "What kind of power?"

Frowning as if searching for the right words, he gesticulated. "Power. You know. Control. Jeanne told me things."

"What kind of things?"

"She was obsessed with royalty. And with Hildegard."

So there definitely was a connection. There was a silent moment where I tried to process that. I must have been very still because Guillaume thought my screen had frozen.

"Are you still there?"

"Yes," I said, shaking away the cobwebby feeling that had come over me. "Sorry. You mean up here? Sabine was obsessed with the college?"

"Sure. She thought it was her ticket. I figured you knew. That's why you're asking about her, no? Because of the school?"

"It makes sense that she would know about this place, but I didn't realize that she'd come up here."

"Well, she did," he said with a hint of defensiveness. "I don't know what she did, but I know she was up there. She told me about it."

"What did she say?"

"Not much. Just that it was very nice. She seemed very happy about it." Suddenly Guillaume looked shiftily around the room he was in, and I couldn't help but wonder if he was alone or if there was someone else there, just off-screen and out of view.

"Is everything all right?"

But he didn't answer my question. Instead, he stared at me with heavy-lidded eyes. "You don't think it was a bear, then?"

"Excuse me?" I said, still focused on my paranoia that he was surrounded by a malevolent cabal.

"The police, they said it was a bear attack."

I thumbed through my notes. "Is that true? I don't think they concluded that it was without a doubt a bear, but an animal attack, yes."

"But you don't think it was?"

"I don't think anything, Guillaume. I'm not an investigator. I'm just interested."

"It wasn't a bear," he said with sudden intense conviction.

"What do you mean?" I asked, leaning forward.

"You must know. About what's in these woods. Up at Hildegard. It is a secret, but not very much of a secret."

My heart began to race. "I'm sorry, but I don't know what you mean. Can you elaborate?"

He pursed his lips, and his gaze dropped to his fingers, which I could just make out were tapping in a staccato rhythm on the table in front of him.

"I think you should talk to my grandmother."

"Guillaume, what did you mean about the woods?"

He looked down and to the side, avoiding my eyes. "I will set up the computer for her. She's not good with technology."

"Guillaume," I said, tightness spiderwebbing across my chest, "what's in the woods?"

"I have to go. I'll be in touch. Talk soon."

He left the meeting before I had a chance to reply.

About fifteen minutes later, Lexi knocked on my door, looking slightly haggard, or rather, because it was Lexi, slightly less enchanting than usual.

"I was wondering, do you want to borrow something for the party?" she asked, and the way she was looking at me was strangely intense. I got the sense that there was something competitive coming from her.

"I'll be fine," I said. "I'll just wear my normal clothes."

"Nonsense. Wear something of Isabelle's."

That hit me strangely. "That wouldn't feel right."

"Don't be an idiot. Her things are beautiful, and they would fit you."

Her eyes were trained on me with such intensity that I suddenly had a creeping suspicion that if I said no that I would be wielding a gauntlet I had no intention of throwing.

"Okay," I said uneasily. "As long as you're sure."

"I'm sure," she said with a quick cold snap of a smile, and then she turned and left.

Alone in my cabana, I showered and towel-dried my hair. Then with some trepidation, I opened the armoire and began exploring. Cashmere and chiffon and silk—these were fabrics I had written about, but had never worn. I fought the slight thrill that tugged at me as I selected a green silk dress and put it on. I pulled my hair back into a tight bun at the nape of my neck, slipped on some strappy black heels, and headed up to the house.

Everyone was gathered in the music room when I arrived, looking divine and drinking green cocktails out of sparkling crystal glasses. Aspen, who looked smashing in a little black dress and an Audrey Hepburn tiara, came over when she saw me, her eyes lit up by the fairy lights strung from the ceiling and leading out to the patio.

"Look at you," she said, giving me a cheeky nudge. "You clean up nice."

"You too," I said. "What are you drinking?"

"They're called malevolent pixies. Dorian invented them. They're on the sideboard. Go grab one."

Waving a quick greeting to the others, I started to make my way over to the cocktails, but got waylaid by a tray of the most delightful-looking mini sandwiches—what appeared to be some kind of potato omelet crowned by a vibrant orange pepper. I picked one, and when I bit into it, it was like an explosion of flavors, the potato, egg, oil, and spices combining in such a way as to far exceed the sum of their parts.

I had a few cocktails, which is more than I was used to, and soon the evening devolved into charades, at which I did not excel, and finally that disbanded, and we all ended up on the patio smoking clove cigarettes like dumb teenagers from a bygone era. I was leaning against the balustrade tipsily laughing with Finn when I began to feel eyes on me. Turning, I saw Lexi sitting at a table shooting daggers at my back. Shivering a little, I tried to ignore it, but when Finn went back inside and I saw that Lexi was still seated in the same spot, I decided to go over and talk to her.

"Mind if I join you?" I asked, setting my drink down before she could answer.

"Please," she said, sitting up straight and trying to reaffix her hair.

Although she still looked beautiful, she looked deeply sad, and I wondered why she seemed so unhappy so much of the time.

"Are you worried about Isabelle?" I asked. "You must be. With everything that has happened in the area, that girl who was mauled and whatnot." I lifted my glass to take a sip.

"Or the girl who ran away," she said curtly.

"Excuse me?" I said, pausing before the rim touched my lips. "What girl who ran away? I'm talking about Sabine Étienne, the girl from the village who was killed by a wild animal."

Suddenly she locked eyes with me. "Have you ever read 'Bisclavret'?"

I shifted around in my seat, noticeably uncomfortable. "Sure, it's one of the first werewolf stories."

"Then you know it. A woman runs off with a knight because her husband is a werewolf. Who can blame her? Maybe that's what happened here. Maybe the girl's fiancé was a werewolf."

"I think we can safely assume that he wasn't. Also, who are we talking about? Sabine Étienne was killed by a bear," I said, but she just shrugged.

Not sure how to respond to this especially prickly version of Lexi that alcohol seemed to bring out, I excused myself, but as I was leaving the patio, I turned and saw that she was still staring at me, that same fixed intensity in those haunting eyes.

The others were now gathered around the piano caterwauling and swaying back and forth. Finn tried to call me over, but I held up a finger as if to say I would be there to join in a minute, though I had no intention whatsoever of doing so. Instead, I decided to hide for a bit, so I slipped through the house to the exterior walkway that led to the library. By this point, I'd searched the library as much as I could without drawing undue attention, but I felt emboldened to try once more.

Maybe it was the liquor, but the place felt especially magical to me that night. The warm caramel glow of the lamps brought out the soft red tint of the wood, and the vast array of books, instead of feeling overwhelming like they did some days, created the impression of endless possibility and an expandable sense of time. Slowly I walked the room, looking for nooks and crannies, anything that might be large enough to conceal the artifact. I pulled out a book here and there to make sure there was nothing behind it, but there never was. On a lark, I pulled out a copy of Linnaeus's *Philosophia Botanica*.

It was a beautiful copy, and momentarily I wondered if I

could just borrow it and sneak back down to my cabana without causing a fuss. I could hear them up there now performing a terrible rendition of Steve Miller's "The Joker." Maybe the party was over for me.

I was just starting to replace *Philosophia Botanica* when I noticed something familiar on the shelf—the book with the blazing sun on the cover. Isabelle had pointed to it in my dream. I walked over and grabbed it off the shelf. *Ficciones* by Jorge Luis Borges. It turned out to be a first edition. Nice. I thumbed through it briefly, then replaced it before heading back out of the library and sneaking off down to my cabana.

The night was still lovely out, and I was humming Steve Miller against my will when I reached my cabana and froze. My door was open, a shadow cast onto the stones outside. I crept quietly forward, slowly making my way until I was able to see through the opening.

It was Dorian, standing by my bed, examining the box I'd found in the storeroom. Surprise quickly turned to anger as I stormed into the cabana, slamming the door open. He startled, nearly dropping the box.

"Robin," he said, looking guilty.

I noticed he'd draped his jacket over the back of my desk chair. "I see you're making yourself comfortable."

"You're angry," he said, taking a step back. "I'm sorry if this looks bad, but I didn't come in here to snoop, if that's what you're thinking."

"Well, what else am I supposed to think? Enlighten me."

His shoulders fell. "I came here to ask you something, but you weren't here, and then this box caught my eye. I'm sorry, I shouldn't have intruded. I know how women can be about their privacy."

"What does my being a woman have to do with anything? It's not like I can't handle you trespassing and going through my things because I have ovaries. I promise I will not get the vapors. It's just general courtesy not to snoop. Also, I was at the party at *your* house. You could have just talked to me there."

He gave me puppy-dog eyes. "But you disappeared."

"I just went to the library. I was coming back."

My anger reaching a crescendo, I picked up the box and held it to my chest, but then I saw the sadness in his eyes, the genuine contrition that seemed to simmer there, and my rage began to subside. Maybe I was overreacting.

"I'll go," he said softly. "I really am sorry."

"No, wait, Dorian," I said, stopping him. "I'm sorry. I'm not happy that you invaded my privacy, but I shouldn't have yelled like that."

"No, really, I'm in the wrong, and I'm sorry. I shouldn't have come in here."

I thought that was going to be that, and then he would leave, but instead he pointed to the box, a wry smile forming on his lips. "These things, these cards, you don't believe in them, do you?"

I could feel myself blush. "No. Of course not. But also that's none of your business."

"They're for your research?"

I stared at him blankly. I couldn't really lie and say that they were part of my research because if he pressed, it would become clear that I hadn't the first clue what they were. Of course I also didn't want to reveal that I'd basically just stolen the lot of it from his house.

"No," I said carefully.

He laughed. "You don't use them, do you? Because this is hokum. Ridiculous. For the small-minded."

I crossed my arms in front of my chest, seeing an opportunity. "Do you know what they are?"

"Of course. Locals use them. They are much like tarot, but with older roots."

"What about these?" I asked, showing him the tiles. "Do you know what these are?"

"They're called widows' keys."

I grimaced. "Morbid name. Do you know how to use them?"

He shook his head. "I think you need a book."

"I assumed as much. I'll look into it."

"Let me know if I can help," he said.

"No need," I said. "Now, if you don't mind, I'd like to go to sleep."

He didn't budge, so I physically turned him around and pointed him toward the door. He tried to give me handsome-boy sad eyes, but I wasn't falling for it. Looks only counted for so much.

Reluctantly he left, closing the door slowly behind him. It was only a moment or so later that I noticed he'd left his jacket draped over my chair. I picked it up and started toward the door, intending to call after him, but then something fell out of his pocket. Reaching down, I grabbed it, and was stunned to discover it was a key card. My mind flashed to the building I'd found in the woods. Ask and ye shall receive, apparently. I bit my lip, thinking, and then set the jacket back on the chair where I'd found it. Did I want to go down this road? I decided I did. I set my alarm for three A.M. and went to sleep.

When my alarm went off, I arose and got dressed. I then stepped out into the darkness. Around me, the night was warm and violent, a hot wind playing in among the leaves. I moved quickly and quietly, much more so than I'd expected of myself, slipping along the garden paths, hiding in the shadows.

The woods were quiet as I made my way past the night-blooming flowers and over toward the building. I broke into a jog as I made my way along the path, watching my step as it shifted from stone to brick. When I reached the entrance, I found the key slot and swiped Dorian's card; the door buzzed open. Inside, the atmosphere felt different, as if it were somehow pressure controlled.

As I walked down the hall, a strange pulsing sound seemed to surround me. I noticed a sign on one of the doors that read SNG LAB. It appeared to be a traditional lab, but I didn't recognize some of the equipment. Not that I necessarily would, but there was something a little strange about it. In the corner, I noticed what looked like an MRI machine—almost, but not quite. I tried the door, but it was locked.

Down at the end of the hall was a set of double doors. I tried the handle, expecting them to be locked, but instead, they swung open to reveal what appeared to be a mix of offices and living quarters, though the living quarters definitely weren't dorm rooms. They felt more like something one might find at a research outpost somewhere remote. Ernest Shackleton and Antarctic expeditions came to mind.

There was enough moonlight to illuminate my way, but just barely. The doors to every room were open. I peered in one and found it empty. The covers on the bed were thrown back and there were books on the floor. It looked like the occupant had gotten up to use the bathroom and would be back any second. In each room I passed, I noticed a similar scene. Empty, in disarray, looking as if someone had been awakened from sleep and fled.

I stopped and stood in the center of the hallway and just

listened. I began to realize slowly, and with some horror, that something terrible had happened here. When I passed a bathroom, I stepped inside and flipped on the lights. With a low hum, fluorescent light flooded the area. Pale green tile lined the walls. Against one wall stood a row of cubbies, each filled with bathroom caddies, toothbrushes and shampoo poking out of them like flowers in an artistic arrangement. On one sink sat a single toothbrush. On the floor in front of it, a tube of toothpaste lay abandoned.

"What the hell?" I whispered to myself.

Turning out the light, I headed back into the hall, moving as quickly as I could until I stopped suddenly outside one of the offices. There was something familiar about it. Poking my head inside, I noticed a painting of a toad on the wall. When I stepped inside, I was overwhelmed by a familiar scent—oaky and calming.

Stunned, I stood there and closed my eyes, transported. I knew this scent. Charles Danforth. The room smelled exactly like him. I was gripped by a wave of sadness. He was the last person I wanted to think about. I got out of there before I devolved into a blubbering mess. Continuing on down the hall, I reached a room at the end that appeared to be a conference room.

The space was lined with dry-erase boards, and a microwave and a coffeemaker were over in the corner next to an army-green filing cabinet. A *Resident Evil* poster hung at the far end of the windowless space. On instinct, I tried the filing cabinet and found that the top drawer was locked. The bottom two, though, were filled with maps of what looked like the campus and surrounding area. I thumbed through them but didn't find much of interest. At the center of the room stood a large circular table with blueprints strewn around it. Examining them more closely,

I saw they seemed to be plans for repairs or an expansion of some kind. As best as I could make out, it might be for an irrigation system. The strange thing about it, though, was that the plans seemed to correspond to the island. Was this why they were keeping me away from it? They were doing some kind of agricultural project out there? I went back into the central hallway and headed out a large metal door off to the side. As I'd hoped, it led into the woods on the other side of the building.

Around me the warm night winds tore through the trees, creating a sound like a distant train. It felt like a storm might be on the way. As calmly as I could, I headed back toward my cabana, lost in thought as my mind spiraled with possibilities. It wasn't until I was almost to my cabana that the truth of the situation occurred to me. The island was off-limits, and yet they were building some complicated irrigation system for it. Suddenly it all came into view. They must be growing weed out there. Was that what all the secrecy was about? A cannabis operation? Wasn't pot legal in Colorado? I felt a wave of relief wash over me. No wonder Isabelle was hanging bottles in her basement and making nonsensical treasure hunts all over the campus. She wasn't under psychic attack or being hunted by the Illuminati. Perhaps the good scientist, like many before her, was simply getting too high on her own supply.

As I headed into the cabana, the night felt particularly alive around me, as if the animals themselves were excited by my discovery, and for the first time since coming to Hildegard, I felt curiously at one with the environment. I almost felt like I could disappear into the ecosystem and no one would be the wiser.

Yawning, I opened the door to my cabana, and when I saw the divination tools on my bed, I absently picked them up. If I was honest with myself, I wanted nothing to do with the cards.

They might be interesting anthropologically, but they also gave me a bad feeling. It wasn't just the excessively violent imagery; there was also something uncanny about them, like they were snapshots from a dream I wanted to forget. The widows' keys, though, fascinated me. Taking the velvet bag over to the coffee table, I spilled them out on top. Although they were vaguely familiar, I still couldn't make sense of them. It was impossible to decipher them without a key text, but that didn't stop me from admiring them. They seemed to throb with an indiscernible kind of meaning. I picked up the bright crescent moon, and holding it in my palm, I stared at it like a woman scrying into a mirror. Still, it gave no secrets away. Sighing, I left the widows' keys on the coffee table and got ready for bed. When I climbed back under the covers, the tension eased from my body and I relaxed into the pillow.

It happened almost instantly, that sickening sense that something was wrong. Around me, the room grew a distant kind of gray, as if I were a denizen of another plane, a reality laid directly on top of our own. I tried to move, but my muscles only tensed with panicked futility. Acid rose up in my throat as I realized that once again, I was trapped in my own body. I tried to scream, and although my vocal cords burned with effort, no sound issued from them, and my lips remained still.

As I lay there in that gray, unreal world, it took every ounce of my control not to let the fear overtake me. My mind drifted to the figure I'd seen standing over my bed the night of the sirens. I imagined it now crouching by my feet. I imagined it leaning over me with a slavering maw, opening an expansive jaw to reveal a set of dagger-like teeth. The powerlessness was overwhelming. I told myself that it had to pass eventually, but in the moment, that didn't seem possible. It felt like I would be trapped in that state forever. So I breathed slowly and deeply. I told myself that I would be okay because I had no other choice.

I don't know when reality shifted, but at some point, I realized I must have fallen asleep.

I dream of the gardens, vast and twinkling in the mists of twilight. Clusters of fireflies constellate the horizon, and I can see someone up ahead—a flitting of white fabric, wind-rippled as it floats around scurrying feet, pale and bare. Soon she comes into view, jet-black hair, a moon-white dress.

"Isabelle," I whisper.

I try to follow, but the night grows darker, and I know I'll never catch her in time. All around me—a buzzing sound.

"Are you sure it's Isabelle?" asks a voice to my left. It's Aspen, bathed in moonlight and stretched out on an elegant chaise longue. She wears an evening gown made entirely of peacock feathers. "Or is it Sabine? They let her die. We all let her die. So that she might be reborn."

"It's Isabelle," I say. "She has my relic."

"Better catch her quick, then. Before Les Terribles get her. They're all around, you know." Aspen plucks a feather from her dress and holds it up to her face, its jade eye obscuring her own. "Just out of sight."

I'm at the lake now, the sand between my toes. Water laps against the shore and through the fog I can see them—thirteen figures all in a circle. A living relic. At the center stands a woman in white, black hair hanging down in wet waves. Now I'm in the circle, too, part of the coven as it begins to snow.

Isabelle stands perfectly still, her back to me. Her hair is stringy and tangled now, the hair of a madwoman. Her dress is in tatters, more gray than white, and her arms, hanging limp at her side, are covered with scratches. Some of the wounds are slowly oozing blood, crimson rivulets dripping into the snow that now blankets the ground.

I reach out to touch her, but she's no longer there.

The snow falls on my outstretched arm. Not snow—ash.

I'm on the pier now, perched at the edge, and I can see something in the lake, circling in the depths. Slowly it begins to rise, silvery and white, up through the water. A sea creature, gelatinous and massive. Up it comes, a mass of pulsating tentacles. Only when it nears the surface do I see that its tentacles are no more than diaphanous sleeves. Isabelle. Around her, hair swirls out and away like obsidian snakes. One slips up and around my ankle. A tug and I crash through the water. She pulls me down into the deep. All the while, I can see her smiling beside me, her mouth split into a cruel grin—rotten teeth and tangled lake moss—as she drags me down to the subterranean depths, down to the Terrible Ones.

Suddenly I was no longer dreaming. Water slipped between my toes and rain cascaded down my shoulders, the sensations all too real. With horror I realized I wasn't in bed, but standing outside at the edge of the pier, rain thrashing down around me.

With a jolt, I seized, my body wrenched out of that half-dreaming state and back into the sharpness of reality. I stumbled from the edge and looked around, searching for some explanation. It had happened again. I had no memory of how I'd gotten here.

Staring out at the shadowy water, I tried to make sense of what was happening to me. I hadn't . . . I hadn't actually been in the lake, had I? Lightning slashed through the sky, imparting a sudden vivid clarity. Once again, the world was just the world. Coming to my senses, I turned and raced through the rain back to my cabana.

Once I was safely inside, I dried myself off and changed, and then got into bed, staring out the window at the storm outside.

2.4

NEGATIVE IONS:
THE LINK BETWEEN UFOS
AND BODIES OF WATER

A spokesman for a special and little known Royal Canadian Air Force department in Ottawa for the investigation of Unidentified Flying Objects said last night a series of bright lights which glided into the ocean off Shag Harbor, Shelburne County, Wednesday night may be one of the extremely rare cases where "something concrete" may be found. The spokesman, who identified himself as Squadron Leader Bain, said his department was "very interested" in the matter.

—Halifax Chronicle Herald, *October 7, 1967*

The next morning when my alarm woke me, the previous night's jaunt felt like no more than a hallucination. If I hadn't felt the dampness of my clothes hanging over the back of my chair to dry, I might never have believed it. As I dressed, my heart was heavy. I felt like I was losing control of my consciousness, and I knew I needed to seriously consider the possibility that I had a sleep disorder. Since coming to Hildegard, I'd had instances of both sleep paralysis and sleepwalking, and while the former was frightening, the latter, I knew, could be dangerous. What if I hadn't awakened when I did? What if I'd fallen into the lake?

Would I have woken up when I hit the water? Or would I have just continued on, dreaming a liquid death as I slowly sank to the bottom?

In something of a haze, I managed to make myself some coffee. After pulling on boots and a robe, I started out to the garden, but still groggy, I stumbled on the path and went careening into a lilac bush. A string of expletives followed.

"You okay over there?" Finn called from beyond the wall.

"Fine," I called, standing up and dusting myself off.

"I made cinnamon rolls," he called again. "You want one?"

"You made cinnamon rolls?" I asked, incredulous. "Like, you *made them* made them? Like, with dough?"

"Yeah. I'll meet you at your front door. They're still warm."

I didn't ask him how early he must have gotten up to make the rolls, though I was curious if this was some essential part of his character or if it was an aberration. I stuffed down two warm, delicious cinnamon rolls while sitting on the couch, legs tucked underneath me, blanket over my lap. It was the most at home I'd felt in . . . well, in a long time.

Together, we sipped coffee and we chatted about books and pop culture, the conversation light and healing. He must have known something was wrong—I was so exhausted from the previous evening that I could barely keep my eyes open—but he didn't mention it or ask about it, which I appreciated. And when I asked him about the others, he was happy to oblige, regaling me with stories about the time he and Aspen accidentally took mushrooms, or when Lexi once set a barn on fire.

"I didn't even realize you had a barn here."

"Well, we don't anymore," he said, throwing us both into a fit of laughter.

As we laughed, though, I started to feel uneasy again, like someone was watching me. Dr. Casimir, wild woman of the woods?

"This is going to sound crazy, but are you sure Dr. Casimir isn't still here?"

"I'm pretty sure one of us would have noticed," he said with a flash of a smile.

"This is a big property. Couldn't she be out in the woods somewhere?"

"There's no way she could have survived the winter." He took a sip of his coffee. "Though I suppose she could have come back. Is there a reason you think she might be here?"

"Wishful thinking, maybe. I'm still really hoping to get my hands on the artifact she found. If you had to guess where she might have put it, what would you say?"

"Honestly? I would guess she took it with her."

"Really? But what if it's an important artifact? She wouldn't just take it with her and disappear, would she? What if it got damaged?"

"You have to remember, she was kind of a dick."

I laughed. "You say that, but I'm having the hardest time trying to understand her. Some of you loved her, while some of you didn't. She was a hard science person, but maybe she also believed in magic. The whole thing gives off a 'madwoman in the attic' vibe. What was she really like?"

He lowered his eyes. "You don't want to know about that."

"No, but I do."

He sighed. "You say that now, but someday you're going to look back on this conversation and wish you hadn't had it."

That unsettled me a bit, but I decided to press on.

"I won't hold you to anything you say. And I won't repeat it. Please? We're neighbors."

He leaned back in his chair, hands behind his head. "Okay, fine. What do you want to know?"

"Well, I'm having trouble getting an accurate picture of her. Everyone seemed to have been in awe of her except for you."

"Yeah. I told you before, I didn't care for Isabelle."

"But why not?"

"Can't I just dislike someone?"

"Sure, but you must have had your reasons."

He seemed uncomfortable, crossing his arms in front of his chest, and if I wasn't mistaken, his voice raised half an octave. "She was a phony. She was charismatic and beautiful and amazing at what she did, so everyone wanted to ignore the rest of her. But I couldn't. I saw right through her the whole time, and I didn't like what I saw."

"Why were you the only person who saw this?"

"Because I was the only one who would let myself see it."

"And you said the feelings were mutual? She disliked you, too?"

He grinned proudly. "Hated me. And you can imagine how that went, sharing a wall with her."

"How long did she work here? How long have you worked here, for that matter?"

"Isabelle was relatively new. She'd been here maybe five years. The rest of us grew up here."

I stared at him, shocked. "What? Who grew up here?"

"All of us—me, Dorian, Lexi, Aspen."

I sat in stunned silence. An uncomfortably eerie feeling settled over me. I tapped my notebook. "I don't understand. You all grew up together and then somehow, magically, all ended up with jobs at Hildegard College?"

From what I knew about how difficult it was to secure an academic position, this seemed not just impossible but almost laughable.

"Our parents were all professors here. They still are, in fact. Just gone for the summer."

My stomach dropped even further. What Finn was saying sounded completely ridiculous. I decided to change the subject.

"So Isabelle's research, do you have any idea what that research involved?"

"Not really," he said with a noncommittal shrug. "Neurocognitive stuff."

I stared at him a moment, hoping to break through some barrier, to force myself through whatever wall he had put up, but I saw no openings. Then something occurred to me.

"She didn't do anything with parasomnias, did she? Sleepwalking, sleep paralysis, anything like that?"

He looked up at me suddenly. "Hey, want to go hiking?"

"What?" I couldn't hide my shock. The invitation had come completely out of left field.

"Hiking. I'm going. Do you want to come?"

"Now?" I asked, befuddled.

"Yeah, now. Why not?"

"Okay," I said, trying to adjust. "Sure. Why not?"

His abrupt change in mood wasn't lost on me. I asked about sleep paralysis and suddenly he was inviting me hiking? Clearly I had touched a nerve. I didn't really want to go hiking, but I did want to see what else might happen if I kept pushing.

"Where are you going?"

"Just a little hike up the mountain."

"Isn't that off-limits?"

"Naw, I stay on the trails. Besides, the mountain is fine."

"Yeah," I said. "I'd love to."

On Finn's instruction, I brought a swimsuit, but I couldn't find my sunglasses, so he lent me some. Soon we were walking toward the far edge of campus, out past the apiary, and started up the tree-lined path. It was a slow incline, switchbacks cutting a leisurely path up the mountain until the trail began to narrow and grow steep. We passed some lovely groves of silver pines and several gently burbling streams. The mountain air felt amazing, the way it filled my lungs and coursed through me. I could almost feel it energizing my cells.

The birds were incredibly active up there, and as the morning began to lengthen into an ever-brighter day, I saw some spectacular avian specimens—red-tailed hawks, northern flickers, and even a great blue heron. Finn pointed it out as it soared overhead, its two-toned coloring on full display, its wings spread out into an impressive span.

After a final, very steep climb, we reached our destination—a rocky outcropping from which we could look down on the expanse below. From up there, Hildegard College seemed so small, so insignificant. Even the lake and that island looked fairly modest and inconsequential. But what struck me was the isolation. We really were terribly alone, weren't we? And from this bird's-eye view, the woods that spread out and away from campus looked positively menacing. The foliage appeared unusually dark, and the forest itself seemed somehow too thick. There was also an odd sense of motion to the trees: as if windblown, they bent en masse toward the college—a great creeping Birnam

Wood intent on swallowing up the only man-made structure in its path.

After pulling our water bottles from our packs, we sat on the ground, drinking and chatting. I tried to press him more about Isabelle, but he clammed up, so I got him chatting more generally, hoping it might lead somewhere. We talked about women (apparently he liked them) and books (not so much). But when the subject of family came up, a melancholy seemed to wash over him.

"I have a sister, you know," he said, shifting his weight forward so he was kneeling. "She used to work here, too."

"Really? But not anymore?"

"No. She left." He shifted his gaze, staring into the distance, wrapping his arms around his knees.

"Can I ask why she left?"

"Things aren't as friendly here as they might seem. Some of us have to get out."

"I've heard that about academia. It isn't for everyone, apparently."

He took a swig of his water. "I don't mean academia. I mean this place in particular."

"Why? What is it about Hildegard?"

"It's old, really old. And it has roots that go back even further. And there is always a kind of schism between the old ways and the new—two paths, if you will—and my sister got really paranoid about one of the paths, let's just call it a heavier one."

"I'm not sure I understand what you're talking about."

He looked at me squarely. "We're starting to see this all over the world in all kinds of different groups. What was once secret and taboo is coming to the fore, unafraid to hide anymore, and that's what she feared was happening with Hildegard, with the governing bodies of the institution." He gazed out over the trees below. "She just decided she didn't want to be part of it anymore—of any of it." Pursing his lips, he looked over at me and then shook his head.

"You must miss her."

"I do. But," he said, clapping his hands, "listen to me going on. We came up here to swim. The lake is off-limits, so this is the closest spot for free swimming. Might as well take advantage."

I looked at him sideways, deciding to see what I might be able to tease out of him. "Seriously, no one ever goes out to that island?"

He shook his head. "The lake, the island, it's all off-limits. The higher-ups don't want us going near any of it."

"And you never question that?"

"It's not my job to question it. Come on," he said, jumping up. "Last one in's a dialectical materialist!"

The watering hole wasn't much to look at, but it was a dream to swim in. There was a low rock with a trickle of a waterfall spilling into the pool below, and although it probably wasn't safe, we spent the afternoon jumping off it, cannonballing and drenching each other. A relaxed sort of exhaustion settled over me as we headed back down the mountain. We made it home just as the midday sun crested and began its descent into afternoon.

<hr/>

I spent the rest of the day leisurely perusing my research and trying to think about anything I might be missing. Eventually I found myself thinking about silphium. I knew it had to have some significance somehow, but as far as I could tell, the topic led nowhere. Every source I consulted told me much the same thing: It was an extinct wonder drug. What was I supposed to get from that? What could an extinct plant have to do with Isabelle? Eventually I got hungry, so I closed my computer and got cleaned up for dinner.

Up at the house, I found the others on the terrace, sipping champagne from delicate flutes. They were laughing, and Aspen, her hair done up in an elaborate twist, looked decidedly like a 1920s socialite. Her charm bracelet, dangling from her delicate wrist, glinted in the dying summer sun, and as I approached, the sparkle from it caught my eye.

"There you are," she exclaimed, holding up her glass. "Your ears must have been burning."

"Champagne?" Dorian asked, motioning to the bottle cooling in a bucket of ice.

"Finn tells us you had a nature excursion today," said Dorian.

"We did," I said, taking a glass of champagne. "We hiked up to this cool overlook and then went swimming for a bit. It's such a pretty area."

"I love that spot," gushed Aspen, pressing her mostly empty flute to her heart.

"I despise nature," said Lexi, elegantly slouched in a rattan chair. "So nature-y. It's disgusting."

"Did you see any birds?" asked Dorian. "I'm something of a secret birder."

"Is there any other kind?" Lexi laughed, raising her glass in a faux cheers, sending champagne sloshing out onto the stones.

Finn began enumerating birds (red-tailed hawk, rosy finch) while I sipped my champagne (dry, very bubbly), but soon I could feel Lexi's eyes on me. "So, Robin, we were just discussing the nature of evil."

"Breezy topic."

She shrugged. "It passes the time. What are your thoughts?"

"On evil?" I laughed. "I don't think I have any."

"But surely you must have some. You study witch hunts," said Dorian. "Do you not think the people who burned innocents alive were evil?"

"I don't know. I really don't. I think there are evil acts, and I think people can behave in evil ways, but I don't know that a person can be, like, evil exactly. Only flawed enough to commit an evil act."

"Oh, people can be evil," Dorian said with a disconcerting grin. "I know it for a fact."

"How can you know something like that for a fact?"

"Because I have stood here on these very grounds and I've looked it in the eye. And let me tell you, once you see it, there's no way to mistake it for anything else."

The group grew quiet. A straggler bee buzzed around the flowery weeds that sprouted up between the flagstones at our feet. High in a tree, a bird called—a quick whoop followed by three short trills.

Finn cleared his throat. "On that note, let's go in to dinner."

Later that night, I was cleaning up around the cabana when I realized I still had Finn's sunglasses. I decided to return them and say good night. I was starting to feel like we were becoming friends, and when you're stranded in the middle of nowhere with a bunch of weirdos, that's no small thing.

I found him sitting on his couch drinking a beer. He seemed different, pensive, and I realized he probably didn't want me bothering him. Just because I was lonely and wanted to hang out didn't mean he felt the same. So I put his sunglasses on the sideboard and was starting to leave when he said something odd.

"There was no dig."

A thick silence enveloped the space around me. "What?" I said carefully.

"There was no dig, Robin. There wasn't even a blog post."

It was the same story Aspen had tried to foist on me, but this was different. His words hit me hard. Annoyed, I pulled out my phone and searched for the post. I would just show him. But when I tried to find it, I couldn't. It didn't seem to be there anymore.

"It's gone, isn't it?" he asked with a cruel smile.

"I know what I saw. I read it myself."

He closed his eyes, frustrated. "No, I'm not saying it didn't exist. I'm saying it was a plant."

"A plant? To what end?"

"To get you here."

I stood there, stunned. "What? You're joking."

"I'm not."

"Why are you telling me this?"

He raised his beer. "Better to live a short noble life than a long selfish one."

"What is that supposed to mean?"

"It means be careful of the company you keep."

I stared at him, a heavy suspicion sinking into my bones. I'd thought he was my friend, but clearly I was wrong. For some reason he wanted me to stop nosing around about Isabelle and the relic. If anything, that only made me more determined to find it.

He stood up and set his beer bottle on the counter with perhaps too much force. "I gotta go to bed."

He walked me to the door, but once he opened it, he looked at me pointedly. "You don't believe me. I can see that. But let me ask you this. What happened to you right before you found the blog post?"

"I don't know. I was working on my dissertation."

"Were you with anyone?"

"Yeah. I was staying with my cousin Paloma."

He put a hand on his hip. "And did Paloma start acting strange?"

My spine went ice cold. "How do you know that?"

"Look," he said, shaking his head, "it wasn't housekeeping that cleaned up those witch bottles. And my guess is they were serving a purpose. I would watch my back if I were you."

When I left Finn's, I didn't go back to my cabana, but instead walked down to the lake and stared across the dark expanse to the island. I was beset by a confounding mixture of emotion. I didn't believe for a second that Finn was telling me the truth, and I found myself feeling unexpectedly angry, but I was also hurt—too hurt for this to really be about Finn. Once again, I was back to Charles Danforth and the sickening sadness that enveloped me whenever he came to mind. It was ridiculous the way my heart refused to let go of him, how desperately I clung to the pain of it, as if moving past the pain would mean losing him forever, but that's where I was. It was sad but true. A friend can break your heart more brutally than any lover.

Staring out at the island, I began to grow increasingly frustrated. I'd been told repeatedly not to go in the lake and that the island was off-limits, but why had I listened? Clearly Finn was lying to me. Probably the others were as well. They were stopping me from finding the relic, they were making me doubt the post I'd seen, and from the beginning they had directed me to stay out of the water and away from the island. But just because the boat was missing didn't mean I couldn't get to the island. I was a strong swimmer, and it wasn't too far. Screw their rules. I was going out to that island if for no other reason than those assholes told me not to.

2.5

CRYPTOZOOLOGY AS A
PRECURSOR TO BIOLOGY

Further verification for this comes from the fact that a considerable number of officially accepted, well-known animals were cryptids prior to their "official" recognition . . . The mountain gorilla—officially recognized in 1901—had been reported to European explorers during the 1860s but, like the lowland gorilla, had been dismissed as legendary.

—DARREN NAISH, PHD, PALEONTOLOGIST

I was up before dawn, slipping on my bathing suit and heading down to the lake. A few mourning doves were just starting to coo, but other than that, the noises and scents belonged to the night. At the edge of the lake, I dropped my things and waded out. I was shocked by how temperate the water was. Hadn't someone told me it was freezing? When these people lied, they didn't even bother to come up with good lies. When I was about up to my waist, I sank the rest of the way down into the water and started a slow crawl, careful to splash as little as possible. As I slid through the water, I found a sense of peace settling over me. There was something about being out alone during the early hours that was incredibly restorative. I was used to feeling lonely when I was alone, but as I crossed that lake while the first glimmers of sunlight crept over the eastern mountains, I felt comforted and loved in a way I'd rarely experienced.

About three-quarters of the way to the island, I thought I felt movement in the water beneath me—like something large had shifted. I froze, treading water and looking around me. A moment later, I thought I heard an inexplicable noise, almost like someone exhaling. My heart racing, I pushed on rapidly toward the island, my leisurely crawl changing to a sprint. I didn't stop to think. I just pulled myself through the water until I reached the rocky shoreline of the island.

Out of breath and shaking as much from the adrenaline as from the chill of the morning air, I pulled myself up on the rocks. Finding my footing, I quickly made it the rest of the way up. When I'd reached level ground, I stared back at the water behind me. It was smooth and still. I shook my head. If there had been some monstrous creature in the water with me as I'd imagined there was, I would see signs of it. But the water was so placid that nothing could possibly be hiding in its depths.

But I knew I couldn't waste time thinking about a giant fish. I had to work quickly. The island was small, but it was dense with cypress and pines. Ivy blanketed the ground, and shrubs of English lavender dotted the area. I started walking toward the center of the island, but I could see nothing out of the ordinary, definitely not a well-organized grow operation.

At one point, I heard something up above and stopped to listen, frightened that I might not be alone on the island. But then I heard a whoosh of air and looked up to see an enormous owl swooping down on me. Its eyes shone like glass in the early-morning light, and I lost my breath at the sight of its beauty. But then it was gone, and I was left feeling like a dizzy fool standing by myself, still dripping with lake water.

I'd been walking for a while and the sun had fully risen when I saw something unusual. It was just about dead center in the middle of the island—a large clearing filled with billowing plants. Like the fields of tall grass I'd seen on the mainland, this area was cut through with paths lined with paper lanterns. In this case, though, each path led toward a central stone column rising up from the earth. That was strange. Why would there be a plinth in the middle of a field? I waded through the tall grass toward it, my mind racing to understand what I was seeing. It was about four feet high and had an almost ominous, other-worldly glow to it. Or maybe it was just the way the morning light hit it.

When I neared the column, I realized this looked very familiar. I'd seen all this before in the manuscript illustration—the woman with the blue robes sitting atop a pillar, surrounded by plants. When I touched it, I was surprised to find that it was intensely cold and unexpectedly smooth. I ran my hand along the top of it. Marble. It stood defiantly in that field like the single remnant of an ancient ruin, but what kind of ruin would be out in such a remote location? And how ancient did things get in Colorado? I looked all around the pillar, hoping to find some kind of inscription, but there was nothing. Carefully I climbed up to sit on it (because one can't very well see an illustration of an oracle sitting on such a stone and not give it a try oneself), and stared out over the sea of tall grass. And then it struck me—the plants weren't just ordinary plants.

Sliding down from the pillar and lunging for the grass, I took the leaves delicately in hand and examined them. The plants had thick black stalks with leaves similar to celery and yellow flowers sprouting from hearty stems.

"Oh my god," I whispered even though there was no one nearby to hear me even if I'd yelled.

Leaning closer, I inhaled. It smelled strange, heady and musky all at once with hints of lavender and leather. I'd seen this plant before. It was the botanical drawing someone had left me. It was supposed to be extinct, and yet here it was, a field of it growing out in the middle of nowhere.

"Silphium," I whispered again.

My thoughts shifted to the blueprints I'd seen, to the irrigation system, and a curious fluttering sensation alighted in my heart. Good God. It wasn't cannabis that they were growing after all. It was silphium.

For just a moment I thought I saw something in the dirt. But when I bent down to examine more closely, I noticed the sun glinting off something in the distance.

I stood up abruptly. There was a domed structure a short way through the trees. My heart racing, I started through the tall grass toward it, careful now not to trample on anything. Soon I found myself on a stone path that led through the woods to what appeared to be a small circular building not much larger than Jim's garden shed, but fashioned out of the most beautiful stone. It almost resembled a Grecian temple, but in miniature, and had an intricately carved blue door.

Turning the handle, I found it unlocked. The door opened onto a circular room with stone walls. A blue writing desk sat in the center of the room, and there was a low-slung couch against one of the walls and an indigo throw rug on the stone floor. The color of the stone in the center was slightly different from that of the rest of the floor. As soon as I stepped inside,

I had the strong feeling that this was Isabelle's space. I don't know how I knew, and there was nothing to provide immediate confirmation, but somehow I just knew. The office off the scriptorium had never been hers. They'd been lying to me right from the start.

The remarkable thing about the room was that from about the height of three feet up, the walls were completely covered with books. Shelves of them circled up as high as the domed ceiling, and a sliding oak ladder was affixed to the wall to allow access. It was clear, though, that these weren't ordinary books. With ornate spines and lustrous color, they were unlike anything I'd ever seen, even more spectacular than the manuscripts in the scriptorium. They bore names like *Liber Ignium, Book of Mercy, Mutus Liber,* and *Mappae Clavicula.*

I pulled out one called *Atalanta Fugiens,* and opening it, I turned to a bizarre illustration that upon first viewing made me recoil. It showed a heavily pregnant woman nursing a child while next to her another infant suckled on a goat, and beside that, another two suckled on a wolf. As I studied the illustration more closely, though, I realized that these images were symbolic. The woman's belly was the earth, so she most likely was Gaia, mother of the Titans. And the twins with the wolf must be Romulus and Remus, the founder of Rome and the brother he slew. I wasn't sure about the goat, but I hoped it had an equally benign explanation. I slid the book back on the shelf.

I stood, hands on my hips, trying to understand just where exactly I was. I had no idea what this room could be, but it looked like a perfect place to hide a relic. Isabelle's description had given me no sense of its size, but there was no reason to think it was large. My eyes fell on the desk.

I moved over to it and tried one of the ornate handles on the drawers, but it wouldn't budge. When I tried the others, I found them all locked as well. I searched for a keyhole that might fit the key I had back in my cabana, but there was nothing. Turning my attention back to the books, I climbed up the ladder and made my way through the upper shelves, but found nothing. Eventually I climbed down from the ladder and looked back at the desk.

On the top of it, next to a writing pad, was a little wooden box affixed to the surface. It held thirteen rotating letter tiles. Tingles ran up and down my arms as the thrill of the hunt overtook me. This had to be it. Another puzzle. I needed to rotate the letters to release the lock and open the drawers.

Right from the beginning, nothing at Hildegard had made any sense. My unremarkable reality had been shifted askew, turned on its head. Was I part of some experiment? Some cult initiation? It stood to reason that the bounty yielded from the previous leg of this bizarre treasure hunt should provide the clue to solve the desk lock. That was how this worked, wasn't it? Someone was leading me from clue to clue, wanting me to progress. So most likely I had all the information I needed to get into that desk.

I examined the lock more closely. Thirteen letters. I thought back to the botanical drawing. The words scrawled on the back had been *the very deep did rot*. I'd assumed this would provide the base letters for another anagram, but that phrase was seventeen letters, and there were only thirteen here. Still, it was worth a try. I entered those first thirteen letters: *the very deep di*, but as expected, that did nothing. Then I tried *Coleridge*, but that was four letters too short. What was

I missing? I ran my palms over the smooth blue surface and tried to think.

Scanning the room, I searched for anything that might serve as a supplemental clue, but with the wealth of books and little else, there was both too much and too little in terms of options. No, I had to work with what I had. Returning to the desk, I sat down, tented my fingers under my nose, and exhaled deeply. *Think, Robin. Think.*

I tried a few more ineffective permutations of anagrams for *the very deep did rot*, leaving off letters mostly at random, but I knew this wasn't the path. The previous clue had reveled in the playful use of language. So Isabelle liked words. She liked poetry. Maybe she herself was a poet. I needed to refocus on the poet himself, on Coleridge. What did I know about him? I knew he was one of the Romantic poets along with Shelley and Keats and that lot. I knew he was a hopeless opium addict. I knew he claimed that his great poem, "Kubla Khan," had been interrupted by a *person on business from Porlock,* but that had too many letters as well. No. It needed to be simpler. I closed my eyes and counted letters.

Samuel Coleridge = 15 letters
Samuel T Coleridge = 16 letters
Sam T Coleridge = 13 letters

Bingo. I tried it, but still nothing, so I got to work looking for anagrams. I wrote out *Sam T Coleridge* and began rearranging the letters. The first few I came up with didn't work: *domestic regal, dogmatic leers, disco telegram*—I quite liked that one.

And then there it was, sitting right on the page. It practically jumped out at me as if I'd seen it before. I hadn't exactly seen it, but I had heard it: *Latecomers dig.* The words Jim had said to me at the shed.

I entered the letters, and when I slid the final one into place, a shifting sound issued from inside the desk, and the drawers unlatched and sprang open a centimeter or so. Carefully I pulled open the top drawer to find an ancient-looking book and a manila envelope. I opened the envelope and slid its contents onto the desk.

It was a single photo from the same series as the photo Dorian had shown me, that same glittering gathering of flattering candlelight and stylish cocktails. A pair of large male hands flashed in front of the camera, though, partially obscuring Lexi and Finn. I exhaled. I had been expecting something awful—dismembered limbs, a throne made of skulls—but this was just a photo of a group of friends.

Setting the photo down, I turned my attention to the book. I saw that it was called *The Book of Widows,* and when I opened it, I was elated to see the symbols that corresponded to the widows' keys I'd found. So this was the text that explained those keys, laying them out like a chart with almost mathematical precision. The left side of each page showed a set of three of the symbols followed by an explanation. I ran my finger along the top line. Similar to a chart to help a diviner understand a selection of runes or even the hexagrams in the *I Ching,* this seemed to give an interpretation for a trio of tiles when pulled together. As I stared down at the images in the book, I could almost find meaning in them, but not quite.

Vibrant Earth, Desolate Moon, Stable Sea
From a mountaintop, he sees three new goats.
A wolf attacks. It takes only meat. The <u>toad</u>
looks on.

Flipping the page, I selected another:

Desolate Earth, Stable Moon, Desolate Sea
The fox hides in its den. It must not reveal it-
self until the danger passes. It will not want
for food.

Flipping further through in the text, I saw one that seemed appropriate:

Vibrant Moon, Desolate Moon, Stable Sea
Beneath the water, the eye watches the stars.
When the mistress calls, it will make itself
known.

As I turned the remaining pages, I was once again struck by a vague sense of recognition, though I couldn't place it. As I examined each entry, a whisper of meaning drifted past me, but expired before I could catch on to anything. I closed the book.

Standing there, I felt a nagging sensation in the pit of my stomach. Something wasn't right. Something my body knew but my mind did not. Again, I picked up the photo. The hands, was there some clue for me there?

After examining the hands closely, I came to the conclusion that they were unrecognizable and bore no distinctive features. But then something in the background did catch my eye. A young woman dressed as a maid, head bowed, ducking out of the room.

"What?" I whispered as I peered down at the photo, trying to get a better look at the face. "No, it's not possible."

I felt like I'd been kicked in the gut. The woman in the photo, this anonymous maid ducking out of view, I knew her. It was my cousin, Paloma.

My heart beat so loudly that it was almost deafening. Paloma had been here? A wave of cold settled over me as the world seemed to turn upside down. Paloma had been in Colorado? When could she possibly have been here? Discordant emotions and realities clashed into one another and seemed to coalesce in my heart, which had begun to beat wildly out of control. Unable to put a name to the kind of fear I felt, I decided the smartest thing to do was to get the hell out of there. In a panic, I realized I couldn't take the book and the photo with me, because I needed to swim. I would just have to return for them later. Still shaking, I put everything back as I'd found it and closed and locked the front door.

After leaving the little office, I started back the way I'd come, but when I got to the marble pillar, I felt an odd pull to it. I walked through the plants toward it, and when I reached it, once again I hoisted myself up to sit on it. From my perch, I looked out over the trees and couldn't fight the sinking feeling that something terrible had happened here.

Again, something caught my eye, something in the dirt, down at the base of the plants. I hopped down from the pillar and hurried over to it, pushing aside the foliage. There was something down there. As carefully as I could, I dug down until I had a clear view into the dirt. Suddenly I hit it.

Dried blood. A lot of it. All caked into the dirt in patches, fanning out in all directions from the pillar. I stood up, my spine straightening. It was possible there was some other explanation, but from my current vantage point—the remote location, the ritualistic-looking pillar—it looked a lot like the site of a human sacrifice.

Sick to my stomach, I started quickly toward the lake. The sun was all the way up now. People would be waking soon. At a healthy pace, I made my way back to the shore, and when the water came into view, I noticed something glinting down below. I could see it for only a second before the clouds shifted and it was obscured once again. I scrambled down the rocks and slipped into the water. Again, it felt warm in comparison to the brisk morning air. I started swimming across the lake, hoping to get about halfway to shore before I dove down to see what I could make of the lake bottom. By then the clouds should have passed and the sun would help me see what, if anything, could be seen. When I reached a good halfway point, I treaded water to catch my breath, and then, taking a big gulp of air, plunged quickly down through the water, my eyes fixed on something strange below me. Despite the clarity of the water, the bottom was hard to see. It was as if something was blocking my vision, a kind of sheen. Squeezing my eyes shut and then reopening them, I finally saw what it was that had glinted in the morning light.

Instead of a lake bottom, the place was lined with an enormous metal grate. Kicking hard, I continued down until my hands nearly grasped it. The visibility wasn't great, but as far as I could tell, the entire lake was lined with some kind of metal, and down below it, the basin extended into total darkness, an unknowable abyss beyond.

I didn't understand and I was running out of breath, beginning almost to panic. I would need air very soon. I ran my hand along the top of the grate, feeling the algae-covered metal. And when I plunged my hands through the openings, I saw that the other side of the grate was dotted with huge iron spikes. And then I understood what I was seeing. I was up against the mouth of some kind of a cage. The metal spikes were meant to keep something in.

Instinctively, I let go, and my chest nearly bursting, I kicked off the metal and swam up as fast as I could. As I surged through the surface layer, air flooded my lungs, and I had a momentary sense of complete and total gratitude before remembering that I still had to make it to the beach. Gasping for air, my head straining out of the water, I raced for the shore, doing whatever I could just to propel myself to safety. My thoughts spiraled, but I tried to calm myself. Whatever was going on here, I could think about it later. For now, all I needed to think about was getting out of the lake.

As soon as I was in waist-deep water, I stood and pushed through the rest of the way to the shore, where I collapsed on the sand. I lay there longer than I should have, my chest heaving, my body shaking. Staring up at the early-morning sun, I tried to reorient myself.

When I finally pushed myself up to sit and gazed out at the water, myriad questions flashed through my mind, but they were all drowned out by two overriding ones: What the hell was at the bottom of that lake, and why were they trying to keep it from getting out?

I took a nap when I got back, sleeping fitfully into the late morning, and when I awoke, I was disoriented and confused. Rattled by everything I'd found out on that island, I barely knew where to begin. They were growing an ancient plant, there was something seriously messed up going on with the lake, and these people knew Paloma. I needed answers, but I also knew that getting them was going to be next to impossible. I'd discovered all of these things by doing the main thing I'd been told not to do. If they found out what I'd done, they could rescind my residency at any time and send me packing, and then I'd never find the relic.

When I went up to lunch, I was in something of a state. Unhinged, angry, I decided it was time to stop being polite. I knew I couldn't mention the silphium or the lake, but I could figure out a way to find out about Paloma. I had to. I still hadn't been able to get ahold of her, and although I'd been telling myself that my fears were unfounded, I now had reason to believe she was connected to this place, connected to Isabelle. What if she was in danger as well?

I must have seemed distracted as I toyed with my grilled branzino and potatoes lyonnaise.

"Are you feeling all right?" asked Aspen. "You're quiet today."

I looked up from my food to see the four of them staring at me. "As they say, *Celui qui ne comprend pas devrait apprendre ou se taire.*"

"Who does not understand should learn or be silent," Finn translated.

"I saw it out front when I first arrived. John Dee, isn't it?"

"Yes," said Dorian.

I set my fork down. "Why John Dee?"

"He was a prominent mathematician," said Aspen.

"He was also an occultist. Seems like a strange choice."

Aspen laughed. "He was the court advisor to Elizabeth I."

I turned and looked toward the kitchen. "I've been wondering, I never see any kitchen staff. Who is making all this delicious food?" I didn't mention that I'd seen Paloma dressed as a maid standing in this very room. I would leave that out for now.

"Why do you ask?"

"Curiosity," I said, but then I had an idea. "Also, I've been thinking about writing an article about Hildegard."

They looked at me blankly.

"What?" Lexi said after a moment.

"I'm just interested in the history of the place, and until I can find Casimir's artifact, I think this might be a good use of my time. I find Hildegard fascinating. So really, where is the kitchen staff? Can I meet them?"

Finn, Lexi, and Dorian looked unnerved, but Aspen was unfazed. She slid some fish onto her fork and lifted it to her mouth. "There is no kitchen staff," she said after she'd swallowed.

I laughed. "Then who is making the food?"

"Lexi is," said Aspen with an authoritative nod.

Looking remarkably like a deer caught in headlights, Lexi took a generous sip of her wine. "Yes," she said uneasily. "It's me."

It was such a ludicrous lie that I didn't even bother to hide my disbelief. "My compliments," I said, and she raised her glass in thanks before brushing a lock of blond hair nervously behind her ear.

"What about during the school year? Surely a tenured professor of behavioral psychology isn't making food for the entire campus."

"Of course not." Dorian laughed.

"So the regular kitchen staff, would it be possible to get a list of their names?"

He shook his head. "No. I'm not at liberty to share their contact information. It would be a breach of privacy."

"I'm sorry," said Lexi, her tone thick with sarcasm, "but you're writing an article about Hildegard? How can that possibly intersect with your current research?"

"I'm a historian," I said stiffly. "I'm interested in the history of the college. For instance, Finn tells me you all grew up here, but I'm having trouble understanding this. You all grew up here, went to school here, and then what, started teaching here? This is beginning to sound a little culty."

"No," said Dorian. "We went away for our undergraduate and graduate degrees, but this is our home, and we return to care for it."

That seemed like an odd turn of phrase. "You realize this is strange, though, right? That's not how academia works. You don't grow up together at a college and then all get jobs at that same college. What about the postdocs, the visiting jobs, the hellish adjunct positions? You have to admit this isn't normal."

The others were growing increasingly agitated as I spoke, but Aspen seemed calmly interested, like she wanted to see where I was going with my line of inquiry.

"What about Isabelle? Did she grow up here as well?"

"No, she came to us much later," said Aspen. "Recruited because of her exceptional talent."

"But what did she do exactly?"

"That's not something we can disclose," she said. "She worked with very sensitive material. It came with her position."

"I see. And what sensitive material would that be?"

Dorian held up a chiding finger and laughed. "That is exactly the kind of information we can't disclose."

My thoughts drifted to the night I was awakened by the siren, back to the idea of animal testing. "Did it have anything to do with the dogs?"

He looked confused. "Dogs? No."

"I was just thinking about that night, about the siren. It seemed like something of an oversize reaction for a dog getting out. It got me wondering exactly how dangerous these dogs of yours are."

He looked at me straight on, unblinking. "They are for security. They are only dangerous when they are supposed to be."

"That's the weird thing, though. If they're for security, why do I never see them? What exactly are they guarding?"

In response, though, he just gave me a broad smile, and then turned his attention to his meal. Lunch wrapped up quickly after that, the others scattering like I was Typhoid Mary. Clearly I was hitting some nerves.

A storm rolled in that afternoon. It came down hard and fast beginning around four. I holed up in the scriptorium during the worst of it, but even though I was belowground, I could hear how loud it was—terrible, lashing rain and ominous thunder. I worked until well past what sounded like another raucous dinner and on into that time of night when the house was beginning to shut down for the evening. Finn and Aspen separately came in to say good night, and I assured them that I would turn off any lights and lock up before I left.

The storm was still raging when I did finally give up for the night, and as I hurried from the library and out into the night, I had a feeling once again that I was being watched. The storm had brought with it frigid temperatures, the likes of which I'd yet to feel at Hildegard, and by the time I made it into the cabana, I was soaked and shivering. After changing into dry clothes, I made myself some tea and then double-checked that all the doors were locked before sitting at my desk. Rain lashed against the windows, and thunder echoed through the mountains. When lightning lit up the sky a few seconds later, I thought I caught movement in the garden just out of the corner of my eye.

Quickly I turned off the lights and stared out at the patio. But there was nothing there. Just torrents of rain splashing against the flagstones. Sinking onto the couch, I cradled my tea, and despite the warmth, I shivered. I felt like a fawn isolated from the herd as a pack of wolves slowly surrounded it, closing in, preparing for the sacrificial feast.

THE UNQUIET EARTH

3.1

SKY GODS AND EARTH MAIDENS

Astronomy compels the soul to look upwards and leads us from this world to another.

—PLATO

The next morning, I awoke to a crisp blue sky and the heavenly freshness of recently fallen rain. I had a new plan and was ready to implement it. When I'd mentioned writing an article, that had clearly flustered all of them, so I decided I would keep on plying them with invasive questions until one of them cracked. I took a hot shower, had a light breakfast of toast with butter and honey, and then filled a to-go mug I found in the cabinet, setting out to find Aspen. After a short and pleasant search through the rain-kissed grounds, I found her working in one of the greenhouses, her gloved hands deep in the soil.

"Hey," she said. "Sorry, I'm kind of busy right now."

"I can see," I said, setting down my coffee and taking out a notebook. "But we can just chat casually, can't we?"

"About what?"

"Like I said at lunch, I'm writing an article about Hildegard, and I wondered if I could interview you."

She raised an eyebrow. "Are you seriously writing an academic article about Hildegard?"

"Yes," I said, taking a seat on a nearby bench. "This place is such a unique institution. I was wondering about the faculty's social life."

"None of us *have* a social life."

"Okay," I said, pretending to look down at my notes. "But someone mentioned that Isabelle might have been friends with one of the custodians who worked here?"

Aspen frowned. "Who mentioned that?"

"Maybe not a custodian, maybe kitchen staff?"

Aspen looked confused. "No. Who told you that?"

"I can't recall."

"Sure you can," she said, pulling her hands out of the soil and removing her gloves. "You must have it in your notes. Look through them and figure out who said what."

"I don't want to waste your time with that," I said with what I hoped was professionalism.

"I'll wait," she said, crossing her arms with an air of great patience.

She had me there, so I just stared at her, unsure how to get out of this.

"You know," she continued, "whatever it is you're trying to do right now, you are exceptionally bad at it. Is there something you want to ask me?"

I tried to seem casual, but she was right. I was bad at this. I was an academic, not a spy.

"How do you know Paloma?" I asked at last, realizing that bluntness was probably my only option at this point.

Aspen shook her head slowly, her eyes searching me. "I don't think I know anyone named Paloma."

"Really?"

"Yes really. Why are you asking all these questions?"

"The relic—" I started to say, but she cut me short with an exasperated breath.

She closed her eyes and rubbed her forehead with obvious exhaustion, and then all but ignoring me, she turned her attention to some startlingly yellow blooms.

"Marigold?" I asked, and she looked at me like I'd just spread mud all over a new carpet.

"Dianthus. For someone who studies herbalism in any fashion, you know shockingly little about plants." She tilted her head and stared at me like a doctor trying to diagnose a puzzling disorder. "Robin, do you know what the doctrine of signatures is?"

"The doctrine of signatures?" It was an ancient theory that the physical appearance of a plant gave an indication of what it would treat. I'd heard of it, but knew very little about it. "Was that Plato?"

"It was put forth by Paracelsus and taken up by myriad scholars, including Thomas Browne. I am something of a fan myself. You know," she said, gently touching the dianthus, "according to the doctrine of signatures, the color of a plant can signal its use. For instance, yellow corresponds to urine and phlegm, so you could use a yellow plant to treat diseases of the kidneys or lungs."

"If I'm not mistaken, using plants that way has killed people."

"True," said Aspen. "But the theory itself isn't wholly without merit. Think about ginseng. It's a whole-body tonic. And it's especially effective as a virility enhancer."

I shook my head. "Next you're going to tell me that ginseng looks like a man?"

"Because it does."

"So does that tree," I said, pointing at a vaguely human-shaped sapling in the near distance.

"I'm not saying that it's a replacement for modern scientific study. I'm just saying it's hubris to think that just because we have more knowledge now that we should obliterate all past thought."

"Well, if I get pneumonia, I'll come straight for your dianthus."

She stared down at the flower and then smiled back up at me, a sly twist to her lips. "I think it's time that we stopped fucking around, don't you?"

"What?" The word came out garbled and strange. This was not what I was expecting. "Stop fucking around how?"

With a cold smile, she climbed up to sit on the edge of one of the planters, her face suddenly shifting, looking much older and more dangerous than the person I'd thought she was. The woman sitting before me wasn't the same person I'd first encountered in the apothecary garden, all friendly smiles and *just call me Aspen*. She was calculating and cold.

I could barely move, but I tried to smile, my lips quivering as I managed a poor simulacrum of the real thing. "I don't know what you're talking about."

"Don't you?" she asked, leaning back again, crossing her legs like a university lecturer congratulating herself on a job well done. "You're telling me you really have no idea what's actually going on?"

"I'm sorry, but I don't."

She laughed. "Let me ask you this, Robin. What exactly do you think we do here?"

"Well, Hildegard College is obviously a college. It's in the name."

"Tell me the truth. What do you really think?"

I exhaled, my breath shaking as I thought back to the darkened building in the woods and to the plans I'd found in the conference room, to the state of disarray I'd found the rooms in, to the blood on the island.

"Is this some kind of cult?"

"What makes you say that?"

"Apparently you all grew up here. That doesn't make any sense."

"Tell me more. I'd love to follow your thought process."

"I'm sorry, but why play games? If you're just going to tell me some big secret, then just tell me. There's no reason to be coy."

"Testy!" she said with approval. "It's nice to see this feisty side of you start to come out. But I'm not being coy. I'm genuinely interested to see how much of the puzzle you've pieced together."

Tingles traced my spine as she said that. This was what I needed. *Just play it cool, Robin. Don't scare her off.*

"Okay, I'll play," I said carefully. "What have I pieced together? I think you're up to something here, something covert. Hildegard College is a cover of some kind. I think you do research, but I'm not sure it's what you say it is. Maybe you work for the government."

"Ah, but which one?" She raised her eyebrows.

"So I'm right, then?"

"I didn't say that. Tell me more. Do you suspect espionage? Do you think we're in the Company?"

"I can tell you're making fun of me, but I don't think my suspicions are completely unfounded. I mean, the remoteness, the secrecy, all the tech. This place could easily be some kind of government-run enclave where you do testing. And Isabelle, she was your best research scientist. I think she discovered something she wasn't supposed to. Or maybe she saw something she wasn't supposed to see."

Aspen scratched her chin. "Is that really honestly what you think?"

I thought for a moment. Deep down, that was pretty much exactly what I thought. "Am I close?"

The edges of her lips crept up into a hint of a smile. "Not even remotely," she said, fighting back obvious laughter.

"I give up, then," I said, unable to hide how annoyed I felt.

"Listen, Robin, I think it's time."

"Time for what?"

"To tell you the truth. Meet me tonight at Isabelle's office on the island. Seven-fifteen."

"The island?"

"Don't play dumb. And there's no need to swim this time. The boat will be tied up at the dock. Go back to your cabana and rest up. Tonight is the final act. We're going to lay all our cards on the table and so, I hope, will you."

"But I don't have any cards," I said, doing my best to hide my panic.

"Sure you do," she said. "Don't be late."

"Can you give me a hint?"

"Let's just say there are more things in heaven and earth than are dreamt of in your philosophy." Aspen picked up her gloves and put them back on slowly. "Now get the hell out of my garden."

With a mixture of excitement and annoyance, I returned to my cabana. I was just walking in the door when I got a notification that Guillaume Étienne had entered my Zoom meeting.

"Shit!" I'd forgotten about Guillaume and his grandmother.

I grabbed my notebook and set up my computer. Trying to

appear professional and prepared, I logged in and entered the room. When they turned on their video, the image on the screen made me feel like I'd been transported to a fairy-tale cottage.

"My apologies for being late. I was having problems with the internet," I lied. I didn't like lying, but I'd found recently that I was curiously good at it.

The old woman who sat beside Guillaume was ninety if she was a day, but there was glimmer to her cat's eyes that hinted at a much younger woman lurking somewhere inside. Around her shoulders she'd wrapped a mint-green shawl that sparkled when the light hit it just right, and a large amethyst hung pendulous from a chain around her neck.

"We weren't waiting long," said Guillaume. "Can you hear us all right?"

"Just fine. Thanks for agreeing to talk with me, Madame Étienne."

"My pleasure," she said in a deep, husky voice.

There was nothing overtly frightening about Jeanne Étienne, but as I looked at her, I noticed fear blossoming in my chest. This woman had elements of Little Red Riding Hood's grandmother and the big bad wolf all rolled up into one.

"Grand-mère, this is Robin," said Guillaume. "She wants to ask you about Sabine."

The woman squinted at the screen, an inscrutable smile playing on her lips.

From what I could see of the room they were in, it was decorated with shawls and doilies. Fringed lampshades sat haughtily atop the many small tables that dotted the space. Jeanne sat in a green wingback armchair, and with a flourish, she produced a cigarette holder and lit the slim pink cigarette she'd inserted in the tip. She inhaled, and when she exhaled, a great billow of what I imagined to be lavender-scented smoke exploded into the room.

"Tell me," she said in a thick French accent, "up at Hildegard College, what kind of food do you eat?"

"Excuse me?" I said, leaning forward. "What kind of food do we eat?"

"It's a simple question, my dear."

"I don't know," I said, perplexed. "Normal food. Why do you ask?"

"When I was a little girl, my grand-père was the cook at Hildegard. His position, it was a very elite position, very high class. Everything he did there was secret. He had to sign an agreement that he would never disclose the truth of what he saw there. But I never signed a thing."

She leaned back in her chair as a sly smile spread across her lips.

"She visited as a child," said Guillaume.

She nodded. "Several times. My grand-père took me with him to see the parties."

"There were parties?" I asked, feeling strangely uneasy, almost like I was choking—as if even over Zoom the smoke in the air was getting to me.

"Oh yes," Jeanne said, eyes wide. "The most opulent parties. There were kings and queens, the aristocracy. All the best people. When I was about, oh, five, there was one out in this enormous temple. It was deep in the woods. Lights hanging everywhere, sparkling, magnificent. It was like being in the realm of the fairies. Or on the moon. And my grand-père made a lavish feast with suckling pig. Clark Gable was there. I sat on his knee."

"Clark Gable?" I asked, perhaps a little too overtly suspicious. "The actor?"

"Not just an actor," she said, brandishing her cigarette like it was a wand. "The most famous movie star of his time. Handsome like you wouldn't believe."

I smiled, trying to be genial. Kids and old people made me nervous, so old people lying about what happened when they were kids left me in a panic.

"Guillaume said that Sabine came to talk to you shortly before she died."

The old woman plumped out her bottom lip in a pout. "She did, poor creature."

"She wanted to know about Hildegard?"

Again, that wry, slightly malevolent grin trembled across her lips. "You know how girls are. They want to wear fancy dresses and go to balls. They want to meet princes."

Again with this. At least I could see now where Guillaume had gotten his dismissive attitude toward young women. But I decided to forgo the lecture.

"But there aren't parties like that here anymore, are there?"

"Maybe there are, maybe there aren't," she said with a wink. "Anyway, I told Sabine to go up and see what she could find out. That there might be a job for her—maybe in the kitchen, maybe on the grounds, you never know."

"Did she talk to anyone here?" I asked.

"She met with a woman, and this woman paid her to do something. Started paying her lots of money, more money than kitchen work should be. Sabine was very excited about it all—by what was to come. I did not like this woman, but she said she had more jobs in store from Sabine, that she wanted to include her in some kind of secret enterprise. Unfortunately, that never came to pass."

A shock rode through me as I listened to her speak. Was it

possible Sabine had met with Casimir? Lexi's face also flashed through my mind.

I was getting lost in the possibilities, but the old lady was talking now, monologuing about various celebrities she'd met as a child. If she was telling the truth, then the scope of the college's connection to the elite strata of society was even greater than I had imagined, but why would the rich and famous have congregated at a remote monastery in the Rocky Mountains?

Of course she could always be lying. She could have sent Sabine up there with her head full of make-believe. When she stopped talking briefly to light another cigarette, I took the opportunity to get a word in.

"I was wondering how Sabine seemed to you in the days leading up to her death."

"Her death? Non, we still don't know for sure that she is dead."

I cocked my head. "But the article I read said she was mauled by a bear."

"True." She nodded. "However, there is no body."

I froze. "No body? Then how can they know she was mauled by a bear?"

The old woman smiled. "We don't. As far as I'm concerned, my granddaughter is very much alive."

I had no idea what to say. I wasn't sure if she was delusional or if the account I read had been wrong. Either way, I needed to shift the subject.

"Okay, so then in the days before her disappearance, how did she seem to you?"

"I didn't see her much. She stopped by a short while maybe a week before she disappeared. She was in good spirits."

"Did she say anything that worried you?"

"Worried me? No. She was secretive about what she was do-ing, but she seemed happy." Her gaze shifted to me. "You don't believe me about Clark Gable, do you?"

After setting her cigarette holder down precariously on the edge of a too-small table, she pushed her slight frame up and out of her chair, and in a flurry of lace and chiffon, she swept out of the frame. I could hear a cabinet door open and the shuffling of paper. Guillaume, still on the screen, looked at me apologeti-cally. A moment later, Jeanne returned holding a photo album. She sank slowly to the floor like a child playing at fairy princess and began thumbing through the pages.

"Guillaume, hand me my spectacles."

He reached over and handed her a pair of glasses, which she put on, and then slapped the page of the photo album she was looking at.

"There it is. I told you." She held up a photo. "Guillaume, make it so she can see the photo."

He held it up to the camera so I was unable to see anything but the photograph. It was sepia and faded, but the grounds of the college were clear—the garden, the lake in the background—and on a bench sat a mustachioed man with a little girl on his lap. So she'd been telling the truth.

"Very nice," I said. "That's definitely Clark Gable."

I'd been intending to ask more about the woman at Hildegard with whom Sabine had been in contact, but when Guillaume moved the photo, I was shocked to see that Jeanne's expression had changed markedly. Instead of the bright-eyed, ruby-cheeked old woman I'd met a few moments earlier, my computer screen showed a stunned-looking creature, her skin suddenly pallid be-neath the vast quantities of rouge. She looked like a completely different person—upset, horrified even.

She whispered something to Guillaume and then pushed herself up out of the chair.

He looked at me, stunned. "We must go," he said. "Grand-mère is feeling unwell. We must go."

"Now!" Jeanne snapped from somewhere off-screen.

"Can we speak again?" I asked quickly, but Guillaume's window suddenly winked out, and I was left staring at my own confused face.

REVENANTS

It is the question of ghosts.
—JACQUES DERRIDA

My Zoom with Guillaume had left me unsettled, so I tried to distract myself with some light reading. I curled up on the couch with a book, and soon the light through my French doors began to fade. When the time came, I walked down to the beach and found the boat tied up at the dock, just as Aspen had said it would be. Standing there and staring out over that strange blue water, I shivered just a little, but this time it was with a sense of excitement and infinite possibilities. I felt like I truly was on the verge of uncovering something important whether they wanted me to or not. Sometimes we disclose more by actively trying to hide the truth than if we'd just left things well enough alone, and that, I hoped, would be to my benefit. I untied the boat, climbed in, and started rowing. As it glided over the water, I tried to see if I could make out any hint of the metal grate, but the water was too dark to see.

At seven-fifteen, I knocked on the door to the office, and was mildly amused to find them all there. Finn opened the door and the others waved from where they were spread out around the room. Each was sipping from a red party cup.

Finn handed me one. "Drink up," he said with a mischievous grin.

"What is it?" I asked, staring into the pungent liquid.

"Aspen made it. That's all you need to know."

Despite my reticence, I had to admit there was something vaguely magical about the atmosphere in the room.

I set the drink down and sat facing them. "Okay, I came all the way out here. What gives? Is this about the relic?"

"Good God," said Aspen. "What is it with you and this relic of yours?"

"I don't think you understand," I said. "I have to find it."

"You're right," she said with a hint of an eye roll. "We don't understand."

I felt like I was on the verge of losing my mind. I needed them to understand why I needed it so badly, and yet in quiet moments, I had to ask myself the question: Why exactly did I need it so badly? It was true that I wanted to make my mark on the world. I was so close to accomplishing things I'd once only dreamed of, but there was somehow more to it than that. Could it really all go back to Charles? Was everything I did somehow a one-sided competition with him, a silent conversation held just inside my mind?

"Forget about the relic for a second," Aspen continued. "You wanted to know what this place really is and what we really do, right?"

"I do," I said, absently running my hand along the edge of the blue rug at the center of the room.

"First, we need you to clear your mind and open it completely. Can you do that, Robin?"

"I can try."

"Okay, please, drink," she said, motioning to the cup.

"What is it?"

"Medicine," said Finn quickly.

"But what's in it?"

"Trade secret, I'm afraid," said Aspen with a wink.

"Yeah, well, I'm not drinking anything unless I know what's in it."

"That's a shame because we're not talking unless you drink."

I inhaled and grimaced. "It smells awful."

"Things that are good for you usually smell bad," said Aspen.

"Drink up," said Finn with a smile. "I promise it won't hurt you."

I wasn't sure what to believe, but I didn't think Aspen would try to outright poison me, so I decided to trust her. I assumed there might be something slightly hallucinogenic in it, but I'd taken mushrooms before. If they decided to dose me or do something stupid like that, I'd just ride it out.

I took a sip, a single sip, and soon the room began to change. The air seemed to sparkle and my heart began to buzz like it was filled with hungry honeybees. Whatever this reaction was, it was too soon for a hallucinogen to start working, so I assumed my response was due to some kind of placebo effect.

My head spinning, I focused on the blue of the rug, on the tiny tendrils, the softness, the sturdiness. I worried the edge with my fingers, but then I hit something hard underneath.

"What is this?"

"It's a rug," Lexi said with a laugh.

"No," I said, feeling around. "There's something under here. Is this a trapdoor?" I started to peel back the corner and saw that I was correct. Dorian put a hand on my forearm to stay me.

"Leave it. It's a remnant from another time—our predecessors' time. They built tunnels that ran all underneath the grounds here, but the tunnels flooded back in 1890. Now there's nothing down there but swamp water and cholera."

I let the corner of the rug flip back into place.

"Okay," I said. "So tell me, then. What's the big secret?"

Aspen leaned forward and spoke in a low voice, which seemed crazy, since we were in the middle of nowhere. "This place," she said, "these mountains, they're unquiet. Some places are like that. I'm sure you've heard of haunted houses, right? Well, these mountains are like that. We're not alone out here. Do you understand what I'm trying to say?"

I started laughing. "That the woods are haunted?"

"Not just the woods, and not precisely haunted. Unquiet. Occupied."

Unquiet—the exact same word that had occurred to me when I was in the woods.

"Occupied?" I asked.

"Yes. Occupied long before mankind ever walked this earth. Robin, do you know what alchemy is?"

I sat there speechless. Of all the things I'd been expecting her to say, this was not on the list.

"Of course I know what alchemy is," I said, but my voice was shaking.

I stared at them blankly, a sudden understanding washing over me. The book that had so enchanted me in the scriptorium, it had contained an illustration of a woman in robes I'd mistakenly identified as the Oracle of Delphi, but it wasn't the oracle, was it? It was a famous image—Mary the Prophetess, the mother of alchemy. Of course! How could I have missed it? She was one of the first scientists in history, pioneering alchemy, which later became chemistry. The bain-marie we'd all used in high school chemistry was even named after her.

"Alchemy takes many forms," said Aspen.

"Right. Metal into gold. All that nonsense." I was starting to get confused, unable to find the words I wanted.

"It's not nonsense," she said. "Tonight we're going to make you believe. Drink up."

I took another sip, trying not to look as repulsed as I felt. "What am I drinking?"

"A form of alchemy."

"So you're telling me you're, what, alchemists? Alchemists trying to make gold out of metal in the mountains of Colorado? Like the pseudoscience gold rush?"

She narrowed her eyes, a professor who suffers no fools. "Did you know that the great alchemists set out to prove the existence of God?"

"Good luck there."

"Oh, but we've already done it," she said with a smug little smile.

There was an eerie thickness to the atmosphere all of a sudden.

"You've proven the existence of God?" I laughed. "How?"

"By proving His opposite."

For a split second, I thought I felt something moving underneath the ground, something enormous and powerful like a freight train. But I couldn't have. I must have imagined it.

"This is making me feel strange," I said, looking into my cup. "Is it acid?"

"Just herbs," said Aspen.

"No, there is something else in here. Something pharmaceutical."

"Do you know the etymology of *pharmaceutical*?" Aspen asked suddenly.

"Of course," I said, trying to get the words out, but my tongue felt thick. "From *pharmakon*."

"Meaning poison . . . or *spell*." She held my gaze a moment too long and then dropped it.

Things were spinning now. I could barely make sense of the world around me, and yet rising up inside me was a certainty that I didn't need any of this. Suddenly I stood up.

"This is bullshit," I said, and I could feel myself slurring, hear the words coming out all wrong. "I'm the boss of myself, and I'm . . . I'm the boss of you people, too."

I started for the door.

"Lexi, go after her," I heard Aspen say.

I lurched toward the door, opened it, and stepped . . .

. . . directly into my uncle's apartment in New York.

"Holy shit," I whispered, in utter shock. I knew it wasn't really happening, that I was just tripping, but I could have sworn that I was in Paloma's room. I could even smell her perfume.

I walked through the door and out into the hall, but when I turned a corner, I saw someone sitting at my work desk, papers spread out all over.

"No," I whispered, starting down the hall toward her, but suddenly she turned, and I froze in place.

It was me. Pale and terrified, the other me stared down the hall directly at me.

"Hello?" she said, her voice shaking. "Who's there?"

"No," I whispered. "This isn't real."

Shaking, I walked toward my reflection. She sat at the desk holding a pen. Her hand shook, but she put her pen to the paper and hurriedly drew four symbols. They were all images from the tiles I'd found—the disintegrating rectangle, the crescent moon, the stylized S, and a square divided into four parts.

I leaned over her shoulder, my breath moving the hairs on the back of her neck so that they stood on end.

Suddenly the other me stood up, knocking over her glass, orange juice spilling everywhere.

"What the hell?" I jumped back and sprinted back to Paloma's bedroom, and instinctively I flung open the door to her closet. When I stepped through to the other side, I was . . .

Outside in the woods . . . the night was warm, and the sky glittered with stars. It felt oddly romantic, like something beautiful could happen at any second. I kept moving, and soon I was out of that darkness, only to emerge onto the path of a thousand fireflies. No, not fireflies—lanterns. I was on the lantern-lined path that led through the switch grass, the soft glow lighting up the night like the entrance to a mystical realm.

"You okay there?" Lexi asked. She was out of breath. Must have run to catch up with me.

"No. I was just—I was . . ."

Moonlight flooded down, illuminating Lexi's hair so it gleamed like polished brass. I noticed that my stomach was also starting to get fluttery and nervous. "Am I hallucinating?"

Lexi gently touched my arm, but I yanked it away, stumbled, and fell into the dirt.

"Stay away from me," I said. "You put something in my drink, didn't you?"

"Jesus, Robin, I was just trying to help. You looked like you were going to fall . . . which you did."

"I'm fine," I said, and the words came out strange and garbled and required too much effort.

"You don't look fine. Let me help you up."

The more I tried to speak, and the more I tried to stand up, the more out of control I felt. I started crawling forward, closer and closer to the edge of the woods.

"The tea," I mumbled.

"The tea is fine. Aspen knows what she's doing. Your dose was exact."

I pushed myself up to stand, my feet unsteady, but at least I was somewhat vertical. Still, I stumbled toward the woods.

"Don't go that way," said Lexi, and I could detect a note of fear in her voice. "We should head back."

But I didn't listen. I just kept heading toward the woods.

"Robin, come back. It's not safe!"

"I'm fine," I said like a defensive alcoholic.

She called after me, but then I was in the trees. There were branches or fingers or something sharp, and they were clawing at me as darkness whispered in my ears. I moved through, navigating as if by intuition, but with a vague memory of having been in these woods some time in the primordial past. Or maybe it was the future.

Lexi's voice began to fade, and then I thought I could hear others, a chorus of voices rising up through the night calling my name. Or someone's name. Nothing is my name, is it? Or is it that my name is nothingness? Soon, though, other sounds began to muffle those voices. Old sounds, old voices, deep and eldritch, as if issuing from the ground itself, booming, sometimes shrieking. Those other voices were pulling a velvet cloak over reality as I knew it, muffling it, silencing it. Best to keep moving. Because I knew I needed to get somewhere. I just wasn't sure exactly where *there* was.

Up ahead, the moon shone down with aggressive brilliance, and soon it led me through the tree line and I stumbled out in a field with an enormous temple at its center. Standing there in the open, moonlight streaming down on me, I noticed that my shoes and the hems of my pants were soaking wet. How had that happened? Was I losing time? My head was beginning to clear up a little. I noticed a figure standing on the steps of the temple. I'd taken it for a statue initially, but now that it moved, I saw that it was in fact a man—a familiar man. Up ahead of me, standing in the middle of a clearing in the Rocky Mountains, stood none other than Charles Danforth.

"Charles?" I said, stepping toward him, my voice breaking with emotion. "Is that really you?"

I was so relieved to see him that any residual antipathy was eclipsed by pure elation at the prospect of a reunion. I raced toward him, met him halfway up the steps, and flung myself into his arms. Only he wasn't really there, was he? It was a ghost of a memory, wasn't it? It had to be. Still, he smelled the same— exactly the same—and I began to cry.

"Please help me. Please get me out of here."

"I will," he said. "I'm here to help. But first I think you should look inside."

"Inside where?" I asked, my eyes clouded with tears as I gazed up at him. "Oh god, I can't tell you how good it is to see you again."

"You look terrible," he said, laughing a little at the state of me.

I clutched his shirt. "I get it now," I said, feeling all dreamy. "I really do. I understand what plants do. They open up the other realms. They're spells. That's why they're so dangerous. They open you up to the things that want to use you for."

"If you say so," he said.

"Charles, where are we? Where are we really?"

In the depth of the night, the trees seemed to be moving in our direction. Or was it something else?

He kissed my forehead. "Oh, sweetie, we're in the place monsters come from."

"Monsters are real?"

"They always have been. You just need to venture far enough out into the woods." He gestured toward the trees.

"Do you mean here? In these mountains?" I asked, certain now that I had to be dreaming.

"Not just here. But here is very important. You know that."

"I don't understand," I said even though I partially did. I looked up at him, my heart breaking with the memories of a lost friendship. "Charles, who are you to me?"

"I think you know."

"I thought you were my friend."

"I am your friend. I always have been."

"Then why did you leave me?"

He shook his head. "It's you who left. Don't you remember?"

"No," I cried. "I wouldn't do that."

"Listen, Bugbear," he said, gently taking my hand, "I'm going to tell you the truth. I'm the only one who ever will."

Bugbear. My heart felt like it was going to explode. That was his pet name for me. Only not in New York. Somewhere else.

I looked up into the night sky, at the stars swimming like jellyfish above us. Around us the woods were completely silent.

"Why is it so quiet?" I asked, gripping his hand more tightly.

"It's coming," he whispered. "If you listen very closely, you'll hear it out there, moving between the trees."

Once he said that, it was like a switch was turned on. I could hear something. And now I realized that maybe I could always hear it. Maybe that thing, whatever it was, was always out there, just out of sight, moving invisible through the trees.

"What is it?"

He sighed, adjusting his knit burgundy hat. "Let me ask you something. What is the purpose of alchemy?"

"Aspen said it's to prove the existence of God. She said that they'd done that somehow."

"Not them," he said. "Those who came before us. Long ago. They proved the existence of God by proving its opposite. And now it must never get out," he said, raising a hand toward the movement in the woods.

"The devil?"

"It's more complicated than that. It's impossible to put a name to it because we can't comprehend what we can't comprehend. We die in wars, unwittingly offering up libations in its name. Unknowing, unthinking, we kill each other in the name of a god or country or cause, convinced we're doing it of our own free will, but really we are just ants, working in tandem, providing the necessary offerings to placate a monster."

"This monster?" I whispered.

He nodded. "Great slumbering horned gods."

"What happens if it gets out?"

"You mean if *they* get out."

"It's more than just one?"

"It is one, but it's also legion."

I stared into the forest, deep into the movement of the trees in the dark. And for a second, I thought I saw something there, something enormous and cosmic and cruel. All spindle legs and dripping pedipalps, it reared up toward the sky, flashing a muted pale white against the night sky. And then it was gone. And perhaps it was never there. Just a trick of the eye.

"What happens if they get out?" I whispered.

"Sometimes they do. And that's why you have to find your bluebird. You're nothing without it."

"Charles, where are we really?" I was beginning to feel excessively sleepy. I sank to the ground, my eyelids starting to flutter shut.

"In the woods. I'll meet you here again someday. In the dark, amongst the trees. I'll hold your hand so you're not afraid, and we'll go home. I promise."

"No, I'm serious. Where are we?"

"Under the water that isn't water. In the time before the accident."

"What accident?" I barely managed to say.

"This one," he said, and turning, he exposed the back of his head, where I now saw a deep, horrific gash.

"Who did that to you?" I whispered.

He sat down beside me. "I think you know, Bugbear." He put an arm around me, and unable to keep my eyes open any longer, I nestled my head into his shoulder and settled into the deepest sleep of my life.

3.3

SEANCES, TABLE-TURNING, AND AUTOMATIC WRITING

On the afternoon of October 24th, 1917, four days after my marriage, my wife surprised me by attempting automatic writing. What came in disjointed sentences, in almost illegible writing, was so exciting, sometimes so profound, that I persuaded her to give an hour or two day after day to the unknown writer, and after some half-dozen such hours offered to spend what remained of life explaining and piecing together those scattered sentences. "No," was the answer, "we have come to give you metaphors for poetry."

—WILLIAM BUTLER YEATS

I woke up somewhere in the woods inexplicably clutching *The Book of Widows*. Had I taken it from the office and not realized it? My hair was tangled with leaves and my forearms were caked with mud. I wasn't sure where I was, but in the distance, I could see the sky-blue glint of the lake, so, pushing myself up, I started in that direction. On aching bones, I trudged back through the woods, and when I came out onto the main path, I determined by the color of the cloud cover and the stillness of insect activity that the day must be lingering somewhere near dawn.

Back in my cabana, I showered, changed, and then sat out in the back garden with a cup of strong coffee. Was I losing my mind? It was certainly plausible I'd had some kind of break with reality, a hallucination brought on by that concoction of herbs, some of which either singly or in combination must have had psychotropic properties. I knew this had to be true, and yet none of me wanted to believe it. Even though I knew that Charles must have been a hallucination, I wanted to believe he was real just to have him back.

My head was still swimming and I had something like a nasty hangover, so I curled up on the couch and slept for a few more hours. When I awoke again, I went in search of the others. I needed to find out what was true and what I'd hallucinated. I knew that I'd gone out to the island on the boat and that I'd drunk the tea, but beyond these facts, I wasn't sure what was real and what wasn't. Surely Charles couldn't have been real. He was back in New York, probably scamming some other idiot out of their research.

They were down in the apothecary garden. I could hear them laughing. I expected them to react when they saw me, but no one showed the slightest sign of interest in my presence, with the exception of a small wave from Finn.

"Hey, sleepyhead," he said. "I tried knocking on your door earlier, but you must have been out cold. Rough night?"

I balked. "You're joking, right?"

I looked around at the rest of them, hoping for someone to help me feel less crazy, but no one seemed even slightly perturbed. They were all acting like nothing had happened.

"What are we supposed to be joking about?" asked Aspen, slipping off her gardening gloves and tucking them into her back pocket.

"Last night," I said, with eyebrows raised and a shoulder shrug as if to convey *What the hell?*

"What are you talking about?"

"What happened out in the woods." They stared back at me with blank expressions. "You have to be shitting me. Aspen gave us psychedelic mushrooms or ketamine or something. And you all told me you were alchemists or . . ." I tried to find the words, but my head was spinning, confusing everything I was trying to say. "You said there was an evil in the woods. You told me that there was something awful out there."

"It sounds like you had a hell of a dream there, kiddo," said Dorian.

"It wasn't a dream. I woke up in the woods, for god's sake. Lexi, you have to remember. You were there with me."

But Lexi looked away. There was a flush to her cheek and a sadness in her eye, and I knew then that I wasn't crazy. It had all really happened. Only for some reason they were intent on lying to me about it.

Overwhelmed almost to the point of tears, I turned to go, meaning to return to the cabana, but instead abruptly shifted direction and headed down to the lake. On the verge of a panic attack, I sat down on the cool pebbled beach and stared out at the water. How was I supposed to understand what was happening to me if I had no outside source of stability? The philosopher and critic Tzvetan Todorov defines the fantastic as the hesitation between a supernatural and a mundane explanation of an occurrence. For example, in a work of fiction, if a woman in the woods sees a monster and turns out to be crazy, then that is realism. If it turns out that there really is a monster in those woods, then that is horror. But if one can make an argument for either to be true, then that woman occupies the space of the fantastic. It was a space with which I was becoming abundantly, achingly familiar.

I hugged my knees tight to my chest, fighting back tears. I

wanted to be held, to be told I was safe and loved and that everything would be okay. Instead, I was alone, and I had no idea whom to trust. I wiped away my tears and decided to go up to the scriptorium to think.

I was at a crossroads, I knew. Funny metaphor, crossroads. Ancient cultures believed that the meeting place between two roads was a space between worlds, a place where you might have one foot in reality and another in the beyond. Crossroads were where witches went to make deals with the devil. I didn't think I was in danger of making any deals with any devils, literal or metaphorical, but I did feel strongly that the choice I was about to make had the potential to take me in a direction that could change my life forever.

I couldn't put my finger on the precise moment I'd begun to feel my grip on reality slip, but since coming to Hildegard, it was as though I was becoming someone I barely knew. My dreams felt hallucinatory, almost prophetic. I was experiencing sleep paralysis and waking up in places I couldn't remember going. And I'd started considering notions I'd once scoffed at. In my darkest moments I'd half believed that werewolves and lake monsters might be real, I was vaguely convinced that the island was the site of a human sacrifice, and now I was hallucinating in the woods and losing time. I wanted to find out what had really happened to Isabelle (and, of course, to her artifact), but at this point, was it worth it?

No, I decided. It wasn't. Finding the relic would be great and all, but these people were playing with my head, and my life was beginning to feel wildly out of control. I'd seen things I couldn't explain and had experienced mental trajectories so far outside of my character that they were beginning to seriously worry me. Getting a leg up on an academic publication wasn't worth the disorientation and lack of agency I had begun to feel. If this were a movie, I would be shouting at the main character to get out of there. And indeed, nothing was stopping me. I kept feeling as though something was, but it wasn't. I was free to go. And that's exactly what I decided to do.

I bought my ticket that night and then started packing. Grabbing my suitcase, I threw it on the bed and started tossing in clothes. I opened the desk drawer, grabbed the cards and the widows' keys, and went to pack them as well—I'd return them if anyone asked—but one slipped out of the deck and landed on the floor. I picked it up and was about to put it back in the deck when the image on it made me freeze. It showed a cart traversing a steep mountain pass, and in the back, hoisted onto a hook, was a grisly rendering of a flayed animal. I didn't know if I believed in the accuracy of divination, but if there was ever a message from the universe, that was it.

The next day, I headed up to the house to let them know I'd be leaving. I found Dorian in his office sorting through some papers.

He stood up when he saw me, smiling brilliantly. "Looks like you're feeling better."

"Yeah," I said, lingering in the doorway, fiddling with my hands. Why was this producing so much anxiety in me? I took a breath and noticed I was shaking. "But I have to head home."

He didn't seem to understand at first, but then his smile faded, and I felt a knot in my heart when I saw the sadness in his eyes. "Can I . . . can I ask why?"

"It's my cousin," I said, trying to look like I wasn't lying. "Sort of a family emergency. There's no way around it."

He sat back down and looked at the papers he'd been examining. "I see."

I walked over to him and put my hand on his shoulder, but he flinched at my touch.

"I want you to know that I really appreciate everything you've done for me. I just need to go back home."

"Of course," he said, his tone distant and cold. "Family always comes first. Do you want me to make the arrangements for you?"

"I booked my flight already."

"Of course," he said, still not meeting my eyes. "I wish we would have gotten to spend more time together, but you need to go where your heart calls you."

That seemed like a strange turn of phrase. My heart?

"I really appreciated the fellowship opportunity," I said, but he looked away.

"Yes, of course," he said, ignoring me and turning a sheet of paper over. "I don't mean to be rude, but if you'll excuse me, I have work to do."

"Yeah," I said, stepping away awkwardly. "Of course."

Confused, I walked back out into the hall. That was not how I'd expected him to behave.

I wasn't sure if Dorian would inform the others of my impending departure, but later that day, I decided I should tell them myself. I found them gathered in Aspen's cabana sitting around a low coffee table drinking out of steaming mugs, and as soon as I walked in the room, I could tell I'd been a recent subject of discussion.

"We hear you're off," Finn said with a puckish grin.

"Yeah. Tomorrow afternoon. I just wanted to stop by and say it was great meeting you all."

I'd expected some kind of pleasantries, but instead they just stared at me as if waiting for me to explain more. It felt weirdly unsocialized. I looked at each of them, our eyes momentarily connecting, and behind those eyes I saw a singular, completely inexplicable emotion: fear. I had the feeling they were looking at me like I was a wild animal capable of almost anything, and that collectively, they needed to keep me under control.

"Anyway," I said, trying not to show how shaken I actually was by their response. "I just wanted to say goodbye because as I said, I'm leaving tomorrow."

"How are you going to leave?" Lexi asked.

That sounded vaguely threatening. My arm muscles involuntarily tensed in response.

"I've booked my transportation." This was only partially true. I wasn't able to book a ride from the college, so I'd arranged to get picked up in Petit Rouen.

"We'll be sorry to see you go," said Lexi, overcome with emotion, which took me by surprise, because as far as I could tell, she didn't even like me.

But if Lexi seemed sad about my leaving, Finn and Aspen seemed almost panicked.

"It would be in everyone's best interest if you stayed for the entirety of the summer," Aspen said, almost as if she were repeating a scripted line of dialogue.

"I don't think that's going to be possible," I said, nearly beside myself with how weird it was all getting. And without saying another word, I turned and made for the door, giving a perfunctory wave as I departed.

I stayed in my cabana after that. Whatever doubts I'd had about leaving had been more than cleared away by the response I'd gotten. I still needed to figure out how to get to Petit Rouen, but no doubt Dorian could take me. He seemed annoyed, but I was pretty sure he would still give me a ride to the village.

TRANSMOGRIFICATION

Whoever believes that any creature can be changed for the better or the worse, or transformed into another kind of likeness, except by the Creator of all things, is worse than a pagan and a heretic.

—MALLEUS MALEFICARUM, *FIFTEENTH CENTURY*

The next morning, the cloud cover was the color of bruised strawberries and there was an electricity in the air that spoke of an impending storm. I watched the encroaching weather system uneasily, hoping it wouldn't interfere with my travel plans. Just after nine, Lexi and Dorian knocked on my door and invited me up to the house for a farewell breakfast. Sitting there eating sour-sweet berry jam on freshly baked bread and sipping fragrant tea out of heavy ceramic mugs, I found it hard to imagine that I'd ever thought I was in any danger. Still, the meal wasn't totally without strain. There was something going on between them that escaped my understanding. Lexi was irritable whenever Dorian tried to speak to her. Clearly they had fought over something but were putting on brave faces for my final meal at Hildegard.

After securing a ride to Petit Rouen from Dorian, I headed back to the cabana, showered, and dressed, mentally preparing myself for the journey ahead. While gathering up my things, I noticed the peacock key, picked it up, and felt the weight of the cold metal in my palm. I knew I should leave it here, but instead, I slipped it into my back pocket. If they needed it, I would mail it back. My jacket on now, I was just about to grab my phone from where I'd left it on the bedside table before getting in the shower, but it was gone. I began to panic but stopped myself. No, I must have just forgotten where I'd put it. I was being paranoid. There was no way someone had taken my phone, but after thoroughly searching the room, I still came up empty-handed.

Oh god. Could I get out of Colorado without it? My boarding pass was downloaded onto it; all my credit card information and my contact numbers for people back home on it. And then with horror I realized my computer was missing as well. My heartbeat thud-thudded in my ears. I needed a solution fast, because my ride in Petit Rouen was leaving in only a couple of hours.

I went outside the cabana, stepping onto the brick walkway. "Hello?" I called. "Did anyone borrow my phone?"

I walked up and down the path, poking my head into the neighboring cabanas, but they were all silent and empty. As I jogged up toward the main house, a wave of emotion passed through me. Suddenly I felt helpless, utterly helpless. Since coming to Hildegard College, I'd had trouble putting my finger on exactly what it was that bothered me about this place, but in a word, it was that. Something about it made me feel out of control and at the mercy of someone else's whims, though I was hard-pressed to say exactly whose.

Inside, the house was empty. I called out, searched the main rooms, the library, the scriptorium, even the basement and storerooms, but I couldn't find a soul. Outside, I called for the others but came up similarly short. Where the hell was everyone?

Back in my cabana, I could barely breathe. Leaning against the wall, I tried to follow any thread that might explain what was happening to me. How could all of them simply disappear? It made no sense, but then I decided screw it, I would just have to leave without my phone and my computer. There was something wrong with this place and I had to get home. I had credit cards; I could figure out a way to get my flight info and ticket. I'd just grab my things and wait for Dorian in the front hall. Soon I would be gone from this place, and that was all that mattered.

Gathering up my bags, I closed up the cabana and walked up to the main house. And then I waited.

And waited.

Half an hour came and went.

And then another, but there was no sign of anyone. And all the while, a terrible acidic fear constricted my throat. I felt a vague sense of déjà vu, as if this had all happened before. I'd felt powerless many times in my life, but never so obviously trapped—like a caged animal. My desire to escape was nearly overwhelming. Finally, after an hour and a half, I heard a car motor in the driveway. I sprang up from the wooden bench I'd been sitting on and bolted for the door, nearly slipping on the baked tile as I rounded the corner toward the arch that led to the foyer. I didn't care if I'd missed my flight already. I would get another one. I just had to get to Denver. Through the front window, I could see a van parked in the driveway. There was a picture of an anthropomorphic ice cream cone on the side, and below that was written *Bibo!*

My heart sank. It was a delivery person. I stood a moment, considering. Even though this wasn't my ride, maybe I could talk them into giving me a ride to Petit Rouen.

I peered out the window, expecting to find the driver unloading boxes of whatever *Bibo!* was, but instead, I was shocked to see that it was Guillaume from the village. Before I could call out to him, he closed the van door and hurried around the side of the house, toward one of the woodsy paths. In an effort to head him off, I cut back through the music room and slipped through the French doors and out onto the side terrace. Peering over the side of the balustrade, I could see him down below, his copper head bouncing as he walked. Where on earth was he going? I followed along up above until I saw him take a sharp left and start down a covered path. I hurried down the steps to the lower level, careening onto the grassy path he'd taken. He was nowhere in sight. As I walked, the sky grew dark, storm clouds hanging thick and angry above. I ran along as fast as I could, and then finally I saw him up ahead, rounding a bend in the woodsy path.

Thunder tore across the sky, and then heavy rain began to fall.

"Guillaume!" I called. "Please wait!"

On the second shout, he stopped and turned toward me, disgust on his face.

"Please!" I called as I ran to meet him. We were just outside the apothecary garden now, a short way from the mouth of the woods. "Can you take me to Petit Rouen? I can pay."

As soon as I approached, I knew I'd made a mistake. He looked at me with a burning fury.

"*Où est-elle?*" he screamed as he approached, filled with a terrifying rage. "*Où est ma sœur? Sorcière!*"

I took a step back, frozen with terror. Why was he yelling at me about witches?

He bore down on me, towering, seething. "Where is my sister?"

It happened too fast for me to react. A step toward me, a meaty fist flying, a blow to my face, and I crumpled to the ground. Pain tore through me. I could barely see for it. There was blood spurting from my nose, and when I reached up to touch my face, my fingers came away crimson. Adrenaline pulsed through my veins as I stared up at him. Using all my strength, I slammed my foot into his kneecap, pulled myself up, and started running as fast as I could. Along the path, I raced toward the trees. Soon I was under the cover of the forest, sprinting toward . . . toward . . . my mind spun. Where exactly *was* I running? Why hadn't I run to the house? With horror, I realized it was too late to turn around now. If I doubled back, I'd risk running straight into him. He was strong, and I didn't want to try to fight him, but maybe I could lose him if I just kept running. I needed to get far enough ahead and find a place to hide. My face throbbed as I propelled myself through the trees. Down an embankment and through the small clearing, I thought I could see something like a break in the foliage up ahead.

I dashed for it, and under the cover of the woods again, I felt marginally safer. I was flying now, moving faster than I'd ever moved before, branches whipping past me. And then something astounding happened. I broke through the trees and emerged onto a magnificent expanse of rolling green—a massive enchanted glen upon which sat the most astonishing sight. Stretching out in masses of stone and marble stood an enormous structure built to resemble an ancient Greek temple. I gasped. It was just like it had appeared in my hallucination, and like Jeanne had said. So it had been real. I was so stunned that for a second, I stopped running.

I heard Guillaume come crashing through the foliage.

"*Où est Sabine?*" he screamed.

And as he surged toward me, I felt something equally terrible deep inside me howling for release. I stumbled back, fell, and then he was on top of me, leering, teeth like rot.

"*Où est ma sœur?*" he shouted again.

The colors began to blur and congeal.

I tried to scream, but his knees were now on my chest, his hands around my throat. He began to squeeze and the world became flashes of light like single images strung out between gold and gray.

And then there was a figure behind him. A streak of movement, a flash of blond hair, and a hand grabbed his hair, pulled back, slid something across his throat. Clean and clear, there came a bright red line.

His eyes widened and blood spilled out. He gripped his throat, the life bursting out of him like birds bound tight and then released.

Cool hands slid beneath me. Aspen's voice whispering in my ear.

"Shhh now. Everything's going to be all right. We got you. Shhh. We got you."

———

I awoke in a brightly lit room. Every part of my body ached, but something was different. The sense that death was gripping me was gone. I felt different inside. As if something horrid and sick deep within me had been cured, a tremendous fear eased.

I wiped my eyes and looked around the room, but it was empty. It seemed to be some kind of small medical suite. Was it possible I'd been taken all the way to a hospital and didn't remember?

"Hello?" I called softly.

I tried to move, but found that I was too weak. I sank back down onto my pillow and drifted back to sleep again, dreaming of trying to fit an odd-shaped key into a lock, but the lock kept morphing until finally I realized it was never a lock, but a rose, and its petals fell away, broken and bruised.

And then someone touched my forehead.

I opened my eyes and saw Aspen standing over me. She was applying something wet and cool to my face with a cloth.

"You're awake," she said, smiling down at me.

"Where am I?"

"In the infirmary, down below my garden."

"You saved me," I said, my voice breaking with emotion.

"Well, Lexi did the dirty work. I just did a little bit of something to help bring you back from the brink. That psycho did a number on you."

It was only then that I remembered Lexi slitting his throat. A shiver ran through me. Who exactly were these people?

"Oh god," I moaned. "Is he . . ."

"Dead?" I heard Lexi say. Turning my head, I saw her sitting on a couch over in the corner, cool as a cucumber. "Yeah, he's dead."

"Oh god. Oh god, what are we going to do?"

"Look at me," Aspen said, grabbing my chin like one would a fractious child. "You have to forget about that business."

"Business?"

"Yes. It's over now. A man attacked you, you don't know who he was, and he got away."

"But he's dead," I whispered, the loss of human life bearing down on me like a weight I'd never even considered. "His name was Guillaume."

"It was him or you. We made a choice."

"But the body."

She shook her head. "There is no body. You hear me? We took care of it. Don't mention it again, understand?"

I nodded. "Yeah. But could you let go of my face?"

She released her grip.

I tried to clear my head, to understand what I was hearing, but everything seemed too chaotic and unreal.

"I don't understand," I said. "Why did he attack me?"

Over on the couch, Lexi yawned and stretched. "I think he said something about his sister."

"But I had nothing to do with his sister. She was the girl who was attacked by an animal. How could I have anything to do with her? And why were you there? You couldn't have just been there randomly."

"Oh, we weren't," said Lexi. "We were following you."

I frowned. "But why? How could you know to follow me?"

Aspen cleared her throat as if she were uncomfortable.

"We're always following you," said Lexi.

A cold shock shot through me. "What?"

I looked at Aspen, hoping to see her laughing as well, but she looked very serious.

"Aspen?" I said, and it was really more of a plea than anything else.

"Sit up," she said.

With some effort, I did as she directed. She retrieved a small purple cup from the table and handed it to me.

"Drink this."

The liquid in the cup was a strange color, almost blue, and it smelled musty, of herbs and the earth. Bitter.

"Not again. What is it?"

"It's not hallucinogenic, I promise. It will help with the pain, give you strength."

Instead of tasting bitter, it was unexpectedly sweet and clean-tasting.

Staring over at Lexi, I tried to reconcile what I knew of her with the image of her slitting Guillaume's throat.

"You really were following me?"

Aspen nodded.

"But why? Why would you follow me? I don't understand."

She pressed her fingers to her temples and looked over at Lexi. "It's time, isn't it?"

Lexi nodded. "We have to. Finn is wrong. We can't just keep waiting for her to figure it out."

"They'll be pissed if we do this."

"Then we won't tell them." Lexi cocked her head. "You know I'm right."

Aspen sighed and seemed to prepare herself to speak. "Let's try this one more time. Tell me what you know. Everything you know about this place."

Blinking, exhausted, I did my best to reply. "I told you. You do something covert, something with the government or alchemy. I don't know what's real and what's not anymore."

"No," she said, shaking her head, "you know more. Tell me anything you can think of. Tell me what you know."

The pain was subsiding, but I could feel the swelling still, and was having trouble thinking clearly.

"The island," I said. "Something about the island."

"Yes!" said Aspen with wide, excited eyes. "What about the island?"

"I don't know. Isabelle was killed out there, wasn't she? She saw something they didn't want her to see."

"Who's they?"

"I don't know," I said, rubbing my forehead. "The people who run this place. They killed her to keep her quiet."

Aspen sighed and sat down on the stool. "No. She didn't die. She left, and she took something very important with her when she did. Do you have any idea what that was?"

"No," I said, feeling increasingly disoriented. "Why would I know that?"

"It was a code. Do you have any idea what that code might be?"

"What? No. I don't know what you're trying to do to me, but I know what really happened. There's blood out on that island, all around a pillar. That's her blood, isn't it?"

Aspen shook her head. "That's not her blood. No one killed Isabelle."

My mind raced, desperately trying to piece something together, but my head throbbed and my body ached.

Above us, the fluorescent light started to flicker. Now off, now on.

"Listen to me. I need you to remember," she said, and the room became deadly still except for the light, which dimmed and flared, shivering like the beat of a thousand straining insect wings.

"What?" I asked, my voice catching, breaking.

"Focus," she said. "I asked you before what you thought we did here and I'm going to ask you again. What do we do here?"

"Alchemy," I said, my head feeling strange, like I was swimming, like the entire world was somehow turning inside out.

"No," she snapped. "What do we do here? What does Isabelle do here?"

"Cognitive neuro-programming."

"That's right. And what does that mean?"

I was feeling increasingly on edge, like electrical currents were zapping through me, lighting up my spine, setting the base of my brain on fire.

"She studied the brain—perception, cognition, memory." I paused when I said that word, *memory*, and I looked up at Aspen, suddenly terrified. "No," I whispered.

"Who do you think you are?" She was standing over me.

My head was throbbing, and I could hear my heartbeat in my ears.

It was coming together now. All those bits and pieces, all those things I'd blocked out, that I hadn't wanted to see.

I stared down at my hands. I touched my swollen cheek.

"Come on. This isn't that hard, is it?"

All the subtle things I'd recognized, all those things I shouldn't have known—the way Jim seemed to know me when he picked me up at the airport, the way I'd instinctively known how to unlock the basement gate.

"No," I said, tears spilling from my eyes.

The way they'd all looked at me right from the start, as if I was something dangerous, but also something familiar.

"Tell me," Aspen commanded.

They'd looked at me like they'd known me. Because they *had* known me.

Silence filled the room as the light shuddered and beat.

"I'm her, aren't I?" I said, breaking.

Aspen started laughing, a broad smile slitting her face.

The light flickered off and then burst back on.

"Welcome back, Isabelle," she said. "Now, where the fuck is Charles?"

IV

THE OTHER SIDE

4.1

MASS HYSTERIA
AND CONSPIRACY THEORIES

*Can we get control of an individual to the point where he will do our bid-
ding against his will and even against fundamental laws of nature such as
self-preservation?*

—CIA DOCUMENT, PROJECT *ARTICHOKE*, 1952

I sat stunned, disbelieving, and in such shock that I could barely
feel my limbs. What the hell was happening to me? I was Robin
Quain. I was a historian. Wasn't I? No, I was someone else.
Whatever had been done to my memory, it hadn't worked all
the way. Things had crept through in my dreams, and it was
those dreams more than anything that made me sure I really was
Isabelle. And there were other clues. I thought back to Finn, to
his telling me how someday I'd regret asking for the truth about
Isabelle. Even my favorite *Twilight Zone* episode was a clue, as if
I was trying to shout the truth at myself, though it consistently
fell on deaf ears.

"Charles?" I whispered, and memories flashed before my
eyes—the two of us laughing in his office at NYU, only it wasn't
NYU. It was here, in some kind of lab. Drinking vodka in the
Russian bar, only it wasn't a bar, was it? It was my cabana, and
we were elated about the progress we were making. We were

geniuses, weren't we? Going to go down in history. Then staring into his eyes near the sundial in Washington Square Park, only it wasn't a sundial, and it wasn't Washington Square Park. Still, the snow fell in thick, mournful waves.

"I'm Isabelle?" For some inscrutable reason, I looked over at Lexi for confirmation.

"Whip-smart, this one," she said with her characteristic snarkiness. "Took you long enough."

"Who is Charles?"

"Your best friend."

"Well, other than me," said Lexi.

"She's joking," said Aspen. "Lexi hates you."

"Honestly," said Lexi, examining her nails, "most people hate you. I was one of the few who didn't until, you know, I did."

Blinking slowly, as if trying to see through a thick haze, I asked, "If I'm Isabelle, why do I think I'm Robin?"

"Hell if we know. Something happened to your brain. You and Charles disappeared the night of the breach, which is unfortunate because you're the only ones who know the code."

I tried to make myself understand what Lexi was saying, but my eyes were gritty, and I had no clue what was happening to me.

"But Charles is in New York. He was my best friend in grad school."

"No," said Lexi. "He was your best friend here, but there is something you're hiding from yourself about him. We think that's why he carried over into your screen memories."

"Screen memories?" I tried to sit up, but my head was spinning, so I lay back down. "I don't know what you're talking about. I am completely freaking out right now. I don't understand what's happening to me."

Aspen looked over at Lexi. "I don't know how much we can tell her."

Lexi shook her head, a warning.

"Please." Desperately, I looked over at Aspen, hoping she could throw me some kind of lifeline before I completely lost touch with reality.

"Okay," said Aspen, calmly sitting down and making eye contact with me. "Listen to me carefully. I know this is hard to understand, but you aren't Robin Quain. You're Isabelle Casimir. You're a neuroscientist and you used to work here with your best friend, Charles. There was a security breach. I can't tell you more about that until you remember it yourself. The night of the breach, you and Charles disappeared, and we need one of you to tell us the code so we can seal the breach."

"What are you talking about? A breach of what?"

She looked over at Lexi, hesitant. "There are some things I can't tell you yet, but there is a barrier we need to maintain. In some ways, it is our one and only job. It's why Hildegard is here."

"What kind of barrier?"

"A fortification," said Aspen, and I could tell she was searching, choosing her words very carefully. "It's expansive, meticulously constructed—a Hadrian's Wall, if you will."

"Where?" I asked, but she just shook her head.

"I can't tell you that yet."

"All you need to know," said Lexi, "is that there was an accident and part of that barrier was damaged. We need to repair it, but we can't without the code."

"Does any of this ring a bell?" asked Aspen.

I looked around the medical suite at the sterile equipment, the sharps container on the wall, the harsh fluorescent lights.

"No. It all sounds completely fucking crazy."

Lexi let out a peal of laughter, and I nearly joined her. The entire thing felt unbelievable, like an uncanny dream where the world is almost as you know it, but something indefinable had suddenly changed. And yet what Aspen said about the code sounded right to me on some deep level. I didn't know any code off the top of my head, but I did have—had always had—a sense of hidden knowledge somewhere inside me. And I could almost feel that night. The sirens. The howls. The screams. I looked at Aspen, something cold and commanding coming to the fore.

"Clarity," I snapped. "I need clarity. This fortification, what's its purpose? We're in the middle of nowhere. What are you trying to keep out?"

"There she is," said Lexi. "The bitch is back."

Aspen smiled. "You are starting to seem more like yourself, but we need to be careful. If we tell you too much, it could jeopardize the reacclimating process, possibly even irreparably damage your cognitive function. We aren't even supposed to have told you this much. You'll have to remember on your own."

"Where is Charles?" I had seen him in the woods that night, but I thought it was a hallucination. Nothing about it felt real, and yet it could have been, couldn't it? For now, though, I would keep it to myself. I didn't trust these two, not completely. Not yet. But if Charles was here, it meant he wasn't the Charles who had betrayed me. He was still my best friend, and the only person I was going to trust. I just needed to find him.

"We have no idea where he is. We haven't seen him since that night."

"Exactly how long have I been gone?"

"Since February."

A sudden paroxysm shook me, and I started laughing. It wasn't exactly that I thought this was funny. It was more like someone was poking some receptor in my brain that induced uncontrollable laughter.

"You need to get yourself together," commanded Aspen. "You are partially responsible for getting us into this, and you have to understand that there are stakes involved."

"I'm not responsible for anything. I just met you people."

"She still thinks she's Robin," said Lexi, sounding defeated.

It was only half true, though. I knew that they weren't lying to me. I was Isabelle Casimir, and yet in my bones, I still felt like Robin.

"You need to cut it out," said Aspen, her voice suddenly firm. "You need to start getting your memory back because we are all in deep shit if you don't."

I breathed deeply, trying to contain my bizarre urge to laugh. "But why exactly? I don't understand why this is happening to me."

She looked over at Lexi, uncertain, but Lexi shook her head. "Not yet. Too risky."

"Look, all I will say is that there is an evil here, and it is imperative that it stay controlled. Right now, there is a chance that we are about to lose control, and we need you to help us have that not happen."

"Could you please be clearer?"

"We can't, unfortunately," she said. "We all have different security access here, and our disciplines are siloed, but no one knew as much as you. All we know is that you need to remember the code. We aren't supposed to be involved in that aspect of the memory retrieval. We are only supposed to provide familiarity and direction with your research."

"Okay, but who did this to me and why?"

"We have no idea who did it, but our best guess is they wanted your research."

"Wait, my research," I said, rubbing my temples. "Is my research even real?"

"Not your Salem witch trials bullshit. Your real research."

My heart sank as I understood what she meant. Whatever I did here, that's what made me me. The person I thought I was never existed.

"We might be wrong," said Lexi, and standing, she walked over and looked down at me like a slightly disgusted bird of prey. "It's possible she gravitated toward her subject naturally because it was familiar, but it's also possible that there is something real hidden away in there."

Lexi and Aspen exchanged an intense look I couldn't quite understand, and then Aspen stared at me as if still trying to assess if I really was as clueless as I maintained.

"Okay, look," she said. "There's more going on than just you skipping town. There were undercurrents of something disturbing in the months leading up to your disappearance. Hildegard as a whole is experiencing something of a splintering. There are those of us who want things to go on as they always have. We are a research institution that prioritizes knowledge above all else. We don't play politics. We don't work with governments, especially not ones that commit human rights violations."

I tried to follow what she was saying, but I felt like my brain was filled with spiderwebs, a thousand vicious arachnids scurrying around in there, envenomating my synaptic connections.

"But that's changing?" I asked.

"There are some who think the way to continue to exist, to expand even, is to change these basic tenets."

"Who are these people?"

"Key members on our board and of our upper administration, but they are by no means a majority. And for the most part they are off-site. But we know that you had begun to be suspicious of someone here. We know it isn't either of us."

I began to understand. "But you're not sure about Finn and Dorian."

Aspen bit her lip, looking uncertain.

"We should tell her," said Lexi. "She needs to know."

"They're more connected to the administration than we are, and regrettably, the old boys' network is still very much alive and well at Hildegard. We still don't know who did this to you, and until we know more about how this happened and what you know, it's best not to involve them directly yet."

Slowly I looked around the room, still trying to get my bearings. I blinked, trying to focus, but I was incredibly tired.

"So I should keep it a secret? Just go on pretending to be Robin?"

"For now, yes. And we'll keep referring to you as Robin. You also need to pretend to still be doing your research. Meanwhile, you need to actually be trying to figure out what you know. And we'll help you as much as we can without drawing attention. That's the best path forward at the moment, but we can adjust as needed."

I put my head in my hands. "And this is all about some code? Why are you talking about this like the stakes are through the roof?"

Aspen sucked in a breath. "You really don't remember what's out there, do you?"

"No. What is it I'm supposed to remember?"

Aspen looked at Lexi, but again, she shook her head. "Not yet."

"Look," she said, "for right now you need to trust us that this is big, really big. And time is of the essence. You need to start getting your memory back as soon as possible."

I could feel a strange energy coursing through my body. It was close to rage, something like adrenaline, like a powerful angry person was clawing at me from within, trying to spring to life. If this was who Isabelle was, I wasn't sure I wanted to meet her.

"And if I don't figure it out? If I don't remember? What happens?"

Aspen sighed. "Something very bad."

"Catastrophic," said Lexi.

I stared deep into their eyes and was struck by what I saw there. Whatever it was they feared, it was something that went down to their cores.

When I was feeling well enough to walk, they helped me to an elevator that took us up two flights to a darkened corridor.

"Where are we?"

"Back of the garden house," said Aspen, and she opened a metal door for me to step through. We emerged into a familiar space, the sitting area with the walls lined with books. Still partially dazed, I stared around the room and back at the metal door. I now remembered how curious I'd been when I'd first seen it. Some part of me must have known where it led.

"Okay," Aspen said. "One more time. Tell me what you're going to do."

I recited my instructions. "I'm supposed to go to Finn's cabana and tell him I was attacked by a strange man. I will continue to be Robin, but I'm going to spend all of my time and energy trying to remember the code and what happened to Charles."

"And you're not going to trust anyone but us."

I smiled at her. Not only was I not going to trust the others, I had no intention whatsoever of trusting these two. As far as I was concerned, it was every man for himself. I would try to find the code, but that was secondary to figuring out who did this to me and why. Maybe Robin was easily influenced, but Isabelle was a lot more stubborn and calculating. I could feel her rising to the surface even then.

"Pinkie swear," I said.

We decided to leave separately so as not to attract attention. I was the last to go, and as I stepped outside into the waning dusk, the coolness of the evening air hit me like knife blades, and I remembered my face was covered in bruises and cuts.

Walking through the apothecary garden, I stared down at a collection of vividly yellow flowers, barely able to breathe. There was no Robin. Only Isabelle. Whatever else I had expected to find at Hildegard College, this was not it, and in many ways, it was too much for me to even begin to unpack. Because I was unable to process it intellectually, my body seemed intent on responding physically. I felt dizzy and like my head might explode.

Without meaning to, I sank down to the ground, my heart beating erratically. Whatever this emotion was, I didn't want to stay in it. I wanted to return to those windswept empty hallways in my mind and feel nothing again. And then briefly, I wept. I kept the grief and self-pity to a minimum, though; I knew I couldn't sit out in the garden curled up fetal and weeping.

At least now I knew what I didn't know. That terrible uncertainty always gnawing at me, that feeling that something wasn't right—at least now I knew why it was there. But even as I tried to accept this new truth, the horror of my reality began to dawn. If I wasn't Robin Quain, then there was no escape. There was no home, nowhere to return to. I *was* home. I already *had* returned.

Sadness swelled in my chest, a longing for someone to make it all better. To take the confusion away. I needed someone or something. Charles? My bluebird? And then a sudden thought—what if Charles was the one leaving me the clues? I just needed to find him, and then I would be able to figure out what to do.

I wiped my eyes and looked up at the darkening sky. In the distance, like a call to arms, a radiance of cardinals burst from a tree, tufts of red smoke. Taking a deep breath, I started out of the apothecary garden, steeling myself for the battle to come.

When I reached Finn's cabana, I could see him sitting on his couch, drinking a beer and reading what appeared to be a book in Cyrillic. When I knocked, he invited me inside, and when he saw me, he dropped the book.

"Holy shit."

"I'm okay," I said, shuffling in and leaning against the back of a chair for support.

"You don't look okay. What happened?"

"I was attacked," I said simply.

"Oh my god. By whom?"

"Some man. I don't know. I didn't get a look at his face."

"Let me get Aspen," he said, starting for the door. "She'll know what to do."

I limped over to the couch, and taking a seat, I fought back tears as a wave of relief swept over me. I hadn't realized just how terrified I'd been until I was back somewhere safe. I was shaking, a subtle tremor running the length of my body.

When Aspen appeared at the door, she did a great job of

feigning surprise. She and Finn helped me back to my cabana, and soon Lexi and Dorian were there as well. Aspen brewed me some herbs on the stove while I showered, and then I drank the strange, bitter yet cloying concoction while sitting freshly bandaged on the couch, trying to answer questions without giving too much away. Whatever this new batch of herbs was, they were quite a bit stronger than what she'd given me before. The full strength of them didn't take effect until about fifteen minutes after I'd finished the thick, dark brown tea, but when it did, I felt a pleasant numbness wash over me. The pain became a distant worry, as if it were all happening to someone else. For what it was worth, the group did a fair job of seeming concerned about the attack. Maybe some of them really did care? Or maybe they were all great liars. Finn fussed over me and Lexi patted my hand. My head fuzzy from the herbs, I smiled at them distantly, trying to remember why I'd been so upset earlier.

Dorian seemed especially distraught, several times moving as if to hug me again, but then stopping himself, seemingly embarrassed by his emotions.

"Robin," he said, "what has happened to you today is beyond regrettable. That it could have happened on our secure campus is shameful. We have alerted the authorities about the incident, and we intend to search the premises ourselves at first light." As he spoke, I had the distinct feeling that his words had been rehearsed, but I tried not to let my suspicion show as he continued. "Earlier today we'd been alerted that our alarm system had been breached. Finn and I went out to examine the quadrant breach out at the far northwest edge of the perimeter. That must have been when you encountered the assailant. We take this very seriously, and we intend to do everything we can to rectify the situation."

"Thank you," I said, rubbing my numb lips with the surface of my hand.

"I think given the circumstances, the most prudent thing would be for you to stay on at Hildegard with us a while longer," he added as if he'd just remembered his line. I had a feeling that sentence had been on a different page, and he'd forgotten to memorize it along with the rest of his speech.

Looking around the room, I found it difficult to believe that none of these people were who I'd thought they were. Every moment I'd spent with them had been a lie. And now I had to become part of that lie. The thought of it was making my palms sweat.

"Yeah, I'd like to stay," I said, trying to sound much more fragile than I felt. "I think that makes sense."

Dorian couldn't keep the surprise from registering on his face.

"After what's happened to me, I don't want to travel yet. I want to stay and finish out the residency if possible."

"Of course," he said, obviously stunned. "Anything you need."

"I saw something out in the woods. A temple. I know that sounds crazy, but I saw it, I swear. Why is there a temple out in the woods?"

The room fell uncomfortably silent.

"Oh, the folly," said Dorian suddenly, and the atmospheric tension eased.

"Folly?" I asked. The term was familiar, but I wasn't sure exactly what it meant.

"Sure. You must have heard of follies before. The Conolly Folly, Needle's Eye. They're ornamental architectural elements added to grounds purely for fun. They were all the rage at one point. And in Ireland they're strewn all over. Right, Finn?"

Finn looked startled but nodded. "Yeah. Famine follies, they're called. They were built by the poor during the Great Famine because no one believed in handouts back then. So they paid the poor to build useless structures, miniature castles without proper interiors, towers in the middle of swamps, things like that."

"That enormous thing out in the woods is a folly?"

Finn nodded, and I decided to drop it. There was no way I was getting the truth out of them anyway. I sat in silence for the rest of the evening, observing the others as they came up with various plans to try to find my assailant. It was odd, trying to track their thought processes. At first I'd been unsure whether Guillaume was somehow in league with them, but seeing the genuine disquiet in their eyes convinced me he was an outsider. However, it didn't convince me that they were wholly unaware of his motive. They didn't know him, but they didn't seem especially surprised by the fact of him.

Plans to search the grounds were made, and Dorian pretended to call the police. I was under no delusion that this was the case (shocker—there was a problem with the phones), but it was a nice bit of theater. After a while, I told them I needed to rest, and the group disbanded.

That night I tried to sleep, but tossed and turned, uncomfortable in every position. Whatever the others might believe, I could barely sense the part of me that Isabelle occupied. I knew that I was her, but I didn't feel like it. It was true that there was an unfamiliar strength lurking somewhere deep inside me, influencing me certainly, but it wasn't as if I was suddenly a different person. It didn't take away the sense of self that I knew. But was that going to change now? Sometime soon would I become a person I didn't know, or would the process be barely perceptible, Isabelle gradually eclipsing Robin until one day I would simply be gone?

As I lay there, tears swelling in my eyes, I felt a crushing grief for the life I'd never known, for the me that never was, and repeatedly, thoughts of Charles floated to the surface, bringing with them surges of emotion so strong, I could barely breathe. It was as if my heart was imprisoned in a belt of barbed wire and someone had just cinched it tighter. There I was again, standing in the snow, the anger and humiliation so cutting I'd needed to lash out. I'd pushed him. I remember that. Only none of that had ever happened. So why was the heartache so heavy I felt like it might smother me? I missed him terribly. I'd never stopped missing him. Only the world in which I was now missing him was a hell of a lot scarier.

Stifling a howl of frustration, I sat up and turned on the light. When I'd first moved into the cabana, I'd seen some booze somewhere in the kitchen—nothing that had seemed especially appetizing at the time, but right now anything would do. I began searching through cupboards until I found what I needed. Back behind the blender was a bottle of expensive-looking cognac. I wasn't even sure what cognac was, but it would suffice.

It tasted like rotten peaches, and I suspected it had turned, but took another swig anyway. The alcohol slipped through my system, and my nerve endings began to light up. I was feeling something other than loss now, wasn't I? Granted, it was a burning sensation, but at least it was different.

I took another swig, wincing at the flavor, and searched every crevice inside my soul for the memories I knew had to be there, but it was as if some kind of physical barrier was blocking anything from rising to the surface. Something, some path to memory, was blocked on purpose, wasn't it? Whatever it was that lingered inaccessible inside of me, it must be so dark and deep, so sullied, that it was somehow safer not to remember it just yet.

I needed to distract myself, so, opening the drawer beside my bed, I retrieved the divination cards. They had been bothering me. I understood how to use the widows' keys (if not why exactly), but I wasn't sure what the cards had to do with anything. I shuffled through them, trying to understand what they were. Similar to the tarot, except they lacked a major arcana, they were composed of five suits: angels, demons, peasants, flora, and beasts. As I sipped the probably poison cognac, I sorted the cards, organizing them into suits.

"Oh . . ." I whispered, suddenly seeing.

Jumping up, I pulled the coffee table away from the couch and pushed the armchair back to make room on the floor. I got down on my hands and knees. Shaking with excitement, methodically, I placed each card as if assembling an enormous jigsaw puzzle. Now I understood. When arranged in ascending order, each suit revealed a narrative. My heart racing, I began to see that if I arranged the cards correctly, they told one huge, overarching story.

It began with a series of images showing ordinary peasants living typical agrarian lives. That was followed by cards that showed black rain falling and plants growing. The next set showed smokelike demons rising up from the soil and the villagers dying off in horrific ways. Next came the monsters—hideous beasts, subterranean nightmares, and a malevolent horned god. The end of the series showed angels coming forth to rescue the survivors and helping them to flee across the sea to a new, safe land. And finally—and here it was hard to tell—the last two cards seemed to indicate a peasant planting a yellow flower in the soil of the new earth, and finally, the return of the monsters. It was some sort of a cycle.

Stepping back, I looked over the entire sequence, and suddenly I saw. My mind flashed to Pliny the Elder, to what he'd written about the black rains: how in antiquity, they'd brought forth the silphium, that panacea that I now knew grew plentifully here at Hildegard. I looked at the bloodshed depicted in the cards, at the images of people being torn limb from limb, at the burning skies, the fallow fields, and I had a depth of knowledge so strong I knew it could only have come from Isabelle. These cards, whatever they were, they weren't just used for divination or carnival fortune-telling.

This wasn't a game of any kind.

This was a warning.

4.2

SECRET SIGNS:
THE HIDDEN REALITIES
OF EVERYDAY EXPERIENCE

The truth needs the trick, the fact the fantasy. It is almost as if the left brain will not let the right brain speak (which it can't anyway, since language is generally a left-brain function), so the right brain turns to image and story to say what it has to say (without saying it).

—JEFFREY J. KRIPAL, PhD

The next day I found myself thinking about my bluebird. That longing had been with me since the start, emerging in dreams and lingering just outside of view. In my dreams, Charles had told me I needed to find my bluebird, so it couldn't be him, but it was related to him somehow; I could feel it.

I wasn't ready to see the others just yet, and I was supposed to be looking for Charles, so I decided to do just that. Now that I knew he was here, I needed to reconsider all those times I'd had a sense that someone was watching me, in case it might have been Charles. I dressed and set out through the crispness of the early-morning fog for a walk out into the woods. The woods—always the woods, as if there was something specific out there that I sought. And perhaps there was. It was possible that there were dangers in the woods, but at this point, ignorance seemed to pose the biggest threat to me. I wasn't looking for anything in particular, but I did deviate from the set paths, and soon I found myself on an unmarked trail.

The morning was pretty glorious in a brisk, misty way, and for a short while I was able to lose myself in the meditative rhythm of my stride. If pressed, I wouldn't be able to pinpoint the exact moment when I realized something was walking beside me, just on the other side of the trees. Instead, it was more a growing awareness of a feeling that I wasn't alone. I was walking along a woodsy path that cut through a grove of cedars, and I could hear it: footfalls, crunching of leaves, the stray snap of a twig. I stopped, and the movement stopped in tandem. When I started up again, it started up as well, and when I picked up speed, so did the mysterious presence.

I had the distinct feeling that someone or something was pacing alongside me in the woods, perhaps trying to keep me from stumbling onto something I wasn't supposed to see. Of course its intentions could be worse, much worse. The only thing I knew for sure was that I didn't want to find out what that worst-case scenario might entail. Turning, I started back the way I'd come, and the movement shifted with me. My breath was shaking and raspy now, and a swelling terror in my belly was making itself known. I needed to get the hell out of there, and fast.

To my horror, the movement suddenly shifted, and I could tell that whatever was right on the other side of that dense foliage was coming straight through toward me. I backed away, nearly senseless with terror. Something was coming to get me. I wasn't typically given to childish terror, and yet I found my fingers in my mouth stopping a scream.

"Hello?" I called, my voice shaking, but there was only silence. "Charles?"

The bushes shook violently, and a figure stepped through.

It was Dorian, leaves in his hair, a fun-house horror smile on his lips. For an instant, I thought he was going to reveal a butcher knife and stab it directly into my heart.

"Hi," he said, and for the first time, I noticed something vaguely unhinged in his eyes.

"What are you doing out here?" I took a step away, but immediately he closed the gap.

"Just walking. You?"

"Same," I said. "Just walking."

I desperately wanted to leave, but I didn't want to turn my back on him.

"Do you want to walk together?" I tried to make it seem like a casual suggestion, like I didn't think it was even remotely strange that he was in an expensive suit in the middle of the woods, smiling at me like a goddamn serial killer.

"No, that's okay," he said. "I have some things to do out here."

"Right." I kept my eyes locked on his.

"Right." He smiled, and suddenly he was himself again. Nothing dangerous there. Nothing to fear.

"I'll be seeing you around, then," I said, turning to go.

I took only a few steps, but when I turned back around again, he was gone.

As I walked back, I couldn't shake the anxious sense that I was somehow in danger. When I'd thought Isabelle was someone else, her life and work had sounded vaguely romantic, but now that I was Isabelle, it didn't feel that way at all. I longed for Robin Quain's boring life, with her concerns about tenure and dumb publications.

As I walked, I mulled over the name Quain, rolling it around on my tongue like a lozenge. Why was my name Quain? Had it been given to me by whoever did this, or had I chosen it for myself after the fact? Either way, it was a strange name, one that stood out for sure, and therefore not necessarily great for anonymity.

And then I stopped on the path, the woods suddenly feeling so large, I thought they might envelop me. I knew the name Quain, recognized it. It was in fact someone else's name. Jorge Luis Borges had written a story called "An Examination of the Work of Herbert Quain." The story takes the form of a critical review of the work of a fictional writer named Herbert Quain. That must have been where the name came from. But what did it mean?

Suddenly I understood. The dreams of the blazing orange sun, Isabelle pointing to the book. There was a clue for me in that book, wasn't there? I'd barely looked at it when I'd first found it. There had to be something I missed in there. I needed to get to the library.

Rushing back along the main path, I passed by my cabana and went straight to the house. Up there, it was dimly lit and silent. The sound of my shoes echoed off the tiles as I walked across the main room, past the entryway with that big golden heart and the vase of fresh flowers—birds-of-paradise—and over to the exterior passage that led to the library. As I walked, it was like seeing everything with fresh eyes. Each brick, each window I passed, I wondered if it had a special meaning to me. I wondered precisely what memories had been born within these walls.

When I stepped into the nave, I felt a shift in the air. It was always so much colder and damper than in the rest of the monastery. Slowly, feeling almost as if I were approaching a danger-ous beast, I made my way to the corner where the Borges book was. Carefully I pulled *Ficciones* off the shelf and held it in my hand, staring for just a moment at the blazing sun on the cover, before opening it up to the story in question. But when I paged through, I found no clues.

Crestfallen, I let the book drop between my knees. I'd been so certain. No, I told myself. There had to be something more. And then I had a thought. Borges's stories were often self-referential and metafictional, and in "An Examination of the Work of Herbert Quain," Borges credits Quain's work as provid-ing the source material for another one of his stories, one called "The Circular Ruins."

I opened the book up again and found "The Circular Ruins." There it was, the clue I was looking for. Right beneath the title was a handwritten set of numbers:

(39.2525233,-107.48774090)

My heart leapt. They were coordinates. Finally, something concrete. No puzzles or anagrams or word games, just some solid information that I could actually use. But why had I left them here instead of in the Quain story? It was true that "The Circular Ruins" was my favorite story. I even had a quote from it in my of-fice back in New York. Flipping farther on, I located that quote and found that someone had underlined it: *With relief, with hu-miliation, with terror, he understood that he also was an illusion, that someone else was dreaming him.*

Written beside it were the words: *Uta Hopper Symon.* Was that a person? I wondered. Another anagram? Or was it just an unrelated note some long-ago reader had left in the margin?

And then a rush of understanding washed over me. There was something about the content of the story, wasn't there? Something I was trying to communicate with myself. A cold shock gripped me as I saw the truth unfold before me. "The Circular Ruins" told the story of a wizard who made a man simply by dreaming him into existence. After the wizard created this man, he destroyed his memory so that in the end, the creation had no idea who he really was. In the end, the wizard burned himself alive after realizing that he, too, was simply someone else's dream.

Aspen and Lexi said they didn't know who did this to me. They said they thought it was someone who wanted to steal my research. I was told repeatedly that the work I did here was unmatched, that I was a singular genius. Clearly the man in the story was meant to represent me, but what if I was also the wizard? Had I done this to myself—played with memory and destroyed myself in the process?

But there was another possibility still. Maybe this clue wasn't meant to be an answer; maybe it was meant to be a warning. Because it was possible that the wizard was someone else, someone still out there, someone who still posed a threat.

Around me, the heavy quiet of the library began to feel oppressive, and I found myself wondering what exactly Hildegard College was. Aspen and Lexi had spoken of a barrier, but what kind of barrier, and what was it keeping out?

For the first time, I felt like the library wasn't a safe place to linger. I finally had a direct piece of communication, and I needed to put it to use. Those numbers were coordinates, and I was fairly sure they would lead me somewhere on campus. I just needed to find it.

Replacing the book, I left the library and headed into the

main house. Without my phone or computer, I would need to find something with a map function, and knew there was a computer in Dorian's office. Thankfully, it wasn't password protected, and I was able to look up the coordinates with ease. Zooming out, I saw that they put me squarely at the apiary.

Momentarily, my heart sank. I couldn't go rummaging around the apiary with a bee allergy. Then I remembered that Finn had said Isabelle used to steal his honey to mess with him. That meant that Robin may have been allergic to bees, but Isabelle was not. Useful to know before I plunged headfirst into a beehive.

I was about to leave the office when I had a sudden thought: I could reach out to anyone with the computer. I could contact 911 and be rescued in an instant. But then I thought better of it. If I called the police, I would be calling them on myself. Sometimes no rescue is possible—not when you're the problem.

Despite the darkening sky, the apiary looked especially gorgeous that day. I tucked in my clothes to cover any naked skin, grabbed Finn's bee veil and gloves, and started poking around. After a quick visual scan of the area, I zeroed in on the little bee houses. Would it be possible to hide something inside one of them? It seemed like that could disrupt honey production, but what if it wasn't inside the hive? What if it was underneath the house?

Getting on my hands and knees, I inspected the first house, even going so far as to put my face to the ground to see if there was anything underneath. It wasn't until I searched the third house that I found it. Something small and metallic was affixed to the underside with duct tape. Reaching, I slid my nails under the edge of the tape and tore. When I pulled it out, I saw that it was another key. A glimmer of excitement lit up my nerve endings as I

stared at the key. It was embellished on the bell, like the peacock
key that opened the storeroom on the second floor of the library.
Only in this case, the embellishment was a rendering of an owl.
I was almost certain this would open the door I'd been unable to
open at the back of the storeroom.

Cautiously hopeful, I climbed out of the protective gear and
stowed it back where I'd found it, my heart racing with excitement. This was it. I knew it. Thunder groaned across the sky, and
the atmosphere sizzled with electricity as I slipped the key in
my pocket. As I hurried back toward the library, fantastical sce-
narios played out in my head. Opening the secret room to find
Charles waiting there with a glass of champagne ready to inform
me everything would be fine and he'd just wanted to play a little
game. *Did you like my treasure hunt, darling?*

Dark clouds, heavy with rain, began erupting just as I made
it under the covered walkway that led into the old monastery.
The library was empty, and as I started up the stairs to the
closed wing, I felt especially unsteady and nervous. Upstairs in
that lonely corridor, rain lashed against the stained-glass window, drawing my attention to the image of Mary and the olive
branch. Only, what if it wasn't the Virgin Mary? And what if it
wasn't an olive branch?

Slowly I walked toward it, taking it in as if for the first time.
All it took was a perspective shift, and the woman was no longer
the Virgin Mary, but Mary the Prophetess, cloaked in blue, staring back at me as if she could see through space and time right
to this moment. I took a step closer, and reaching out, I traced
a finger along the outline of the plant she cradled. This wasn't
necessarily an olive branch, was it? With those flecks of yellow,
it could just as easily be silphium. It had been here all along right
in front of me, a message encoded within a seemingly ordinary

work of art. What else, I wondered, had I missed? What messages still lurked just outside of my line of sight?

A streak of lightning flashed, bringing the image to shocking life, and as the thunder rumbled in its wake, I turned and hurried back to the antechamber, opening the door and rushing inside. I switched on the light and made my way through the maze of file boxes until I reached the door at the back of the room. When I slipped the key in the door and heard the ward lock turn, a giddy relief washed over me. I was close now; I could feel it. Floorboards creaked beneath me as I stepped into the darkened space, and I caught a whiff of extinguished candle.

Inside, I was met with an astonishing sight. It was a large room, big enough to hold at least forty people fairly comfortably. Through the light filtering in from the antechamber, I could make out what at first appeared to be stalactites and stalagmites, but which, upon closer inspection, were glass bottles. Multicolored, and by the looks of them, very old, they hung from the ceiling just like the ones in my basement, but here they were matched by similar bottles secured to the floor, each rising up to meet its twin. The entire installation spooled out in matching concentric circles, their openings aligned as if they were exchanging energy somehow.

A quick search for a light switch proved fruitless, so carefully, I walked around the bottles until I came to an enormous altar. It was strewn with candles and various quasi-religious paraphernalia—stone gods and metal goddesses, twig structures and prayer candles. It felt cluttered and haphazard, but it gave me a bad feeling. There was nothing overtly diabolical, no pentagrams or Baphomets or anything like that, but whatever this was used for, I knew in my bones it wasn't good.

At the center of the altar was a set of books, one of which

lay open like a holy text. Leaning over it, I could just make out
images on the open pages, but the light from the antechamber
wasn't enough to see any detail, so I grabbed a match from over
by the candles and lit it. Under that flickering illumination, the
chilling illustration became clear. It was similar to the drawings
I'd once seen in the codex in the scriptorium. The left-hand page
featured the woman in the blue robes, Mary the Prophetess,
but where the images in the other book had been meticulously
rendered, this had none of that beauty. It was inexpertly exe-
cuted and had a squalid malevolence to it. And then there was
the right-hand page. It showed the horrific details of a bloody
massacre—a blindfolded victim and hordes rising up from the
underworld coming to collect her. What followed on subsequent
pages were depictions of bloodshed, of monsters, and of unthinkable torture and pain. The final page showed a crude depiction of a man in a robe feeding a yellow plant to horrific beasts.
Below the image, the text read *Les Terribles.* The Terrible Ones.

I knew that phrase. I'd heard it in my dreams, but I'd also
seen it once before. *Help!* Paloma's email had begun. And then
it had gone on to describe being kidnapped, having her memory erased, and nightmarish creatures she had called the Terrible
Ones.

A wave of disgust washed over me, though I couldn't say exactly why, and I took a step back from the book. I didn't want to
be in this space anymore. It felt toxic, spoiled somehow. Satisfied
this was what I meant to find, I started from the room, but then
stopped and turned around slowly. Something had caught my
eye. There was something else on the altar, wasn't there? Among
the carved wooden figures and the candles was something I'd
passed over initially. Since discovering who I was, I had been
focusing solely on Charles and the code. I'd all but forgotten

about the relic, had thought it was no more than a red herring, but there it was, sitting on the altar between a bundle of foul-smelling dried herbs and a statue of what might be Anubis.

It was much smaller than I imagined it would be, only a bit bigger than the palm of my hand, and where I had imagined graceful figures, the thirteen bodies were twisted, distorted, with holes for eyes, large, terrible sunken things. In the center was Janus, but it was also something else, wasn't it? It had two faces, but it also bore horns, and it had a hostile wickedness to it that made me finally certain that whatever magic or science was practiced at Hildegard, there was some arm of it that bled fiercely into the occult.

Time was running out—I'd been in that room far too long already—but I was now faced with a dilemma. Take it with me and risk angering whosever space this was, or leave it and assume it held no deeper importance? A beat and then it was decided. I slipped it in my pocket, bolted from the room, and locked the door behind me.

4.3

BLACK HELICOPTERS, PROJECT BLUE BOOK, AND MK ULTRA

Thousands of government-sponsored experiments did take place at hospitals, universities, and military bases around our nation. Some were unethical, not only by today's standards, but by the standards of the time in which they were conducted. They failed both the test of our national values, and the test of humanity. . . . So today, on behalf of another generation of American leaders and another generation of American citizens, the United States of America offers a sincere apology to those of our citizens who were subjected to these experiments, to their families, and to their communities.

—PRESIDENT BILL CLINTON, OCTOBER 3, 1995

Back in my cabana, I locked the door, covered all the windows, and set the relic on the coffee table, half expecting it to magically transform itself into a marvel that would explain everything, but it just sat there.

Retrieving a magnifying glass from the desk, I lifted the artifact and examined it, looking for any kind of markings or defects, anything that might serve as some kind of clue, but there was nothing. I turned it upside down, looked at it from the side, and took it into the windowless bathroom in a misguided attempt to see if it had any kind of luminescent qualities. I even shook it, and while it did seem like there was a faint rattle inside, that got me no closer to understanding what to do with it. So I just sat and stared at it for what seemed like hours, hoping some epiphany would come. It never did.

There was still so much I was missing. I felt like I was close to some kind of solution, but that it was just out of reach. Then it occurred to me that since the very beginning, everything that had happened to me at Hildegard had felt like a video game. I would discover a clue that would lead me to a location where I would discover either another clue or a locked pathway. Then I would receive yet another clue that would lead me to a key that would open that lock, and so on. Now that I was almost certain that I had done this to myself, I had to assume that I'd left those clues for myself. It stood to reason, then, that if I searched through any clues I had yet to solve, that they would lead me to the next step toward whatever I was supposed to find.

One thing that bothered me was why I had made Robin allergic to bees when Isabelle was not, but as I sat there staring at the relic, the answer came to me. It was so simple I'd almost missed it: I hadn't wanted to find the missing owl key, and thus the relic, until I had recovered enough of my memory to know that I was Isabelle. For some reason, Isabelle could go in the apiary, but Robin couldn't. I had essentially locked that part of the path until I had enough information to use it wisely. But the problem was, now that I had what I'd been looking for, I had no idea what to do with it. Then it occurred to me: I hadn't figured out I was Isabelle on my own. Whatever clue was supposed to lead me there had been skipped over when Guillaume attacked me. Aspen and Lexi told me who I was. I hadn't been the one to figure it out. No clue had led me here, which meant there was still a clue out there for me to find, something that I was supposed to have found *before* the owl key. I was almost there, but not quite, and my inability to cross that threshold was nearly driving me mad.

Frustrated, I walked outside and sank into a chair, staring up at the sky. Dusk was coming in fast, but the moon was already visible, an alabaster crescent ushering in the night. As I stared up at it, I was reminded of the strange feeling I'd had when I'd first found *The Book of Widows*—that vague, eerie feeling I was being watched.

I sat up suddenly, my memories unspooling back to the island, back to the night Aspen had drugged me and I'd gotten lost in the woods, and finally all the way back to my time in New York.

There I was again, sitting at the desk, feeling someone standing behind me, and when I'd come back to my senses, I'd found I'd drawn four symbols. These four symbols:

Since I'd first seen the tiles, I'd sensed that they were vaguely familiar but had quickly dismissed that instinct. Moon symbolism, after all, was fairly common, but now it was clear to me. I'd drawn them back in New York when I was in some kind of hypnotic state. They'd been important enough for me to carry them through from my time here as Isabelle to my life as Robin. They were a message to me; I was sure of it. I just didn't know what they could mean. The widows' keys were used for divination. I knew that much. You selected three tiles, probably tossed them in the air (or something similar), and saw what order they landed in. Then you consulted the text to see what the combination meant. But I had drawn four symbols, not three.

Thumbing through the book, I tried to make sense of it, but nothing came to me until I landed on an entry I'd noticed before but glossed over. There was a single mark in it. Someone had underlined the word *toad*.

   Vibrant Earth, Desolate Moon, Stable Sea
From a mountaintop, he sees three new goats. A
wolf attacks. It takes only meat. The <u>toad</u> looks on.

Why would that be underlined? I thought through everything I'd encountered up until that point, and then I landed on something. Back in the abandoned building, there was an office that had reminded me of Charles. The painting in there had drawn my attention. It was a painting of a toad. It couldn't be a coincidence. With absolute certainty, I knew that this must be the clue I'd missed. I had to get back into that office and examine that painting.

As I hurried back outside, I thought I heard Finn call after me, but I didn't answer. I had a singular purpose now and couldn't be distracted. There was a strange charge to the atmosphere as I started into the woods and along the trail to the abandoned building. When I reached the front door, I used Dorian's card to open it and started down the hall to the office.

Inside that small room, every surface seemed to scream *Charles*. I could honestly still smell the ghost of his cologne. So where the hell was he? Ignoring the papers spread out over the desk, I went directly to the painting of the toad. I stood before it a moment, looking closely to see if there might be a clue somewhere in its design, but nothing immediately jumped out, aside from the fact that it was a pretty bad painting. Carefully I felt around the edges of the canvas, then lifted it down from the wall and turned it over. There on the posterior, I found exactly what I sought. A small key was taped to the canvas backing.

I removed the key and hurried back out into the hall, but as I started toward the conference room, I had a feeling I was being watched.

"Hello?" I called, but I was met with only silence. Shrugging it off, I hurried into the conference room and tried the key in the filing cabinet.

It turned with ease and opened to reveal a wealth of folders and a single white binder. When I grabbed one of the folders, a Hildegard brochure slipped out. It was a few years old and seemed to be fundraising material. Flipping through it, I saw a bunch of bland promotional photos and then a list of names at the end. They appeared to be the members of the board of directors. A few of them were circled. Something about the brochure gave me a bad feeling, but I couldn't quite put my finger on why. I was about to look through it a second time when my gaze fell on the white binder, and I could barely believe what I was seeing.

It was large and white, with a plastic cover, and it had a label on the front: *Project Bluebird.*

My bluebird! I nearly screamed.

With tension in every muscle of my body, I sat down and opened it. I could barely believe what I'd found. Project Bluebird was a binder? It had never been a person. All along, it had been more research collected in one of Charles's Luddite binders. I started reading, the minutes ticking by as I plunged into the only world I used to know. I tried my best to understand what I was reading. It was the work Charles and I had done together, but it was far beyond my current realm of understanding. I found the content completely unfamiliar, at least at first. The more I read, however, the more it felt like an unused part of my brain began to awaken, long-dormant synapses firing again, connections reforming.

Much of our research revolved around the inherent neuro-plasticity of the human brain. We had modified an existing piece of technology called a hippocampal prosthesis, and using electrodes inserted directly into brain tissue, we had done something called deep brain stimulation. We had been breaking down synaptic connections and essentially rewiring them. Through this process, we could alter the way people think, the way they remember. I found myself trapped somewhere between disgust and pride. The invasiveness of the procedure turned my stomach, but the fact that Charles and I had come up with it was pretty exciting to me. I read on, and with a sinking feeling, I began to realize that there had been testing on human subjects, or at least one human subject—Sabine Étienne. A photograph accompanied her biographical information, and when I saw her face clearly, I realized it was Paloma.

I know what you are, she'd said. People were stealing her memories, she'd written in that cry for help. I'd thought she'd been mad, but in reality, she was the sane one. Sabine Étienne really was Paloma. And we had done something to her. Had it been willing? It must have been. There was no way I would have subjected a person to invasive tests against her will. But what if it wasn't against her will? Her grandmother had said she was obsessed with money and fame and desperate to be part of what happened up at Hildegard. If she had volunteered herself, if she had wanted to be part of the experiment, and if I had truly thought the experiment would be beneficial for humanity, would I have done it?

Whatever we'd done, it had begun to undo itself, possibly when I'd shown her the photo that night, the photo of the were-wolf victim, which I now knew was a photo of her. It must have triggered something, and she'd realized I wasn't her cousin.

Instead, I was a very dangerous person she needed to get away from as quickly as possible. Her note had said she'd gone to California, but she'd probably just taken off and hidden somewhere in New York. She was probably still there.

Disconcerted, I stood up and stretched. This was getting to me. I knew I was close now, but there was still so much outside of my grasp. Setting the binder to the side momentarily, I returned to the cabinet and pulled out the pamphlet I'd found earlier. Something had bothered me about it before, but I couldn't put my finger on it. Now slowly I paged through it, looking at the faces, putting names to them. On the second-to-last page was a photo of two men identified as the CFO and the chairman of the board of directors, respectively. The CFO had a name I recognized—Uta Hopper Symon. But it wasn't just the name that was familiar; it was the face. He looked different, much more put together, wearing an expensive suit and boasting a winning smile, but it was the same man who had picked me up at the airport in Denver. It was Jim, the supposed handyman. I'd wondered why he'd been wearing an expensive watch to do yard work. I now knew he never was doing yard work. He'd been wearing a costume, to what? To spy on me?

Feeling increasingly uneasy, I put the brochure back and returned to the Project Bluebird binder, trying to make sense of what I could. The notes were pretty chaotic, and a lot of them would have made sense only to Charles. For instance, I found a loose sheet of paper covered in digits. They were sums, bursts of quick arithmetic, scrawled by a hasty hand—his, not mine. For some reason, I had a rush of anger when I looked at the piece of paper. This was important; I just didn't know how. It was as if it was trapped just on the other side of a wall I couldn't see through. Had I been angry with Charles in this reality, too? And if so, what could a bunch of numbers have to do with it? I folded up the paper and put it in my pocket. I would need to spend some time with it later.

As I read on, there was a lot that went over my head—mentions of hostile material and biohazards, but I couldn't quite understand what any of that had to do with the work that we did. Also, although the hippocampal prosthesis was indeed a known piece of technology, there was no indication of exactly how we altered it. One thing, though, became very clear—this experimental procedure we had engineered involved putting the participant into a state that sounded very similar to sleep paralysis. I paused and stared up at the ceiling. Was this how Robin was created? And was it possible that as my memories started resurfacing, that paralytic state had been reactivated?

My head was spinning so I decided to take a break, but just as I was gathering everything back up, I noticed something in one of the notes that I'd missed on the first few passes. It was a note from me to Charles about an unsecured entrance on the northwest side of the observatory.

The observatory—the one they told me had been torn down. These were recent notes, less than a year old, which meant that the observatory was still standing. I just had to find it. I moved over to the table with the maps of campus and the blueprints of the island and started sifting through them. I couldn't help but laugh when the truth of it struck me—I already knew exactly where the observatory was. It was the temple in the woods.

I straightened out all the papers, put the binder back in the filing cabinet, locked it, and then left to find this unsecured entrance. Dusk was just beginning to fall as I headed outside. I knew I had to find the temple, but I wasn't exactly sure where it was. Despite passing the TO OBSERVATORY sign multiple times, I was pretty sure I'd been on every trail on campus and hadn't found it that way. And yet I'd managed to get there on my own twice before—once when I was out of my mind on psychedelics and once when Guillaume had chased me. Some part of me must have known where the observatory was both times, and for some reason that part had led me there when in a heightened state of consciousness.

As I headed through the woods, I did my best to relax and trust that I knew where I was going. It couldn't be very far from the center of campus because I hadn't run that far the night of my attack. I found the observatory path and started following it, but soon, trusting my instincts, I diverged, setting off through the trees until I came out at a familiar little clearing: the strange space with the yew tree.

Carefully I made my way down the slope and then came to stand at the tree. From there, I surveyed the area, the fence in front of me, the bushes to the side, until I found it—a break in the foliage on the left side of the tree. Hurrying over to it, I pushed through the thicket and cleared sapling branches out of my way until I emerged into a second clearing—the temple clearing.

I began searching the massive structure for this unsecured entrance on the northwest side of the building. Eventually I found a gate and a wooden door. With a heave, I pulled the gate open, and a terrible squeal echoed through the clearing as metal ground against stone. Inside, the hall was enormous, cold, and dark. It stretched out before me like a magnificent cathedral. Throughout the expanse rose odd, vaguely terrifying statues, though from a distance, I couldn't make out what exactly they were. Along the wall were torches mounted like sconces, but they were extinguished. And yet somehow the space was dimly lit, which seemed impossible until I looked up and realized I was standing under an oculus, a circular aperture in the domed ceiling that opened directly up to the night sky.

"Like in the Pantheon," I whispered.

A common feature of neoclassical architecture, the oculus functioned as a light source, but it often served a deeper, more symbolic purpose as well. As an open space, a kind of eye of God looking down on us all, it was meant to serve as a connecting point, a kind of gateway between mankind and the heavens above. For a moment, I wondered what happened when it rained, but then I noticed there was a drainage system, little holes driven into the marble through which the water might collect. I was about to get down on my hands and knees to examine them further, but a large model—a skeleton of some animal—caught my eye. As my vision adjusted, I could see now that that the statues were in fact all skeletons. I was in some kind of museum.

Taking a closer look at the display, though, I realized it couldn't be real. It was a ghastly piece of art—it must have been. Rising up on two legs, the creature was twisted and hunched, a monstrous torso attached to a skull that looked vaguely canine. It brought to mind ancient Norse gods and biblical demons all wrapped in a single putrid package. In fact it brought to mind the thing I'd seen standing at the foot of my bed.

"Isabelle?"

I turned to see Finn standing at the entrance.

He laughed, a low, disconcerting vocalization. "I thought it was you," he said. "When did you remember?"

Backing away, I shook my head. "I don't."

"Yes, you do," he said, moving slowly toward me. "There's no need to lie. I'm on your side. I didn't like Isabelle, but I like you, Robin. I'm willing to help you, especially if you can help us."

"Why do you think I'm Isabelle?" I asked.

"Because you're here. If you're here, then you remember."

I wasn't sure what to say to that, so instead of responding, I tried to buy myself some time. Looking around the massive space, I concentrated on the strange displays, and taking them in, I saw that they were all similarly unnatural: nightmarish iterations of fiends that have populated folklore since the beginning of time—arachnoid monstrosities with skulls like goats, enormous vulpine specimens with scorpionic tails, and creature after creature with grotesque, twisting horns.

I stopped in front of a display of a hunched-over beast that had enormous spikes jutting from its spine. "What is all this stuff?"

"It's a collection," he said.

"A collection of what? From where?"

"From here." He looked at me sideways. "So then you don't remember everything, do you? Have you remembered the code yet?"

As much as I wanted to hold my cards close, I could tell there was no real point in trying to hide it anymore. If he knew, he knew. I sighed, frustration building in my chest. "I don't know any code. If you people want me to remember a code, then just tell me how to remember it. I'm getting incredibly sick of everyone withholding useful information from me."

"But we have to. Otherwise it would be too risky." He walked a few paces and then stared up at a creature with two heads and knifelike talons. "If we told you everything too soon, we might break you, and then all would be lost. Your mind is in a fragile state right now, and unfortunately you are the only person qualified to tell us exactly how fragile. You see the conundrum. Honestly, I expected you to figure it out your first night back when I planted the flashing light near the grave. I never thought it would take you this long."

A shock froze me in place. "The flashing light in the woods? You did that?"

"Of course. I did all of it."

"No. The messages, the clues. I left them for myself."

"Isabelle, they were fed to you like that to get you to believe them. It was all us."

Stunned, a cold certainty settled heavy on my brow. "You're serious?"

He nodded.

"I wasn't the one leaving those clues?"

"If you were trying to convey information to yourself, don't you think you would have left, like, a clear note?"

"I thought I was using the puzzles to encrypt the information and keep you from intercepting it. If it was you, why do all this? Why play games with me?"

"Because it's what I do. It's the only reason I'm involved. My task was to get information from you, and to do that, I needed you to be receptive to the truth, and believe it or not, people are receptive to the truth only when they think they've figured it out themselves."

"But why not just tell me what was going on?"

Slowly he walked toward me, hands in his pockets. "Do you know what an ARG is?"

I shook my head.

"Alternate reality game. It's a kind of game in which the player interacts with the real world. I design them. The way these work is by giving the player just enough clues so that they can connect the dots themselves. See, if someone tells you a piece of information, you often reject it out of hand. We believe what we believe, and we search for evidence that supports those beliefs. Because of confirmation bias."

"What are you talking about?"

"This," he said, motioning around him. "All this. This was how I got you here."

"Why not just tell me?"

"You never would have believed it. The truth is too fantastical to believe. So I had to induce you to piece the information together and figure it out yourself. There is a biological explanation for this. You should know this better than anyone. When you think you've figured something out, something secret that no one else knows, you get an exhilarating rush of endorphins and other neuropeptides that make you feel good. That good feeling then helps your brain believe your body, so you double down on what you think you've discovered. You think you are seeing through an illusion to the incontrovertible truth. In reality, you're being tricked by your own biology. This is why so many people end up believing in conspiracy theories." He smiled. "But in this case, the conspiracy just happens to be real."

So there was a reason this had all felt like a video game to me. Essentially it had been. Everything had been Finn—the grave in the woods, the doll, the puzzles and clues, the anagrams. It had all been him. He had told me point-blank that his field was game theory. And here I had been going along with it, following along in his game while he looked on like a puppet master.

"This was all you? You did this to me?"

He nodded. "Yes, and you were remarkably slow about the whole thing. That very first night you were supposed to see the flashing light, find the grave, dig it up, and be on to the next clue. You weren't supposed to take days to find it, and then you weren't supposed to tell anyone what you'd found. How were we supposed to react to a grave in the woods? We had no idea what to say. The problem is that the sequence was designed for Isabelle to complete in about a day. But you weren't Isabelle."

I tried to clear away the haze that still obscured my consciousness. "Okay, so now I know who I am, but I'm not sure where that gets me. The person I was, I think she might have been doing something bad. I read through the Project Bluebird notes. Finn, was I brainwashing people?" I asked, my heart recoiling with fear at the answer.

His brow creased as he ran a hand through his hair. "Okay, let me try to explain this. In the scientific community, the study of memory creation has always been given priority over that of memory loss. The science behind how we forget has been almost completely untouched aside from the research you and Charles were doing. This is starting to change now, but it's going to take the others years to catch up to the work you two did."

"What did we do?"

"When you form a new memory—like, say you go to a funeral—that memory is then stored in the hippocampus. And it gets reinforced the more you think about it. Every time you think about it and remember the details of that funeral, all that gets encoded. You replay it in your mind and that causes the memory to be further encoded. It gets stored in the hippocampus and then the cortex. This is how memories are made, but how are they *unmade*?"

"I have no idea."

"We used to think that forgetting was just the breakdown of memory, but it's actually an active biological process of its own, and you and Charles and your whole team, you figured out how to exploit that process."

"Why would forgetting be a natural biological process?"

"Think about it. It makes sense. Our brain wants to forget traumatic experiences. Like, learn from them, but not necessarily keep them as memories. Women who have given birth often report that they forget the pain of the experience almost immediately. Because it's advantageous to the species that they do so."

"Wouldn't it be more advantageous just to make childbirth not hurt?"

"That's beside the point. This is a perfect example of how forgetting is an active process that serves the organism. On the flip side, you have PTSD, which is a pathological process where the process of forgetting malfunctions."

I closed my eyes momentarily, trying to take it all in. "We figured out a way to exploit this natural process."

"*Exploit* is the wrong word," he said. "*Manipulate* is probably more accurate."

"So we figured out how to destroy a memory, but how did I create new ones?"

"I have no idea. You and Charles were in a world all your own. Your research was so prized by the institution that you communicated directly with the higher-ups. You had special privileges, and we were left in the dark about the details. I'm pretty sure that you altered the device to suit your needs. Whatever enhancements you made to it, though, I have no idea."

"Okay," I said, rubbing my temples to ease my incipient headache. As I began to think more clearly, fatigue and stress seemed to settle into my flesh, as if the transition back to my cognitive self was too taxing for my physical form. "It seems to me like the key to all this is in whatever we did to alter that device, the hippocampal prosthesis. How did we alter it? What did we use?"

He gave me a broad smile. "I think you'd better come with me."

4.4

ASTRAL PLANES AND
SHAMANIC JOURNEYS

[Historian of religion Mircea] Eliade . . . identified similarities in the practices and concepts of shamans the world over. Wherever these "technicians of ecstasy" operate, they specialize in a trance during which their "soul is believed to leave their body and ascend to the sky or descend to the underworld. They all speak a secret language" which they learn directly from the spirits.

—JEREMY NARBY, PHD, ANTHROPOLOGIST

Finn led me through the giant hall and around the corner to an elevator.

"Where are we going?"

"The observatory."

When we stepped inside, he used a key card and then pressed his thumb against a pad near the buttons. We started moving down and I could barely breathe.

"Shouldn't we be going up? If we're going to an observatory, don't we need to see the sky?"

"It's not that kind of an observatory."

Soon we were stepping out into a brightly lit corridor, the end of which housed another bank of elevators. Inside the next elevator, we followed the same procedure, Finn using his key card and pressing his thumb against the metal beside the buttons. The elevator went down and down and down. I had the feeling of traveling through time, traveling somewhere I was not supposed to go. Something about the process made me feel like I was engaged in a kind of religious ceremony. It wasn't just me, though. Finn also had a solemn expression.

When the door opened, we walked down another dark hall to a large metal door. He took out a key card, then turned and looked at me.

"Do you have any memory of what's behind this door?"

I strained to remember, but nothing came to me. "Did I work here?"

He nodded. "You didn't just perform research on human test subjects."

"What are you talking about?"

"I suggest you prepare yourself."

I swallowed and nodded. He swiped his card and pressed his thumb. The door buzzed, and we stepped inside.

What I saw there defied logic. At first I almost thought I was looking at a painting—it was that unreal. I was in a dark room, a control room of sorts, and on the opposite wall was a bank of windows looking out into a vast sea of dark blue. In each window, floating in that bluer than blue liquid, was a monstrous creature, pinkish gray with shiny, almost translucent skin. They resembled manatees, but they weren't. Long spindly ducts of flesh issued from their bodies like tentacles, and on their backs were terrible growths like stunted angel wings. Next to them was what looked like an air lock.

I backed away, my hand covering my mouth. "What are they?"

"Call them what you want. Old gods, Nephilim, demons.

They don't have names. We still don't know what they are. Not really."

I tried to look away, but my eyes drifted back to the creatures. They were real. I knew they were real. And on some level, I recognized them. Their smashed, swollen white faces. Their long twisted clawlike appendages, horrid tentacles. I knew them much more than I wanted to.

"This is the nymph stage," he said. "Practically newborns."

"The water. They come from the water?" I asked, breathlessly trying to remember all those terrible things I'd blocked out, trying to piece together too much at once.

"Oh, that's not water," Finn said, and a chill traced up my spine. "That's just one of the paths that connects our world to theirs."

"How deep does it go?"

"All the way," he said, and then he swallowed. "It goes all the way down."

Leaning in, filled with a mixture of disgust and horror, I stared at them. I began to realize what I'd first thought were tentacles were actually tubes affixed to them, pumping something in. Or were they taking something out? I tried to see where the tubes were going, but I couldn't figure it out.

Glancing around, I saw that I was in some kind of command center with various control panels scattered throughout the room, but they showed no activity. It looked like the power had been shut down. Against a far wall was a collection of protective gear and a display of unfamiliar-looking instruments. Long, odd-shaped, and sharp-edged, the instruments appeared as though they were used on the creatures somehow. I walked over to the wall and examined an instrument that looked like an old-fashioned harpoon, barely able to imagine what they might use such a horrible thing for.

"What is this place?" I asked, indicating the apparently nonfunctional control panels.

"This is where we observe them. It's how we control the barrier that separates their world from ours."

The barrier, Hildegard College's own Hadrian's Wall—this was what Aspen had been talking about?

I took a step toward the creatures, a horrifying thought flashing through my mind. "If these are nymphs, where is the mother?"

Finn swallowed. "She's down there . . . somewhere."

I shuddered. "And the father?"

"We've never seen him."

Intrigued, still unable to believe my eyes, I took another step toward them. Suddenly the creatures all raised their heads as one. Finn startled. Enormous eyes shifted, and they all stared directly at me.

"What's happening?" I whispered.

These things weren't as harmless as they appeared. They were extremely dangerous.

"They know you're here."

"What do you mean? How do they know I'm here?"

"They recognize you."

One began struggling, shifting around in its watery prison. Suddenly I remembered the water, how it had felt that day, strange and viscous. Only it wasn't water. It never had been.

"We extract something from them, don't we, some kind of substance?"

"You're remembering now."

It wasn't so much a remembering as a deep understanding.

"Is that what we used to alter that device? Is that possible?"

"The harvest gives us many gifts" was all he said.

"What are we extracting?" I spoke with Isabelle's cold self-assurance. In that moment, I had total confidence that I understood more about this than Finn did. I just didn't remember. "Is it organic?"

"It's a kind of ferromagnetic alloy. It has a number of biological and technological uses."

"Like cobalt?" I asked. "That's what everyone is after these days, isn't it? The future of technology is supposed to depend on it."

I remembered the images of the tech moguls on the website and began connecting the dots. How long had this been going on?

"Similar to cobalt. But not cobalt."

I shook my head. "What does any of this have to do with alchemy?"

"We told you before. Alchemy is just the forefather of chemistry."

"Not witchcraft, then?" I asked, thinking back to the strange room I'd found.

He gave me a sly smile. "Witchcraft and science aren't as far apart as we'd all like to believe. Some say the supernatural is just natural phenomena for which we don't yet have a scientific explanation."

"So which is it that you do here?"

"Science," he said flatly. "Now I want you to look at this." He pointed to a complex keypad next to one of the control panels. "Does it look familiar?"

"Not in the slightest." And then it dawned on me. "Wait, is this it? Is this the code I'm supposed to know?"

He nodded. "The entire system has been shut down, and we need the code to gain access. We just need you to remember the code and we can do the rest. We'll be able to repair the breach remotely from here."

"If this code is so important, why do only Charles and I know it?"

He closed his eyes momentarily, frustration showing in the lines around his mouth. "Because you changed it. Or Charles changed it. Now only you two know it."

"How were we able to change the code?"

"Remember when we talked about systems theory? Those rarely used elements of a feedback loop that are important but can become easily neglected?"

A flashback to the conversation, and a sudden understanding of why he'd told me all that. He'd been preparing me for this moment. And I saw.

"The fire extinguisher."

"Precisely. The security access is the fire in the building with no fire extinguisher. We rarely used the code, so no one thought to update it. No one except you and Charles."

Shivering, I felt a rush of something sick move through me. "What's down there, Finn? Is it . . . is it hell?"

He looked at me squarely, his expression barely changing.

"A kind of hell, I think, yes. There's an evil beneath this place. Surely you can feel it. Think of it as a kind of volatile energy source. We need access to it, but we also have to control it. Since the breach, the things that are down there . . . they've started spilling out."

"Like an oil spill," I whispered, remembering his odd speech about Deepwater Horizon.

"The world is in chaos. Don't tell me you haven't noticed. Man's inhumanity to man is at an all-time high, and the banality of evil seems to be slipping into every crack and crevice, doesn't it?"

I thought back to the way I'd been avoiding the news because the violence recently had seemed nightmarishly out of control. *Brutally unhinged* was the term that had come to mind.

"But if there is a breach and these things have been getting through, wouldn't everyone know about it?"

He shook his head. "It's more complicated than that. The physical manifestations we can stop for the most part. For now. But there is a slow leak. Call it energetic, call it spiritual. It's the incorporeal manifestations of evil. Every religion has a name for them—demons, djinn, hungry ghosts—the invisible sources of suffering and the spirits that whisper in our ears, that seemingly inhuman drive to do the unthinkable. Mankind is inherently good. Never forget that. But we are impressionable, and we can be influenced to do horrific things to one another and even to ourselves."

"And that's what we're seeing now, that darkness that seems to be sweeping over the world? The ceaseless conflict and senseless brutality. It's due to the leak here?"

He nodded. "Now can you understand our impatience?"

The sense of urgency that overcame me in that moment was almost visceral, like it was eating away at my insides. I'd known all along that I was in danger, but I'd never imagined the risk extended beyond me. From everything Finn told me, I could now see that if I didn't do something, and quick, I'd never forgive myself. But I needed to think. There was still so much I was missing.

"Uta Symon, he's the CFO here, right? But he's been pretending to be Jim. Why?"

Finn shook his head, confounded. "I'm not sure. He insisted on being here when you returned."

"I think he's mixed up in this," I said, the words feeling true almost as soon as I said them. "I think it's even possible that he did this to me."

"I can't say I'm surprised. He's someone I've had my eye on for a long time. I suspect he might be the main force behind the . . . Let's just call them the opposition. And he has been on campus a lot in the past year."

I was beginning to get a fuller picture now. "I think he did this to me somehow, or forced me to do this to myself, and I think he took me to New York. Can I talk to him?"

"He left a few days ago, quite abruptly actually."

I mulled that over. "That's probably good," I said, looking around. I needed somewhere calmer, somewhere I could have some space to think. "I think I need to go somewhere and be alone."

Finn nodded. "Do whatever you need to do, but I'm sure I don't have to remind you, the clock is ticking."

I went back to the conference room in the derelict building after that. It seemed like a good enough place to start. I searched through files and spent the better part of the night thumbing through every piece of paperwork I could find, and as I read, I began to remember more. There were aspects of the work I now understood that I hadn't on my first pass. Now that I knew about the horrors that lurked below, some of the notes I hadn't understood earlier began to take on new meaning—the *biohazard*, the *hostile material* had now became starkly real. And then there was Sabine. Something had gone wrong with Sabine. We'd—no, Charles, it was Charles, I was sure—had taken something too far. This was why I took her with me. I was trying to protect her. I was trying to make it right.

As I worked my way through the documents, slivers of rec-ollections rose to the surface—late nights with Charles, eating junk food and laughing during a break; the feeling of being at the center of something truly magnificent. But accompanying those memories was a darker presence, a kind of malevolent watchfulness hovering just outside of view. We weren't really alone out here, were we? There had been someone else always, someone looking over our shoulders. The wizard?

I fell asleep at some point, crashed out on the floor in Charles's office, and when I dreamed, it wasn't a dream. It was a memory.

I was in the lab, staring at Charles. I held a sheet of paper with frantically scribbled numbers on it. I knew what they were. It had to do with cybersecurity, with quantum cryptography. But I was unable to believe what it meant.

"Who did you sell it to?" I demanded.

"I haven't done anything," he snapped.

"Not yet, but I heard you on the phone. How could you, Charles? Throwing away your life's work—our life's work—just like that?"

He closed his eyes, clearly frustrated, and held my shoulders. "I did it for us. I'm trying to keep us safe. You have no idea what these people are capable of."

"These people are our friends."

"Bugbear, you have to give up the delusion. These people, this place, it isn't what you think. We're not doing good things here."

"We're advancing science."

"Look, it happens over and over, right?" He adjusted his cap. "Mankind thinks we are smarter than everything around us. We develop a computer program thinking it will help us, and it doesn't; it just destroys our jobs. We develop a medicine to combat bacteria, but it outsmarts us and evolves to become indestructible. That's what we've been doing here. We thought we were containing these things, using them, but we

weren't. We were strengthening them. All along we were strengthening them. They're going to destroy us. It's only a matter of time. If we try to leave, they will stop us. I needed something to bargain with."

"So you're bargaining with Uta Symon? Letting him, what, sell our research?"

He looked at me blankly. "Not our research—the harvest."

And I knew. I saw it all. The notes I'd found had been about quantum cryptography, which had nothing to do with memory, but I saw now that it had everything to do with the substance we extracted, the substance that comes from them.

I awoke with a start, trapped somewhere between my current self and Isabelle, haunted by what I'd just seen. It was almost startlingly basic. The alloy was powerful enough to exponentially scale up the capacity of quantum computers, rendering encryption technology useless. It would mean the end of data safety as we knew it. Of course someone would pay a high price for that—an almost unimaginable sum.

At the same time, I knew somewhere deep down that something wasn't right. Charles was a good man. If he was even considering selling the alloy, then something much darker was going on. And if I was honest with myself, there *was* something else, wasn't there? Something I feared even more than I could articulate. Something I was still blocking out. There was something inside me—that creeping guilt that enfolded me in the middle of the night—and it felt like it was waiting just around the corner. It was the barrier I couldn't get past. But the question arose: Could I truly not get past it, or was it that I didn't want to? Because I felt certain that waiting just on the other side was something so horrific that once I discovered it, I didn't know if I'd be able to survive it.

4.5

THE DOCTRINE OF SIGNATURES

All herbs, flowers, trees, and other things which proceed out of the Earth, are books, and magick signs, communicated to us, by the immense mercy of God, which signs our medicine.

—OSWALD CROLL, TREATISE OF SIGNATURES, *1609*

Leaning back in my chair, I pinched the bridge of my nose to try to ease the tension that had been slowly building. Ostensibly I had everything I needed to get me where I needed to be, and yet I was stuck. I tried to think back through everything I had at my fingertips—all the clues, all the information that seemed to, more often than not, lead me somewhat closer to where I needed to be, but never quite close enough.

I decided I needed a change of scene, so after locking up the cabinet, I started back toward campus, my mind spinning. As I reviewed the clues that had led me to where I was now, I could feel the answer finally within my grasp. The light in the woods had led me to the grave, which gave me the peacock key, which led me to the secret room, which led me to the desk clue, which led me to the photos and *The Book of Widows*. The entry in the book had led me to the cabinet key, which led me to Project Bluebird.

It all seemed so clear and easy, and yet I kept snagging on *The Book of Widows* and the divination tools. There was more to these items. I knew there had to be. On the way to my cabana, I knocked on Aspen's door. When she didn't answer, I decided to go and see if she might still be up and working in the apothecary garden. It couldn't hurt to show her everything. She was the person I trusted most at Hildegard, and although our fields didn't overlap, she seemed to know the most about the occult. She might have insight I lacked.

I darted into my cabana, and after slipping the relic in my coat pocket, I grabbed a tote from the closet and shoved everything else inside. Then I headed down to the apothecary garden. The garden itself was silent and still, but I saw that a light burned in the window of the garden house.

I made my way back, and when I knocked, Aspen greeted me.

"The gang's all here," she said with a smile, and behind her I could make out the others gathered around. Dorian stood over by the bookshelves, Lexi was stretched out on the couch, and Finn sat in a chair, a look of fierce concentration on his brow.

"What are you all doing?"

"Emergency meeting," said Aspen, ushering me inside. "Finn has informed us all that you know that you are Isabelle." She gave me a quick wink, and I realized that whatever suspicion she'd held of the others persisted.

"Welcome back," said Dorian with a smile. "Took you long enough."

Ignoring him, I pulled *The Book of Widows* out of the tote and held it up. "What the hell is this thing?"

Aspen took it from me and started leafing through it. "I've never seen it before. Finn, what is this?"

"No idea. It was with her things. We found it on her desk

like it was one of the last things she consulted before she left, so I tried to use it to jog her memory."

"Did it?" Aspen asked, looking up at me.

"If it did, would I be here asking you what it is?"

"What else is in the bag?" asked Lexi.

I dumped everything out onto the coffee table. "Do any of you know what any of this stuff is?"

"I told you," said Dorian, "the cards are local folk superstition. The rest of it we have no idea. It was with the book."

Aspen picked up one of the widows' keys. "So you draw these and then consult this to get a reading? It's a divinatory text?"

"Has to be," I said. "But why would I be using divination in the middle of a complete catastrophe? It doesn't make any sense."

Suddenly Aspen looked up from the book, her eyes flashing. "I think this book isn't just about divination. I think it might be something much more important."

"What do you think it is?"

She was smiling now, nearly shaking with excitement. "When esoteric knowledge is passed down, it needs to be steeped in secrecy, right? It has to be encoded so that if it falls into the wrong hands, it can't be misused. Historically, there has always been a reliance on symbols. For instance, in alchemy, birds have always been important. Peacocks, for example." She pointed to the key. "The peacock represents a key stage in the literal alchemical process during which a key substance became iridescent, but metaphorically, it also represents a spiritual pivot for the alchemist as well, like a transition to a different, higher realm of being."

Suddenly I was struck by my choice of name. I'd named myself Robin, and Paloma meant *dove*. I'd named us after birds as if I was trying to enact an alchemical transformation on our very identities.

Aspen opened the book and turned it around to face us. "Our predecessors had to find clever ways of hiding information while still getting it across to the intended audience. So it absolutely makes sense that someone could hide information in images like these."

"So it's not a divinatory text?" asked Finn.

"It is. Very much so, in the vein of the *I Ching*, but if I'm not mistaken, it has a secondary purpose as well." She looked at me. "Okay, show me the four symbols you drew."

I pointed them out within the text, but because they only ever appeared in groups of three, they never appeared all together.

"Okay, now do you remember the recipe from the Joan of Arc–Gilles de Rais letter?"

Excitement pulsed through me. We were getting close now. "Of course. It was aconite, angelica, and hoopoe's blood. But what does *The Book of Widows* have to do with the letter?"

"I think it has everything to do with it, Isabelle," she said. With a flourish, she set the book on the coffee table, her charm bracelet tinkling. "I think this is a recipe book. And I would bet that one of these entries corresponds to the recipe for the witch's ointment in your letter."

Shaking with excitement, I leaned over and paged through the book. "This is a recipe book? You've got to be kidding me."

She gave me a sly smile. "The *I Ching* is actually what gave me the idea. It can be interpreted as an alchemical recipe book as well."

"What?" A shock coursed through me. "How is that possible? The *I Ching* is an ancient divinatory text based on cleromancy."

"Yes, but it can also be interpreted as a recipe book. This is common knowledge. I'm not making it up." Aspen smiled, the slant of her cheek almost breathtakingly beautiful. "And I'm also not vouching for the recipes, but there are some alchemical traditions where each of the trigrams in the *I Ching* is thought to stand for an element. The three unbroken yang lines stand for true lead, the three broken yin lines stand for true mercury, and so on. The same might be true here. Look, this crescent moon could stand for one substance, the full moon for another, and so on, and here it probably tells you what order you're supposed to combine them in."

Suddenly I understood what she was getting at. "And you think each of these symbols stands for a different medicinal herb?"

"I think it's very likely. My guess is that depending on the combination of the herbs and the order in which they are decocted, each recipe will create a different effect. Isabelle, I think this is the key to breaking through your last barrier to remembering the code."

Finn looked over at me. "What do you think that is, that barrier?"

Breathing deeply, I took a moment and looked around the room, stared at their eager faces, listened to the faint sounds coming from outside the window, to the creatures stirring, the night world coming to life.

"I think Symon wanted me to make the procedure permanent. But I found a loophole, a way to undo it. I think Aspen is right. I think it has something to do with the ingredients of the witch's ointment, and something to do with the four symbols. Clearly my Joan of Arc–Gilles de Rais letter isn't authentic. It's an encoded message I created for myself. We just have to decode it."

"Unfortunately," said Aspen, "without something to tell us which herb corresponds to which symbol, we're stuck with guesswork. And guesswork can be deadly when it comes to herbology."

"So we're back to square one," I said, tapping my pen against the table. "There has to be a clue I missed somewhere along the line. Finn, check my work here."

Grabbing a piece of paper and a pen, I started working out the order of the clues, drawing a flow chart.

Light→ Grave→ Peacock Key→ Divination / Clue to Desk→ Photo / Book of Widows→ Cabinet Key→ Project Bluebird→ Borges Coordinates→ Owl Key→ Relic.

"This is how I got from the light to the relic. Am I missing anything?"

He took the pen from me and drew an X in the flow chart.

Light→ Grave→ Peacock Key→ Divination / Clue to Desk→ Photo / Book of Widows→ Cabinet Key→ Project Bluebird— X—Borges Coordinates→ Owl Key→ Relic.

"I have no clue what you're talking about. *Project Bluebird* was the end of the game," he said.

The room grew quiet. "No," I said. "What about the Borges book?"

He shook his head. "Seriously, what are you talking about?"

Then how had I gotten to the Borges book? Tracing it back, I realized that Finn was right. The clues that led me to the book hadn't come from him. They'd come from my own dreams. The blazing sun appearing repeatedly had been my subconscious trying to direct me to it, but I hadn't listened until my dreaming mind procured a masked Isabelle to literally point me to the book.

I should have realized why the clue it contained, the coordinates, had seemed so different from the others. It seemed different because it *was* different. Finn didn't leave it for me to find.

"Oh god." Swallowing over a lump in my throat, I looked around the room. "I think I left this clue for myself."

Finn leaned forward. "When?"

"Before I left. It wouldn't have taken much. Just a key stowed in the apiary. The key that led me to the relic."

"But there is no relic!" snapped Dorian. "There's no blog post and no relic."

"But there is," I said, taking it out of my pocket.

"What the hell?" whispered Dorian, leaning in to get a closer look.

"This atrocious thing is the relic from your blog post?" asked Lexi.

"That's impossible, though," said Finn. "We told you, we never left a blog post."

"No," I said, smiling. "But I did."

Lexi slapped a hand over her mouth. "Oh shit."

With mixed emotion, I set the artifact on the table. "The problem is, I don't know what it means."

We all stared at it, and I could sense a wave of excitement coming from Finn, his eyes alight with the possibilities this puzzle presented.

"Okay," said Aspen. "So you left the blog post yourself, but then you locked the path that led to the relic until after you'd gotten your identity back?"

"I think so, yes."

"But why lock that path?"

Finn was pacing now, and behind his eyes, I could see he was making connections. "Whatever this means, it's something you couldn't comprehend until you knew you were Isabelle again."

I picked it up and shook it, and again there was that rattling sound. "Have any of you ever seen it before?"

They shook their heads, but then Lexi nodded. "I think I maybe remember you with it. I think you said you'd gotten it in town."

"So this isn't an ancient artifact?" I rattled it again.

"Honestly," said Lexi, "I have no idea what it is."

I looked closely at the excessively large eyeholes in the figures. They were just large enough to roll something up and slip it inside. I looked over at Finn. He kept saying that there were certain things I couldn't know ahead of time because they might break me. But what if instead, I broke something else? I stared at the relic for a moment, its ludicrously shaped figures, its poor craftsmanship, and then, with force, I smashed it against the coffee table, breaking it into shards of thick clay.

"Jesus!" Aspen screamed, and Dorian jumped back, shielding his face, but I wasn't going to let myself be distracted. Combing through it, I found what I was looking for—a tiny piece of paper rolled up like a scroll.

Unfurling it, I smiled. Aspen was right. It showed nine images, and accompanying each one were two Latin words, Linnaeus's binomial nomenclature:

Glycyrrhiza uralensis

 Angelica sylvestris

 Mentha spicata

 Mandragora officinarum

 Aconitum lycoctonum

 Caulophyllum thalictroides

 Ferula silphion

 Ephedra aspera

 Albizia julibrissin

It was the key to the recipe.

"Holy shit," I said, shaking with excitement. "This is it."

Dorian stood behind me, peering down at the symbols. "I don't understand. What are these?"

"The code to the widows' keys. All I have to do is translate them and I'll have my recipe."

My heart was nearly in my throat as I scanned through. Just as Aspen had predicted, the ingredients from my letter were listed, but there were only two of them: angelica aligned with the disintegrating square and aconite with the crescent moon. The box with the X was something called *Glycyrrhiza uralensis*, and the S was *Ferula silphion*.

Ferula silphion. Oh my god. I looked up at Aspen. "This is silphium, isn't it?"

Aspen took the slip of paper from me and stared at it before meeting my eyes again, a smile playing on her lips. "It certainly is. Holy shit," she whispered. "Isabelle, I think we found our hoopoe's blood. Hoopoe's blood is silphium."

The problem was there were only three ingredients in my recipe, but I'd drawn four symbols. For now I decided to ignore the *Glycyrrhiza uralensis* and to just focus on finding the entry that contained the aconite, angelica, and silphium. When I'd located it, I put my finger on it and showed it to the others.

      Desolate Earth, Vibrant Moon, Vibrant Sea
From darkness, the night birds take flight. They reach the mountain just before dawn. An unexpected passage.

"Night birds," whispered Finn. "Like you and Paloma."

"Okay," I said with a smile. "This is definitely it. I just need to make something with these three ingredients and then drink it like that night in the woods, and I think that should help me remember. I think that's the final step."

But Aspen looked less certain. "Aconite is really toxic. Like, deadly."

"I know, but I'm sure this is right."

"No." She shook her head. "Something is wrong. We don't have enough information. We have the ingredients, but we don't know the order, and the order will determine the spell."

"Spell?" said Dorian through uneasy laughter. "Is that what we're doing here?"

"The root of pharmacology is spell," I said. "Isn't that right?"

"We could try a few permutations and see which works," offered Lexi, but Aspen shook her head.

"That could be dangerous. Already we're dealing with a very poisonous plant."

"What if you just included the *Glycyrrhiza uralensis*?" asked Finn. "We have to assume you drew it for a reason, right?"

"What is *Glycyrrhiza uralensis*?" I asked Aspen.

"Licorice root. Usually it's treated by dry-frying it with honey."

"Why would I want to add licorice root to the formula?"

A slow smile spread across her face. "You were modifying it."

"Why would I do that?"

"Because you didn't want to die?"

"What?"

Aspen nearly sputtered her words she was so excited. "This is brilliant. If you took aconite alone, you almost certainly would have poisoned yourself—potentially fatally. But herbal formulas can always be modified. Aconite is highly toxic, right? But for centuries, honey-fried licorice root has been used to reduce the toxicity of aconite. Isabelle, you modified the recipe to detoxify it."

"Do you have any down here?" I asked, and as I reached out for her hand, she grasped mine with equivalent excitement.

"Of course. It's a common ingredient."

"This is it, isn't it?" I asked, my heart poised somewhere between excitement and terror.

"You ready?" she asked.

I nodded.

It was time for the night birds to take flight.

4.6

OUROBOROS

All things began in order, so shall they end, so shall they begin again according to the ordainer of order and the mystical mathematics of the city of heaven.

—Sir Thomas Browne, The Garden of Cyrus

Aspen and I made quick work of locating the ingredients we needed—first, the beautiful but poisonous purple aconite blossoms, then the licorice root, followed by the tiny white constellations of angelica. That left only one ingredient, the hoopoe's blood.

"Where's the silphium?"

"This way," she said.

I followed her to a secret cache in the back of the garden, where she retrieved a parceled-out portion of silphium. It was dried, and there was only a small amount of it, but still it was stunningly beautiful, somehow otherworldly.

Once we'd gathered everything, I headed into the garden house kitchen, pulled out a pot, and filled it with water.

"You're sure you know what you're doing?" Aspen asked.

I nodded. There were parts of me returning, and although on a superficial level, I found this frightening, a deeper part of me felt like I was finally coming to life, filled with a power and knowledge I could only have dreamed of as Robin.

When the water began to boil, I sprinkled in the angelica, then the silphium, followed by the licorice root, and finally a small amount of aconite. Once the water returned to a boil, I turned the heat down to medium-low.

"Now," I said, with a clap of my hands, "we wait."

We tried to pass the time while the herbs cooked, but the minutes seemed to crawl by. The others were able to settle into a card game, but I kept finding myself in the kitchen standing over the pot. As I watched the dark liquid boil, amber bubbles dancing and roiling, my mind drifted back to the hideous room where I'd found the relic. Why that room? What was I trying to communicate with myself? Something about that room had set off alarm bells for me when I'd walked in, but I'd been so distracted by the bottles that I hadn't processed it. The smell of an extinguished candle. Someone had been in there, and recently. And then I saw it. I sent myself to that room, left the statue in it to make sure that I knew: Someone among us was still living by the old ways, by the left-hand path. Someone here wasn't who they seemed.

As I looked over at the others, no one in particular jumped out at me as fitting this profile. Lexi and I had our differences, but she wasn't a bad person. Same with Dorian. Aspen, I genuinely liked, and although she clung to some antiquated theories when it came to botany, she didn't strike me as malevolent in the slightest. Finn was perhaps the most complicated of the bunch. He'd hated me when I was Isabelle. He admitted as much, and he was also the main architect of my memory retrieval, so he had to be pretty chummy with someone up top. Still, picturing him as some kind of deranged warlock was a stretch.

Eventually the timer went off, and we all gathered in the kitchen as I poured the caramel-colored liquid into a cup. I knew

I would need to take my journey alone, and so with some prodding, they left me by myself in the garden house. I sat in a chair facing the window, the steam from the sweet-smelling potion wafting up and filling my nostrils with a heady, woodsy aroma.

I sipped the tea and closed my eyes, trying to relax my mind. The memories were in there somewhere. I just had to find them. I began taking slow, deep breaths. This would stimulate the parasympathetic nervous system, triggering the vagus nerve, lowering my blood pressure, decreasing my heart rate, and providing a general sense of calm and well-being. I continued like that for some time, first with my eyes open and staring out at the garden, and then with my eyes closed. At some point I reached a state where alpha waves began to predominate. The fact that I knew anything about these physiological processes meant that Robin was really beginning to fade now. Because I was pretty sure she didn't know anything about alpha waves.

Soon time became malleable and I was outside walking toward the woods. Above me the moon shone bright and my brain began to tingle. My feet felt like salamanders licked clean by the dewy grass.

When had I slipped off my shoes?

As I walked the winding forest paths, a kind of fire in my abdomen became increasingly intense. Soon I was in the woods somewhere dark, sweating and shaking. Suddenly my head spun and a pain in my side tore through me, reached a crescendo, and then abruptly stopped.

There was something like a crack and a fracture deep inside my mind. I could actually hear it, as if a physical barrier had been broken. I hurtled over it and into another time, that other me, no longer liminal, but fully myself once again. My body shook as

I stared at my hands—not mine, and yet mine, Isabelle's—and I could feel it inside me now, everything I'd been suppressing.

I'm out near the fence now, near the yew tree, its great spidery limbs reaching out like arboreal claws. I can feel the grass between my toes as slowly I walk toward that gargantuan fence. My fingers slide between the links, grasping at the metal, and as I stare up and up and up, I know that it goes far beyond what I can actually see. Almost like a world laid on top of our own. On the other side of the fence, I think I can see something moving, creaking and lumbering on ancient, splintered legs, appendages like so much rot.

In the moonlight, I can make out something else moving, out near that singular red X, and I begin to remember. Sometimes they get through, slipping through cracks between our world and theirs, crawling up from the depths of hell. It isn't just those squashed pink creatures I witnessed down below. There are more. So many more. A legion of them. "It is one, but it's also legion," Charles had said. The skeletons in the great hall. Finn had called them a collection.

And now I understand. On a deep, visceral level, I finally understand. If these things get through, if they really get through, it will be the end of us all.

"It wasn't the harvest," a voice beside me whispers.

Flinching, I turn and see someone standing next to me. It's me, only it isn't. Isabelle, her hair swept back in an intricate braid, gives me a slow smile. Her dark eyes are smoky and lined with kohl. She also peers through the fence.

"It wasn't the harvest," she says. "It's them."

"You're not here," I say. "I'm dreaming."

"I'm as here as you are," she snaps. "And you need to start listening to me. We don't have long like this. Soon there will be only one of us."

"What do you mean?" I ask, stealing tentative glances over at her.

"*Charlie was giving them the harvest to buy time, to stop them from taking what they really want.*"

"*What do they want?*"

"*Those,*" she says, pointing to the tessellating darkness, to the creatures moving silently between the trees.

"*What are they?*"

"*The physical manifestations, the Terrible Ones.*"

I draw back. "*Why do they want them?*"

"*To control, to destroy, to use them as weapons. But they don't understand. There are so many of them now. Too many. Because we disrupted the cycle. You know all this. Think. Remember.*"

It's all tumbling onto me, through me, in relentless waves—half remembered, half deduced. The black rains, the silphium, Pliny the Elder. But those black rains weren't just confined to antiquity, were they? No, they'd come again in 1816, in the Year Without Summer when a distant volcano all the way in Indonesia had disrupted the weather patterns, had brought black rains as far away as France. That was 1816, and a few years later Hildegard was founded. That was no coincidence. The black rains brought forth the silphium—the hoopoe's blood—and the hoopoe's blood brought forth the monsters.

"*They need the silphium to live, don't they?*"

She nods. "*They go dormant without it.*"

"*And because silphium could never be cultivated, they could never survive at the surface for long. But you figured out how to cultivate it so you could keep them alive.*"

"*We disrupted the cycle nature put into place to keep them in check. Now there are too many, and they're too close to the surface. And then there was the breach. Now it's down there leaking. Slivers of evil slipping into this world.*"

"*Charles,*" I say. "*We need to find Charles.*"

"Charlie tried to stop them, but there was a mistake." She stares straight ahead. "They tried to use him, but everything went sideways. That's how the breach happened. And now only you can stop it."

"Why only me?"

"Because you're the code."

"I'm the code? How is that possible?"

"Not you, your retina."

A wave of relief sweeps over me as I finally see. "A retinal scan? That's the code?"

She nods. "Yours and Charlie's. But I'm afraid Charlie's won't work anymore."

I know what she's going to tell me, but I don't want to hear it. Not yet. I've been trying far too hard and for far too long not to hear it. I'm not letting her tell me like this. Around us the woods are suddenly so quiet it feels like I'm being smothered.

"I want to come back now," she says into the silence.

"Not yet," I say.

She laughs, a bitter laugh. She isn't me, and I'm not her, not fully. Like these creatures we try to contain, we slip between worlds, and the end of her is just the beginning of me. Or is it the other way around?

She gives me a cruel slip of a smile. She's somehow more delicate than I am, more feminine, but there is an acid to her, venom lurking just below the surface. "You don't want me back because you don't want to know the truth."

"I need to find Charles," I say, and yet I don't move. I stare into the darkness beyond the fence. There are more out there now, moving, crawling on all fours between the trees.

"Charlie's dead," she says flatly. "You killed him."

"No," I say, but my negation falls equally flat.

"It's time to remember," she says.

Tears spring forth as I fall back to that night, as I stand there with Isabelle, watching it all play out before me like some horrible dream.

———

We were out near the pillar. The sun hung low and red in the sky like a throbbing pustule, and yet it was just beginning to snow, coming down in flat, heavy flakes just as in my dreams of New York.

And then the sirens. The breach. The look of abject horror on Charles's face as he understood. Someone had opened the gate, and they didn't know how to close it again.

I tried to run. I had to get to the control room. But he grabbed my arm.

It happened so fast, my world came undone in an instant. Me trying to pull away again, yanking my arm, but he wouldn't let go. Me pushing. Pushing too hard. Me reaching for him to undo what I'd done. The fall. His head colliding with the marble sundial—no, the marble pillar. A skull splitting; there's always so much blood from a head wound, isn't there? Me holding him while he bled out, whispering words of love as his blood soaked deep into the soil, nourishing the plants from which we'd derived our greatest potential, "feeding the crops." And all the while, the snow falling silent and bright.

———

"You let him die out there in the snow," Isabelle says. We're back at the fence now, back in the dark.

"It was an accident," I say through my tears.

"You let him die and then you let Symon take you. You wanted to forget as much as he wanted you to."

With everything laid bare before me, I can finally see the truth.

They're not going to let me seal the breach. As much as Finn and the others might want me to, there are powerful shadows standing behind them, just outside of the frame, that are going to make sure I don't.

I think back to the bitter water Symon had given me in the car. It had been drugged, hadn't it? That's why I'd slept so long, that's why I'd been so sick when I woke up. Had he been planning on killing me? Had he changed his mind when he realized I still thought I was Robin?

Through the darkness I can see more of them now, slipping between the trees with jittery, arachnoid movements.

"Are we in danger?" I ask.

"We're always in danger." She gestures beyond the fence. "There are only so many of them we can contain. If that's even what we're doing."

She turns and faces me, her brutal beauty searing into me, her features sharp as icicles. "You're not going to let me come back, are you?"

"Not all the way," I say. "No."

"You'll never be able to do what I do." It's a threat. "You'll never be able to be me."

"I . . . don't want to be you."

Suddenly she slaps me hard across the face. "You need to wake up now."

With a scream, I surged awake and found myself alone somewhere dark and cold. Scrambling to my feet, I realized I was in the cabana basement. But where were the others? Had I lost them during my hallucinatory sojourn? Or were they somewhere just out of sight?

I held my aching head as I tried to gather my senses. Whatever I'd just experienced, it wasn't a dream. It wasn't reality exactly, either, at least not reality as I knew it. I'd been somewhere else, some in-between space, and in it I'd learned the truth I'd been blocking all along. Charles was dead. I killed him. I never meant to, but I had. And although a grief tore at me, eviscerating me with its filthy talons, I now knew what I had to do. Like Isabelle said, I was the code. I just had to get to the control room.

Still somewhat unsteady on my feet, I managed to climb the stairs to the patio garden. The stars were still shining, but the moon was sinking into the western horizon as I walked through the French doors to my cabana. As quickly as I could, I changed, pulling on some sturdy boots, and then I set out.

But if I expected to make this last leg of my journey alone, I was to be sorely disappointed. They were all out there, standing on the path outside my cabana door. They looked awful. Aspen's eyes were red and swollen. Finn was holding her tightly and seemed to be crying himself. Lexi looked pale, almost like she was dissociating, and Dorian just stared at his feet, clutching a travel mug.

"You know," I said.

Finn nodded, grief infusing his every movement. "You were rambling, pretty disoriented, but we could make out most of what you said. We know about Charles."

I bit my lip to try to stanch the flow of tears. "I was wrong about him," I said. "He never betrayed me. He never betrayed anyone. He was trying to broker a deal to save us."

I knew if I kept going, I was going to break down. I missed him terribly and knew that pain would never leave me. He was the only person I'd ever really trusted, and now that he was gone and I was truly alone in the world, I didn't want to pretend otherwise.

"I need to get to the control room," I said, and I surprised even myself with the coldness of my tone. "I think I should go alone."

"No," said Finn quickly. "We should stick together."

I tried to resist, but Aspen pulled away from Finn and wiped her eyes. "He's right. At this point, there's safety in numbers. This is our one goal. We can't let something happen to you right before we accomplish it."

I had a bad feeling about it—the part of me that was Isabelle preferred to work alone—but I nodded and was turning to go when Dorian touched me gently on the shoulder.

"Here, drink this. It will help," he said, and he handed me the travel mug.

Together we made our way out into the woods, out to the temple. When we were almost to the steps, I went to take a sip from the mug, but paused and sniffed. I stared into the liquid, my heart breaking just a little, and then dropped my arm to my side without drinking.

As we were entering the temple, I reached out and placed my hand on Aspen's arm, stopping her. Silently I held out my tea for her to smell. Shock swelled in her eyes, and she glanced at Dorian. A silent communication passed between us, and then I set the tea on the edge of a display and caught back up with the group.

We made our way through the rest of the great hall and down to the observatory. A key card and thumbprint let us into the control room, but when the door buzzed open and we saw what lay before us, my heart leapt into my throat and a small scream escaped me.

It was chaos, annihilation. It looked like someone had taken a hatchet to the control panels. Screens were smashed; wires had been wrenched out like intestines splayed out mid-autopsy. It no longer mattered that I had the code, not if the system it enabled me to access had been destroyed.

"Oh god," Lexi said, looking around at the absolute orgy of destruction.

"Fuck," whispered Dorian.

Aspen's mouth hung open in horror.

Finn's eyes were wild. "What do we do now? What the fuck are we gonna do?"

Lexi was starting to hyperventilate. "Oh my god. Oh my god. How did this happen?"

"It must have been Symon," Dorian said.

"No, Finn and I were just down here," I said, searching the room for something to use as a weapon.

"And Symon's been gone for days," said Finn.

"He must have come back," said Dorian.

Again, a whiff of the acrid scent of that extinguished candle, the traitor in our midst. My gaze flitted to the strange-looking tools on the wall. Slowly I walked over to the harpoon instrument and lifted it off the wall.

"What are you doing?" asked Lexi.

I pointed it at Dorian. "It's him," I said. "It's Dorian."

He took a step away from me, holding up his hands. "Don't act crazy."

"Holy shit, Isabelle," said Finn. "What are you doing?"

"You did this," I said to Dorian. "You're working with them, aren't you?"

"What are you talking about?" asked Finn, his tone more curious than frantic now.

"You're being hysterical," Dorian said.

"You never wanted me to remember the code," I said. "You don't want the breach repaired. You want it opened wider. And once it became clear that I was the code, your instructions were to kill me. Isn't that right?"

"Isabelle, please," said Lexi. "Put that thing down."

"No, she's right," said Aspen. "He put oleander in her tea."

Lexi shuddered, moved toward him, and then pulled away. "Dorian, is this true? Tell us it isn't true."

But he just smiled, his canines slipping below his lip line. "It's going to happen no matter what you do. If not me, it will be someone else."

"No." Lexi fought back tears. "Please tell me this isn't true."

"Whatever they're paying you, it's not worth it," said Finn, rounding on him, but Dorian seemed completely calm.

"You think I did this for money? I did this because I'm not an idiot. I saw which way the power was shifting and I went with it. There's nothing you can do now," he said. "You might as well join me. I don't want to turn you in. I really don't. And I don't want to have to kill you."

Finn squared on him and nodded to the harpoon. "It doesn't look like you're in a position to negotiate right now, Dorian."

"Neither are you!" he laughed, almost maniacally. "There is now no way to fix the breach. There's nothing you can do, so let's just call it a draw."

"And what?" I asked. "Let a plague of monsters descend upon the earth? Let them ravage mankind?"

"We have no other option," he said. "It's no longer a choice for us to make. Now it's destiny."

Lexi began to cry, and a general sense of doom descended on the space. I could feel myself on the edge of giving in to it, too, my arms beginning to sag with the weight of the harpoon. In another life, I might have given in to that urge, but that part of me was gone now. I knew there was something I was missing, some possible solution hovering just beyond my perception. And then I saw it.

"We'll have to repair it manually," I said.

Silence snapped through the room like an electrical impulse.

Finn pointed at one of the disemboweled panels, wires splaying out from it, frenzied. "And how do you propose we do that?"

"This isn't the only entrance," I said quietly, and I could see the muscles in Dorian's jaw briefly tighten. "There's an old entrance. The one the ancestors used."

"No," said Aspen. "There isn't. This is the only one."

"That's not true. There is another entrance. I'm the only one here with high enough security clearance to know about it. Although it looks like someone must have let Dorian in on the secret as well."

"What are you talking about?" asked Finn. "What old entrance?"

"The trapdoor beneath my office on the island. It leads down to it. That's why the office is out there. It's not an office. It's a guard post meant to stop people from knowing what's beneath it." I stared straight at Dorian, holding his gaze. "If we get down there, we could repair it manually."

"No," he said quickly. "It's impassable, flooded ages ago. I told you that already."

"You told me that when you thought I was Robin. I'm not Robin anymore, you dick, and I know that it wasn't flooded."

He squinted, roiled by some emotion I couldn't quite grasp. "Even if you tried to access it from there, it's basically useless. It was built hundreds of years ago."

"It's archaic, but I can still use it."

"No," Dorian said with a quick shake of his head. "You'd never survive."

"What do you care if I survive?" I looked over at the others. "I can fix it."

Panicking now, Dorian looked around at us. "It's not too late. You all could come along with me. Think splendor and luxury beyond your wildest dreams."

"Yeah, I think you can fuck right off there, Dorian," I said.

"You've always been such a stubborn little bitch."

Finn locked eyes with Dorian. "They're going to be on the wrong side of history. You don't want to be on it with them."

"We won't be on the wrong side of history," he said, a slightly crazed look in his eye—the look I'd seen that day out in the woods. "We'll be able to control them. We'll be among the righteous, honoring the Mother like we've always done, just now much more actively."

"You can't believe what you're saying," pleaded Aspen.

Suddenly his face grew red with rage, and the veins in his temples looked twisted and engorged. "It doesn't matter what I believe. They have the power now. We're either with them or against them, and there's no way I'm going against them."

"He's scared," said Aspen, her own features contorting with fear at the prospect. "What are they threatening you with?"

"I told you once that I've seen evil before—true evil—and I have. You don't know these people like I do," he said through gritted teeth. "Like my dad and I do. One doesn't want to disappoint them."

Was that what they were holding over him? His family?

"But you can't believe in what they're trying to do," said Finn.

"Don't tell me what I believe!" he yelled.

"What the hell is he talking about?" said Lexi.

Dorian focused on me. "You've said it yourself. The world is filled with sin."

"I never said that."

"Violence, then. You see it everywhere you look. Vile obscenity, unholy depravity. It must be stopped. And these"—he gestured toward the water—"are our holy vessels, the Mother's sword in the coming holy war."

"Oh god." Aspen shuddered.

Raising his hands, he stepped away from me, toward the creatures.

"What are you doing?" I demanded.

"The only thing I can do," he said, smiling. "I had one task, and I needed to fulfill it. If I can't complete the task, I need to make alternate plans."

"Don't act crazy," Finn said. "We can help you, Dorian, protect you from them. You can tell them whatever you want. All we ask is that you don't stop us."

He laughed, low and bitter. "But that's the only thing I'm supposed to do. If you succeed, I fail. If I fail . . ."

His eyes grew distant, and then he moved toward the flood lock and pulled hard on a lever. He was performing some kind of manual override, but it wasn't quite working. The door was jerky, stuttering, and sparks issued from it in a juddery burst.

"You have me outnumbered," he continued. "And I've never been much of a fighter."

"Stop that," I demanded, moving toward him.

He looked at me straight on and in a matter-of-fact tone said, "They will sing my name. They will celebrate my righteousness as the blood of the sinners floods the streets."

In an instant, he stepped into the chamber, threw a lever, and shoved the door shut behind him.

"No!" Aspen screamed. "What are you doing?"

He gave us a horrifying grin and then threw another lever,

and without utilizing any of the safety straps or equipment, he let the chamber flood. Thick blue liquid rushed in, slamming him against the side of the lock before carrying him out into the indigo expanse beyond.

"We have to do something," Finn yelled, moving to the door. "He's going to drown."

I dropped the harpoon and started to suit up, intent on going after him, my eyes on the nymphs, but they didn't seem to even notice him.

"The outer door needs to close before we can do anything," Aspen said, coming to Finn's aid.

Together they were working on closing the door and clearing the water, and for an instant I thought we might be able to do something, but then they came. Like a flood of darkness, they swept up. Black scales and needle teeth, their eyes almost human but with a sickness to them that spoke of something primordial, something rotten. The legion surged up, surrounded him, tearing his flesh, devouring him.

Our screams filled the room, echoing around that dank, funereal space, and time seemed to expand beyond the laws of physics, each moment bleeding into the next as we pounded against the glass, powerless to stop the bloodshed we were forced to witness.

And then like sated piranhas, they disappeared, undulating wisps of inky darkness, fluttering back down into the depths, leaving nothing but floating strands of marrow in their wake.

No one spoke. The nymphs never even woke up. Still half clad in the suit, I stumbled back, nearly fainting, but Finn caught me.

Lexi was close to hyperventilating, and Aspen wrapped an arm around her. "Deep breaths," she said calmly.

"What are we going to do now?" Lexi gasped. "What the fuck are we going to do?"

Finn looked over at me. "Do you really think it's possible to fix it manually?"

I looked out through the viewing window to the liquid, deep into that cerulean expanse beyond. "I do."

"It's too dangerous," Aspen said. "You saw what those things did to Dorian. We've never even seen those before. Who knows what the hell else is out there."

"The actual repair will take me a matter of seconds. I'll be in and out," I said. "But we need to go now."

We left the woods soon after that. Finn grabbed diving gear from his cabana, and the four of us headed out to the island. No one spoke as we glided across those inky depths, and when we reached the shore, I was shaking with fear. I knew exactly what I had to do, but no part of me actually wanted to do it. The sun was just beginning to rise as we walked through the fields of silphium, and by the time we reached the office, the mountain bluebirds were trilling.

Inside, we removed the rug to reveal the trapdoor. Finn smashed the lock with a heavy stone and we pulled back the bolt. Opening the trapdoor, we saw an expanse of stone steps stretching down in front of us. Antiquated sconces lined the walls.

"Jesus Christ," whispered Finn. "I had no idea this was here."

He lit one of the sconces. We climbed down the long flight of stone steps, and soon we hit a lengthy corridor. It was colder down there, and the atmosphere felt odd, unstable. I almost thought for a moment that I could hear something on the other side of the wall, something undulating and massive.

"You know where we're going?" Finn asked.

"I think so," I said. "It should be at the end of this corridor, and then down another flight of steps."

Soon the firelight no longer reached us, and we switched to phone flashlights. But when we descended the final steps to the old entrance, there were two more sconces. Finn lit them, and warm light blazed forth, flooding the area.

"Jesus," whispered Aspen.

We were in an ancient space, all metal and stone. There was a rusting iron gate that led to a kind of cell half filled with water. On the other side of it, we could see heavy bars with spikes on them, and near the stone ceiling, a small, barred aperture with hinges like a cage door.

"There," I said, pointing. "I need to go through that opening."

The water there was three-quarters of the way up the gate. Beyond that, there was only darkness.

"Isabelle," said Aspen. "No."

"It's going to be fine," I said. "We'll break this lock. I'll suit up and swim through to the second gate over there. I'll get that aperture open—someone will have to go with me and close it behind me right away—and then I'll start the swim down to the breach."

I looked at their disbelieving faces and then at the ancient gates before me, at the gray-black water sloshing against the stone walls, out to the horrors that awaited me beyond.

As I suited up, I thought about Charles, about how he would have laughed to see how ridiculous I looked in flippers. I thought about Robin, about the secret self I'd had the chance to become. And I thought about you, sitting there reading my final words. I wonder what you will make of them. Will you think me mad?

Will you think this all an extravagant fiction? If so, that means I succeeded. And if not, if I've failed, then you will know that every word I've written here is the truth. I hope with my very soul that's not the case.

When I said goodbye to Aspen and Lexi, I had hope in my heart, but as soon as my eyes met Finn's, the reality of my situation came into clear focus.

He put his hands on my shoulders. "You don't have to do this."

"I do."

"We could organize a team."

I raised my eyebrows. "Given the time constraint, given the damage to the observatory, do you really think we have time for that?"

He hesitated. "You know we don't."

"And how many lives would be lost? Finn, you need to let me do this. No one else is going to die because of me."

"You don't have to be a martyr."

"I promise I'm not trying to martyr myself," I said. "I don't want to die, but I don't want anyone else to, either. It's better to live nobly than long, isn't that right, Finn?"

He gave me a weak smile. "I was drunk when I said that."

"And you never know," I said, smiling, wiping a tear that had sprung to my eyes. "Sometimes people have extraordinary luck, don't they? People survive things they shouldn't."

It was more than a question. It was a plea, a plea for him to lie to me.

He looked away and then nodded.

"Finn," I said, my voice suddenly commanding, "if I don't come back, you know what to do?"

He looked at me again, his eyes filled with authority, with

absolute certainty. "You can trust me," he said, and then he took my hand in his. "Safe passage, my dear friend."

I've switched to voice recording now. I'm out here in the water that is not water. I've done it now, successfully capped the well, repaired the breach. We're safe, at least for now. At least until mankind's hubris takes us right to the edge of our own destruction yet again.

I'm on my way back now. I can see hints of sunlight coming from somewhere, but glancing behind me, I can also see something else, something emerging from the darkness, swimming toward me with the fury of a thousand leviathans. I don't know if it's the mother or the father. I don't even know if it's related to the nymphs. All I know is that it's coming for me. I see something like scales, something like fire.

I see a rush of indigo bubbles.

I see what I think might be an eye. It's too large and too close to tell.

I hear myself scream.

In an instant, I'm no longer in the water. I'm deep in the woods, in almost complete darkness. I know this place from its scent, from the cedar and pine.

"Hello?" I call, and my voice echoes back to me.

Somewhere far in the distance, I think I hear a voice cry out, inconsolable sobs.

"Hello?" I call, but again my words are hollow and tinny, and they return only an echo.

Instinctively I start moving toward the sea of darkness, toward a legion of wavering trees and a ceaseless howling wind.

I walk with certainty, and any fear that lingers in my chest is dissolving.

Just before I reach the tree line, I hear something coming through. A rustling of leaves, a body in motion. Soon I can make out a figure. Tall and brawny, a smile and a burgundy knit cap.

"Charles?" I whisper.

"Bugbear," he says with a smile.

He walks toward me, and as he closes his eyes, I see that his lids still hold the ferryman's coins. "I told you we'd meet here again," he says. "In the dark. Amongst the trees."

He wraps his arms around me and holds me tight, the familiar scent of him enveloping me, the breath of forgiveness. "It's time to go," he whispers.

"But the others." I try to turn around but find that I can't. There is only one way to go now.

"They'll be fine. At least for now. And we will keep watch. It doesn't end just because it ends."

I look up at him through the prism of my tears, and I believe him.

He slips his hand into mine, and together, finally home, we step into the void.

ACKNOWLEDGMENTS

Thanks to the amazing Peter Wolverton and everyone at St. Martin's—Claire Cheek, Nancy Inglis, John Morrone—and to Anne Tibbets, whose support means everything to me.

Thanks to Quill Camp, Susannah Nevison, Kristen Kittscher, Joe Sacksteder, David Butcher, Jay Kristoff, Camille DeAngelis, Bri Cavallaro, and duncan b. barlow for everything you've done to support this book.

Thanks to all the people who have kept me close to sane this year: John Gregory Brown, Carrie Brown, Cyndi Fein, Erica Trabold, Fiona Butcher, Betty Skeen, Josh Harris, Chris Penfield, Molly Boggs, Cheryl Warnock, Lynn Laufenberg, Dwana Waugh, Anne Elise Thomas, Zhen Liang, August Hardy, Erin Pitt, Megan Kobiela, John Morrissey, Tim Loboschefski, Megan Perkins, Jessica Wise, Brian Kuhr, Barb Watts, Tracy Hamilton, Hannah Lott, Shawn O'Connor, Claire Stankus, Rudith Butler, and Floyd Butcher.

Thanks to my writing mentors and friends: Khadijah Queen, Natalie Rogers, Thirii Myo Kyaw Myint, Dennis J. Sweeney, Mark Mayer, Rowland Saifi, Alicia Mountain, Alison Turner, Emily Pettit, Erinrose Mager, Justin Wymer, Mona Awad, Sasha Tamar Strelitz, Brian Kiteley, Rachel Feder, Joanna Howard, Selah Saterstrom, Laird Hunt, Clark Davis, Adam Rovner, Scott Howard, Michelle Naka Pierce, Andrew Wille, Nova Ren Suma, Kendare Blake, and the late Keith Abbott.

Thanks to my friends and family: James Camp, Phoebe Camp, Jocelyn Camp, Julie Caplan, Suzanne Motley, Isak

Sjursen, Amy Keys, Clayton J. Szczech, Dave Cass, Leslie Good, Sam Hansen, Brooks Hansen, Kelly Ann Jacobson, Patricia Hernandez, Dylan Rice-Leary, Patrick Tone, Deanne Moore, Kathleen Templeman, Ted Templeman, Teddy Templeman, Ravioli, and Muffin.

ABOUT THE AUTHOR

Phoebe Wolfe Camp

McCormick Templeman's writing has appeared in the *Los Angeles Review of Books, The Dagon Collection,* and the YA horror anthology *Slasher Girls & Monster Boys.* She holds a doctorate in the field of traditional Chinese medicine, as well as a PhD in English and creative writing from the University of Denver, where she specialized in nineteenth-century horror.